LOVE IS DEADLY ...
THE SECOND TIME
AROUND

Waylock put his arms about The Jacynth.
"I've been waiting for you."

The beautiful girl extricated herself. "Whatever your relationship to the previous Jacynth, it does not extend to me. I am the *new* Jacynth. A month ago my previous version was destemporized at Carnevalle. It seems that you escorted me during that evening. Someone evil robbed me of my life... and I want to know his name."

"You suggest I am that Monster!"

"You will answer," The Jacynth said, growing impatient. "Mind search is the means to truth ... and that is how it will be."

"... A FRIGHTENING LOGICAL DEPICTION OF A CIVILIZATION BASED ON IMMORTALITY AS THE SUPREME REWARD FOR A LIFE OF ACHIEVEMENT."
—*Galaxy Magazine*

To Live Forever

Jack Vance

BALLANTINE BOOKS • NEW YORK

Library of Congress Catalog Card Number: 56-12123

ISBN 0-345-25198-9-150

Manufactured in the United States of America

First Edition: September 1956
Second Printing: November 1976

Cover art by Dean Ellis

I

CLARGES, THE last metropolis of the world, stretched thirty miles along the north shore of the Chant River, not far above the broadening of the Chant into its estuary.

Clarges was an ancient city; structures, monuments, manors, old taverns, docks and warehouses two or even three thousand years old were common. The citizens of the Reach cherished these links with the past, drawing from them an unconscious comfort, a mystical sense of identification with the continuity of the city. The unique variation of the free-enterprise system by which they lived, however, urged them to innovation; as a result Clarges was a curious medley of the hoary and the novel, and the citizens—in this as in other ways—suffered the pull of opposing emotions.

There never had been such a city as Clarges for grandeur and somber beauty. From the Mercery rose towers like tourmaline crystals, tall enough to intercept passing clouds; surrounding were great shops, theaters and apartment blocks; then came the suburbs, the industrial purlieus, the nondescript backlands extending out past the range of vision. The best residential areas—Balliasse, Eardiston, Vandoon, Temple Cloud—occupied hillsides north and south overlooking the river. Everywhere was motion, the quiver of vitality, the sense of human effort. A million windows flickered in the sunlight, vehicles darkened the boulevards, shoals of aircraft meshed along the avenues of the air. Men and women walked briskly along the streets to their destinations, wasting no time.

Across the river lay Glade County, a wasteland, drab, flat and dreary, without use or habitation, where nothing grew except stunted willows and rust-colored rushes. Glade County had no reason for being except the fact that it included the six hundred acres of Carnevalle.

Against the dismal background of Glade County, Carnevalle blazed like a flower on a slag-heap. Its six hundred acres held a treasure of color, of pageantry, of spectacular devices for diversion and thrill and catharsis.

In Clarges itself life was confined to the activity of men. Carnevalle knew a life of its own. In the morning there was

1

silence. At noon the swish of cleaning equipment and an occasional footstep might be heard. In the afternoon Carnevalle came to life, preening and shuddering like a new butterfly. When the sun sank there was a momentary lull, then a swift surge into such vitality and emotion as to deny the very concept of oblivion.

Around the periphery swung the comet-cars of the Grand Pyroteck: the *Sangreal Rubloon*, the *Golden Gloriana*, the *Mystic Emeraud*, the *Melancthon* and the *Ultra-Lazuli*, each a different color, each casting a different glow from its flaming train. The pavilions gave off prismatic refractions; the pagodas dripped molten liquid; a myriad lumes floated like a haze of fireflies. Along the avenues, through the alleys and lanes, the crowds streamed and shifted. To the sounds of the thrill-rides, to the hiss and *thwashh* when the cars of the Grand Pyrotek passed over, to the calls of barkers and hucksters, to the tones of plangent zither, hoarse accordion, chiming zovelle, plaintive lemurka, bright ectreen, were added the shuffle of a hundred thousand feet, the undertone of excitement, cries of shock and surprise and delight.

As the night went on, the intoxication of Carnevalle became a thing in itself. The celebrants pressed through the noise, the hundred horns and musics; they breathed aromatic dusts and pastel fogs; they wore costumes and headgear and masks; restraints were brittle films, to be broken with pleasure. They explored the strange and the curious, toyed with vertigo and paroxysm, tested the versatility of the human nerve.

Midnight at Carnevalle saw the peak of tumult. Compunction no longer existed; virtue and vice had no meaning. At times the outbursts of laughter became wild weeping, but this quickly subsided and was in the nature of a spiritual orgasm. As the night grew dim, the crowds became slower, more hesitant; costumes were in disorder, masks were discarded. Men and women, sleepy, wan, stupefied, stumbled into the drops of the tube-system to be whisked home, everywhere from Balliasse to Brayertown, from manse to one-room apartment. All five phyle came to Carnevalle: Brood, Wedge, Third, Verge and Amaranth, as well as the glarks. They mingled without calculation or envy; they came to Carnevalle to forget the rigors and strains of existence. They came, they spent their money, and—much more precious than money—they spent the moments of their lives.

2

A man in a brass mask stood in a booth before the House of Life, calling out to the crowd. Lumes the shape of infinity symbols drifted around his head; above him towered an ideal version of the life-chart, the bright life line rising through the phyle levels in a perfect half-parabola.

The man in the brass mask spoke in a voice of great urgency. "Friends, whatever your phyle, attend me! Do you value life a florin's worth? Will endless years be yours? Enter the House of Life! You will bless Didactor Moncure and his remarkable methods!"

He touched a relay; a low sound issued from a hidden source, hoarse and throbbing, rising in pitch and intensity.

"Slope! Slope! Come into the House of Life, up with your slope! Let Didactor Moncure analyze your future! Learn the methods, the techniques! Only a florin for the House of Life!"

The sound rose through the octaves, building a sense of uneasiness and instability, and shrilled at last into inaudibility. The man in the booth spoke in a soothing tone; if the sound represented the tensions of existence, the man and his voice meant security and control.

"Everyone possesses a brain, all nearly identical. Why then are some Brood, some Wedge, others Third, Verge and Amaranth?"

He leaned forward as if to make a dramatic revelation. "The secret of life is technique! Didactor Moncure teaches technique! Is infinity worth a florin? Come, then—enter the House of Life!"

A number of passers-by paid their florin and crowded through the entrance. At last the House was full.

The man in the brass mask stepped down from the booth. A hand grasped his arm; he whirled with savage speed. The person who had accosted him fell back.

"Waylock, you startle me! It's only me—Basil."

"So I see," said Gavin Waylock shortly. Basil Thinkoup, short and plump, was costumed as a mythical bird in a flouncing jacket of metallic green fronds. Red and gray scales covered his legs; black plumes ringed his face like the petals of a flower. If he perceived Waylock's lack of affability, he chose to ignore it.

"I had expected to hear from you," said Basil Thinkoup. "I thought you might have been moved by our last conversation—"

Waylock shook his head. "I wouldn't be suited to such an occupation."

"But your future!" protested Basil Thinkoup. "Really, it's a paradox that you go on urging others to their most intense efforts, and remain a glark* yourself."

Waylock shrugged. "All in good time."

"'All in good time'! The precious years pass and your slope lies flat!"

"I have my plans; I prepare myself."

"While others advance! A poor policy, Gavin!"

"Let me tell you a secret," said Waylock. "You'll speak no word to anyone?"

Basil Thinkoup was aggrieved. "Haven't I proved myself? For seven years—"

"One month short of seven years. When this month passes—then I will register in Brood."

"I'm delighted to hear this! Come, we'll drink a glass of wine to your success!"

"I have to watch my booth."

Basil shook his head, and the effort made him stagger; it was evident that he was partially intoxicated. "You puzzle me, Gavin. Seven years and now—"

"*Almost* seven years."

Basil Thinkoup blinked. "Seven years more, seven years less—I'm still puzzled."

"Every man's a puzzle. I'm an exercise in simplicity—if you only knew me."

Basil Thinkoup let that pass. "Come see me at Balliasse Palliatory." He leaned close to Waylock and the plumes around his face brushed the brass mask. "I'm trying some rather novel methods," he said in a confidential voice. "If they succeed, there is ample slope for us both, and I'd like to repay the debt I owe to you, at least in some measure."

Waylock laughed; the sound echoed behind the brass. "The smallest of debts, Basil."

---

*glark: (etymology uncertain; perhaps from *gay lark*.) A person not participating in the Fair-Play scheme—roughly a fifth of the population.

"Not at all!" cried Basil. "If it weren't for your impetus, where would I be? Still aboard the *Amprodex*."

Waylock made a deprecatory motion. Seven years before, he and Basil had been shipmates aboard the fruit-barge *Amprodex*. The captain, Hesper Wellsey, was a large man with a long black mustache and the disposition of a rhinoceros. His phyle was Wedge, and his best efforts had failed to raise him into Third. He took no pleasure in the ten years that Wedge had given him; instead, he felt rage and humiliation. With the barge entering the estuary of the Chant and the towers of the Mercery rising through the haze, Hesper Wellsey went catto*. He grabbed a fire ax, cut an engineer in two, smashed the windows of the mess hall, then started for the reactor house, intending to batter in the safety lock, smash the moderator and blast the barge twenty miles in all directions.

There was no one to stop him. The crew, horrified by the desecration of life, fled to the fantail. Waylock, teeth chattering, had gone forward hoping for a chance to drop upon Wellsey's back, but he glimpsed the ghastly ax and his knees gave way. Leaning against the rail, he saw Basil Thinkoup step from his quarters, look up and down the deck, then approach Wellsey, who swung the ax. Basil jumped back, ducked and dodged, talking pleasantly. Wellsey flung the ax, and failing to split Basil's face, succumbed to the opposite phase of the syndrome and collapsed on the deck.

Waylock came forward, stared at the stiff figure. "Whatever you did, it's a miracle!" He laughed weakly. "You'd make slope fast at a palliatory!"

Basil looked at him doubtfully. "Are you serious?"

"I am indeed."

Basil sighed and shook his head. "I don't have the background."

Waylock said, "You don't need background, only agility and good wind. They chase you till they wear themselves out. You've got it in you, Basil Thinkoup!"

Basil shook his head uncertainly. "I'd like to think so."

"Try, by all means."

Basil had tried and in five years broke into Wedge. His gratitude to Waylock was boundless. Now, standing before the House of Life, he clapped Waylock on the back. "Come see me at the Palliatory! After all, I'm Assistant Psychopathist

*catto: subject to the catatonic-manic syndrome.

—we'll contrive to start you up slope. Nothing grand at first, but you'll develop."

Waylock's laugh was sardonic. "Serving the cattos as a kickball—that's not for me, Basil." He climbed back into his booth, pushing up through the swarm of infinity symbols. His cornet voice rang out. "Raise your slope! Didactor Moncure holds the key to life! Read his tracts, apply his tonics, enroll for the regimen! Slope, slope, slope!"

3

At this time the word "slope" was charged with special meaning. Slope was the measure of a man's rise through the phyle; it traced the shape of his past, foretold the time of his ultimate passing. By the strictest definition, slope was the angle of a man's life line, the derivative of his achievements with respect to his age.

The system stemmed from the Fair-Play Act, which had been instituted three hundred years before, during the Malthusian Chaos. The Fair-Play Act had been impending since Leeuwenhoek and Pasteur, indeed had been dictated by the very shape of human history. With disease and degeneration minimized by ever more effective medical techniques the population of the world expanded at a prodigious rate, doubling every few years. At such a rate of increase, in three centuries more, human beings would cover the earth in a layer fifty feet deep.

The problem, in theory, was amenable to solution: compulsory birth-control, large-scale production of synthetic and pelagic foods, reclamation of wastelands, euthanasia for subnormals. But in a world divided by a thousand contradictory approaches to life, implementation of the theory was impossible. Even as the Grand-Union Institute refined a technique which finally and completely conquered age, the first riots began. The century of Malthusian Chaos had begun: the Big Starve was on.

Turmoil spread around the world; foraging raids exploded into petty wars. Cities were plundered and burned, mobs scoured the landscape for food. The weak could not survive; corpses outnumbered the living.

The ravage dwindled of its own violence. The world was scarified, the population reduced by three-quarters. Races and nationalities merged; political divisions vanished, to be reborn in areas of economic polity.

One of these regions, the Reach of Clarges, had suffered comparatively little; it became a citadel of civilization. By necessity its borders were sealed. Mobs from outside charged the electric barricade, hoping to pass by sheer force of will. Their charred corpses littered the ground by the hundreds.

Thus rose the myth of Reach ruthlessness, and no nomad child grew to manhood without learning the ballad of hate against Clarges.

The Reach had been home to the Grand-Union Institute, still a center of research. A report circulated that members of the Institute were investing themselves with extended longevity. The rumor was short of the truth. The end-product of the Grand-Union techniques was eternal life.

The citizens of Clarges erupted with anger when the fact was made public. Were the lessons of the Big Starve to be ignored? There was passionate protest; a hundred schemes were hatched; a hundred contradictory proposals put forward. Eventually the Fair-Play Act was drafted, and won a grudging approval. In essence, the system rewarded public service with years of extended life.

Five phyle, or levels of achievement, were stipulated: Base, Second, Third, Fourth, Fifth. Base became known as Brood; Second, the Wedge; Third, less frequently, Arrant; and Fourth, Verge. When the original Grand-Union group organized the Amaranth Society, Fifth became Amaranth.

The Fair-Play Act carefully defined the conditions of advance. A child was born without phyle identification. At any time after the age of sixteen he might register in the Brood, thus submitting to the provisions of the Fair-Play Act.

If he chose not to register, he suffered no penalty and lived a natural life without benefit of the Grand-Union treatments, to an average age of 82. These persons were the "glarks," and commanded only small social status.

The Fair-Play Act established the life span of the Brood equal to the average life span of a non-participator—roughly 82 years. Attaining Wedge, a man underwent the Grand-Union process halting bodily degeneration, and was allowed an added ten years of life. Reaching Third, he won sixteen more years; Verge, another twenty years. Breaking through into Amaranth brought the ultimate reward.

At this time, the people of the Reach numbered twenty million, with the maximum desirable population estimated at twenty-five million. The population would reach this maximum very rapidly. The ugly dilemma had to be faced: when a member of a phyle lived out his years, what then? Emigration was a dubious solution. Clarges was hated throughout the world; setting foot beyond the border was inviting sudden death. Nevertheless, an Emigration Officer was appointed to study the problem.

The Emigration Officer made his report in an uncomfortable session of the Prytaneon.

Five areas of the world maintained a semblance of civilized, if barbaric, order within their boundaries: Kypre, Sous-Ventre, the Gondwanese Empire, Singhalien, Nova Roma. None of these would allow immigration, except on a reciprocal basis, which made the project impractical.

The Reach might extend its boundaries by force of arms, until, at the logical limit of the process, the Reach of Clarges included the entire world, with the fundamental problem only postponed.

The Prytaneon listened glumly, and amended the Fair-Play Act. The Emigration Officer was ordered to implement the basic intent of the Act. In short, he was empowered to remove from life any citizen who reached the authorized limit of his years.

The amendment was not accepted without misgiving. Some labeled the provision immoral, but others cited the demonstrable dangers of over-population. They emphasized that each man made his own choice: he could live a natural life span, or he could seek, and possibly win to, a high phyle. By the latter choice he entered into a definite contract, and at the end of his time was deprived of nothing which had been his except conditionally. He lost nothing—and stood to gain the greatest treasure imaginable.

The Fair-Play Act became law, together with the amendment. Almost the entire population participated. Attainment to Wedge offered no great problem, especially during the first years. A record of social responsibility, participation in civic affairs, and productive employment was usually sufficient. Across to the higher phyle was more difficult, but possible to men of dedication and ability. Under the compulsions of the new system, these men appeared in great numbers. The effect was to project Clarges into a Golden Age. The sciences, arts and technical crafts, every phase of knowledge and achievement, exploded into new domains.

As the years passed the Fair-Play Act was modified. The life grants of each phyle were given a variable definition, through a formula based on the annual production, the population of each phyle, the proportion of glarks, and similar considerations.

To apply this formula to the record of each individual, an enormous calculating machine called the Actuarian was constructed. Besides calculating and recording, the Actuarian printed individual life charts on demand, revealing to the applicant the slope of his lifeline, its proximity either to the horizontal boundary of the next phyle, or the vertical terminator.

If the lifeline crossed the terminator, the Emigration Officer and his assassins carried out the grim duties required of them by the Act. It was ruthless, but it was orderly—and starkly necessary.

The system was not without its shortcomings. Creative thinkers tended to work in proved fields, to shun areas which might prove barren of career-points. The arts became dominated by academic standards; nonconformity, fantasy and nonsense were produced only by the glarks—also much that was macabre and morose.

Anxiety and disappointment were obvious partners to the climb through phyle; the palliatories were crowded with those who had chosen unreality rather than continued struggle.

As the generations passed, emotional necessity for slope dominated the life of the Reach. Every working hour was devoted either to work, to planning for work, or to the study of techniques for success. Hobbies and sport became rare; social functions were poorly attended. Without a safety valve, the ordinary man could hardly have avoided breakdown and commitment to a palliatory. The safety valve was provided by Carnevalle. To Carnevalle he came once or twice a month, and one or more Carnevalle costumes were essential to a full wardrobe. At Carnevalle the ordinary man, his mind clogged with work, could find release; he could gratify every suppressed longing, ease each frustration.

To Carnevalle, on occasion, also came the Amaranth, wearing gorgeous costumes. Anonymous under their masks, they could ignore the restraints imposed upon them by their own elevated place.

To Carnevalle came The Jacynth Martin, only three years Amaranth, only two weeks out of seclusion.

The Jacynth Martin three times had driven up from Brood, first as a specialist in medieval instrumentation and arrangement, then as a concert flautist, finally as a critic of contemporary music. Three times her lifeline had slanted at a sharp initial angle, then sagged and sprawled toward the horizontal.

At the age of forty-eight she courageously broadened her field across the entire history of musical development. Her slope rose at a decisive angle and she broke through into Wedge at the age of fifty-four. (This now was her static age, until either she achieved Amaranth or until the black limousine stopped at her door.)

She was made a special study of contemporary music, based on an original theory of musical symbology. Her work was such that at the age of sixty-seven she achieved Third.

She became assistant professor of Musical Theory at Charterburgh University, but resigned after four years in order to compose. *The Ancient Grail,* a passionate orchestral suite mirroring the intensity of her own personality, lifted her into Verge at the age of ninety-two. With approximately thirty years in which to attain Amaranth, she set aside a year for contemplation, rest, and a new set of stimuli.

She had always been interested in the delicate culture of the island kingdom Singhalien, and in spite of the apparently insurmountable obstacles and dangers, decided to spend the year she had allowed herself among the Singhali.

She made elaborate preparation, learning the language, the conventions, the ritual postures. She acquired a Singhali wardrobe, dyed her skin. She obtained an air car with a self-contained power source (the usual vehicles of Clarges, which operated by broadcast power, could fly only a few miles past the borders of the Reach). Her preparations complete, she departed the Reach for the barbarian outlands, where her life would be in continual danger.

In Kandesta she set herself up as a witchwoman and with the aid of a few scientific tricks achieved a reputation. The Grandee of Gondwana offered her a missal of safe-conduct into his pirate empire, and she accepted eagerly. Her original schedule was running short, but, fascinated by the Gondwanese artists and their identification of creativity with life, she remained four years. Many aspects of Gondwanese life she found repugnant, in particular the unconcern toward human suffering. The Jacynth was an emotional woman, exquisitely sensitive and all during her time out of the Reach she fought a chronic nausea. At Tonpengh, she innocently attended the ceremonies at the Grand Stupa, and the experience shocked her past her capacity. In an extremity of revulsion she fled Gondwana and returned to the Reach, arriving in a state of near-collapse.

Six months in the well-ordered security of Clarges restored her mental balance, and the next years were her most productive. She published her *Study of Gondwanese Art,* and cinematic essays on various subjects: Gondwanese music; the coral gardens tended by slave divers; the sails of the Gondwanese tiger boats, dyed in patterns of near-microscopic intricacy; the dances on the summit of Mount Valakunai which never ceased lest the sun, the moon and the stars should likewise halt.

At the age of one hundred and four she broke through into Amaranth, becoming The Jacynth Martin.

She went into her seclusion like a caterpillar into metamorphosis, and emerged a transcendentally beautiful girl of nineteen, more or less similar to the original Jacynth Martin at the age of nineteen.

The new Jacynth was a girl nineteen years old, not just a rejuvenated edition of the 104-year-old woman. She was equipped with the old Jacynth Martin's knowledge, memories and personality, although gaps and lapses could easily be found. The new Jacynth, however, was no one else. There were no elements in her character which had not been present in the old Jacynth; she was at once both completely and incompletely the former woman.

The Jacynth Martin, age nineteen, was contained in a slender nervous body of compelling contour. Ash-blond hair swept smooth and bright to her shoulders. Her expression, while mobile and open, was not altogether guileless. According to the convention which relates the beauty of a woman to one of the flowers, The Jacynth might be likened to a ginger blossom.

During the climb up phyle, her sexual experience had been curtailed and desultory. While she had never married she had maintained a sane perspective, and when, earlier in the evening she had arrayed herself in skin-smooth silver, the prompting had been as much from the urge and pride of her healthy body as from the psychic thrust which takes most of the new Amaranth through a stage of abandon. She came to Carnevalle with no conscious design or purpose, untroubled either by currents of foreboding or by pangs of prospective guilt.

She parked her air car, rode a swift disk down a transparent tube and emerged upon the Concourse, at the very heart of Carnevalle.

She paused, entranced by the sound and color, by the spirit of Carnevalle.

The spangled hats, the striped costumes, the hoarse voices; bell tones, musical sounds, the subdued mechanical roar which seemed to come from everywhere; the faint odor of perspiration, eyes peering like intoxicated insects through masks; mouths like pink or purple lilies open to call, laugh, deride; the arms and legs moving in grotesque antics, impromptu capers; the erotic sidling and swaying; the flutter of cloth, the shuffle of shoe or sandal; the tubes and patterns of slave-light; the floating lumes and symbols: Carnevalle! The Jacynth had only to mingle and melt, to drift on the current, to merge with the welter of Carnevalle. . . .

She crossed the Concourse, turned past the Folie Incredibile, into the Lesser Oval, sauntered down Arcady Way, regarding everything with minute interest and the most intense perception. The colors rang in her eyes with the impact of gongs. She heard overtones, sweet, wild, harsh, in sounds which before had seemed quite unexceptional. She passed the sideshows where any kind of freakishness might be inspected; the Temple of Truth; the Blue Grotto; the Labyrinth; the College of Eros, where the techniques of love were demonstrated by men and women with agile bodies and grave faces.

A hundred patterns of slave-light swayed overhead, among them the sign of the House of Life. From a booth a man in a brass mask called out in a voice of great power. A disturbing image entered her mind, a recollection from the Grand Stupa at Tonpengh: the master priest demoniacally handsome, exhorting the moaning crowd of initiates.

Fascinated, The Jacynth paused to listen.

"Friends, what of your slope?" cried Waylock. "Come into

the House of Life! Didactor Bonzel Moncure will help if you so allow! Brood to Wedge, Wedge to Third, Third to Verge, Verge to Amaranth! Why hoard hours when Didactor Moncure will give you years? A florin, I say, a florin! Too much for life eternal?" His voice cut like a brass sickle. "Up with your slope! Learn the hypnotic way to memory! Freeze useful techniques forever, face the future with hope! One florin to enter Didactor Moncure's marvelous House of Life!"

A knot of passersby had gathered; Waylock pointed to a man. "You! You Third there! When do you make Verge?"

"Not me. I'm Brood, draygosser by trade."

"You've got the look of Third, that's where you belong. Try Didactor Moncure's regimen; in ten weeks bid your assassin good-by forever. . . . You!" This was a middle-aged woman. "Good lady, your children—what of them?"

"Young hounds are already ahead of me!" the woman cried in great good humor.

"Here's your chance to outdistance them! No less than forty-two of today's Amaranth owe their place to Didactor Moncure." His eye fell on a girl in shining silver. "You—the beautiful young lady! Don't you want to be Amaranth?"

The Jacynth laughed. "I am not concerned."

Waylock held up his hands in mock astonishment. "No? And why not?"

"Perhaps because I'm glark."

"Tonight may be the turning-point of your life. Pay your florin, perhaps you too will be Amaranth. Then, when you wipe the yellow foam from the face of your first-alive, when you look upon she who is to be you, you will think back and give thanks to Didactor Moncure and his marvelous methods!" A stream of blue lumes floated out of the House and hung over his head. "Inside then, if you want to meet Didactor Moncure tonight; there's only a moment to enter! One florin, one florin to raise your slope!"

Waylock jumped to the ground. He was now at liberty; late-stayers at Carnevalle rarely patronized the House of Life. He sought through the crowd—there, the sheen of silver! He thrust into the jostle, fell into step beside The Jacynth.

The silver glitter on her face concealed whatever surprise she might have felt. "Is Didactor Moncure faring so poorly that his tout must chase prospects through the crowd?" Her tone was light and playful.

"At this moment," said Waylock, "I am my own man, and will be until tomorrow sunset."

"But you hobnob with Verge and Amaranth—what is your interest in a glark girl?"

"The usual," said Waylock. "You're a beautiful sight; do you realize it?"

"Why else would I wear so revealing a costume?"

"And you came to Carnevalle alone?"

She nodded, giving him a side glance, inscrutable through the silver mask.

"I'll accompany you—if I may?"

"I might lead you into mischief."

"A risk I won't mind taking."

They traversed Arcady Way and came out upon the Bellarmine Circus.

"Here we are at the crossroads," said Waylock. "The Colophon leads to the Esplanade. Little Concourse returns to the Concourse. Piacenza takes us out to the Ring and into the Thousand Thieves section. How will you choose?"

"I have no choice. I came to walk and look and feel."

"In that case, I must choose. I live and work here, but I know little more of Carnevalle than you."

The Jacynth was interested. "You live here—in Carnevalle?"

"I have an apartment in the Thousand Thieves; many who work here do."

She eyed him askance. "Then you're a Berber?"

"Oh no. Berbers are outcasts. I'm an ordinary man working at a job, glark like yourself."

"And you never become bored with all this?" She indicated the gay crowd.

"Sometimes to the point of exhaustion."

"Why live here then? It's only minutes to Clarges."

Waylock looked forward along the avenue. "I seldom cross over to Clarges," he mused. "Once a week. . . . Here's the Grand Pyroteck; we shall see all Carnevalle at a glance."

They passed under an arch which scintillated and exploded with sparks; a slideway carried them up to a high landing. One of the comet-cars, the *Ultra Lazuli*, veered and dipped down to a stop. Thirty passengers alighted; as many went aboard. The ports closed, the *Ultra Lazuli* slid up and away, trailing blue fire.

They flew low, dodging among the pagodas and towers,

soared high until Carnevalle was no more than a prismatic snowflake, and at last returned to the landing stage. The Jacynth Martin, flushed and excited, chattered with the fresh joy of a child.

"Now," said Gavin Waylock, "from high to low, from air to ocean." He led her through another entry, down into a dark hall. They climbed upon a mushroom-shaped stand, and a transparent bubble dropped around them. They were lifted, lowered into a channel, and floated blindly through pitch-darkness. Into a watery world, glowing with faint blue and green light, they sank, drifting among coral towers and sea-weed corpses. Fish swam by to peer at them, polyps extended purple, red and pink streamers. Out over a great gulf they moved, and there was nothing below, only a vast black density.

The ball floated to the surface; they re-emerged into Carne-valle.

Waylock pointed. "There's the House of Dreams. You re-cline on a couch and consider many strange things."

"I'm far too restless for dreaming, I'm afraid."

"There's the House of Far Worlds, where you can feel the actual soil of Mars and Venus, touch the moss of Jupiter and Saturn, walk through imaginative conceptions of other worlds. And there—over across the Concourse—is the Hall of Revela-tion; that's always amusing."

They entered the Hall of Revelation and found a great chamber, bare of furnishing except for a number of raised platforms. On each of these stood a man. The first was earnest; the second, excited; the third, angry; the fourth, hysterical. They shouted, argued, addressed themselves to the knots of people who listened with interest or awe, amusement or won-der. Each of the speakers espoused a variety of religious cult. The first proclaimed himself a Manitou; the second spoke of Dionysian Mysteries; the third demanded a return to the wor-ship of natural forces; the fourth proclaimed himself the Messiah and commanded the spectators to kneel at his feet.

Waylock and The Jacynth returned to the street. "They're ludicrous and tragic," she remarked; "it's a mercy they have a rostrum from which they can relieve their internal pressures."

"What else is all of Carnevalle? . . . See those people?" From an exit came men and women, by twos and threes, flushed and excited, some giggling, others pale. "They leave the House of the Unknown Thrill. The thrill is hardly unknown—it is the threat of—" He hesitated over the idea, which those of Clarges considered an obscenity—"the threat of transition. They pay to be frightened. They are tripped into a chasm, they fall screaming, two or three hundred feet. A cushion catches them. Back in the passage, a cauldron of molten metal seems to pour over them, but is diverted—so close that the heat scorches them. A giant dressed in black, with a black hat and mask— a stylized assassin— leads them into a dark room, where he clamps them into a kind of guillotine. The blade starts down and stops with the edge pressing into their necks. They come out—pale and laughing and purged. Perhaps it's good for us to play at—at going off. I don't know."

"That House is not for me," said The Jacynth. "I need no such purge, since I have none of their fears."

"No?" He considered her through the slits in the brass mask. "Are you so very young, then?"

She laughed. "I have many other fears."

"There's a House in Carnevalle to tantalize them. Are you afraid of poverty?"

The Jacynth shrugged. "I don't want to live like a Nomad."

"Perhaps you'd like to Help Yourself to Wealth."

"The idea has its appeal."

"Come on, then."

An entrance fee of ten florins was exacted at the gate to Help Yourself. They were each fitted with a harness and back-board to which were clipped nine bronze rings.

"Each of the rings represents a florin," the attendant told them. "As soon as you enter the passages, you steal any rings you are able. Other players will steal your rings. As soon as all your rings are stolen, a buzzer sounds. You will be conducted to the pay-off booth where you will cash in the rings you have stolen. You may win or you may lose. Stealth and alertness pay better than brash grabbing. Good luck and happy theft."

The passages proved to be a maze of mirrors and glass walls and curtained nooks. At the center was a hall whose walls were riddled with camouflaged recesses. Faces peered around corners, hands reached furtively from shadowed alcoves; the air was murmurous with hisses of exultation and frustration. At intervals the lights dimmed and flickered, and then there came a rush of skittering motion.

Waylock's buzzer at last sounded; an attendant immediately

appeared and led him to the pay-off booth, where he found The Jacynth waiting. He held a dozen rings which he cashed in.

The Jacynth said ruefully, "I'm not much of a thief. I got only three rings. You're a better one than I am."

Waylock grinned. "I stole two from you."

They moved out into the street, and Waylock led her to a Stimmo booth. "What color?"

"Oh—red."

"Red makes me daring," said Waylock. He tilted the mask forward, put the pill in his mouth. The Jacynth looked skeptically from the pill to Waylock. "Suppose I'm already daring?"

"This makes you reckless."

The Jacynth swallowed the pill.

Waylock laughed exultantly. "Now, the night begins." He made a wide gesture. "Carnevalle!"

They wandered down the avenue to the esplanade. Launches and barges moored to the dock were ablaze and loud with wild sound. Across the Chant rose the towers of the Mercery; the lesser buildings up and down the river formed a lesser bulk. Clarges was austere and monumental. Carnevalle was supple and pungent and passionate.

Turning up into the Granadilla they passed the Temple of Astarte with its twenty stained-glass domes, and the Temple of Priapus beside it. Hundreds of masked and beribboned visitors streamed through the low wide doors, from which exuded the scent of flowers and fragrant wood. For a space the avenue was lined with giant grotesques, demons and monsters swaying and nodding, leering and winking; then they were back in the Concourse.

The Jacynth's consciousness had split in two; a small cool kernel, and a much larger area which had become suffused with the personality of Carnevalle. Her faculties were concentrated on feeling and sensing; her eyes were wide, pupils dilated; she laughed a great deal and readily followed all Waylock's suggestions. They visited a dozen Houses, sampled intoxicants at a self-serve dispensary. The Jacynth's recollections became confused, like the colors on an old palette.

At a gambling game, players threw darts at live frogs, while spectators gasped in morbid delight.

"It's sickening," The Jacynth muttered.

"Why are you watching?"

"I can't help it. There's a dreadful fascination to the game."

"Game? This is no game! They only pretend to gamble. They pay to kill frogs."

The Jacynth turned away. "They must be Weirds."

"Perhaps there's a touch of the Weird in all of us."

"No." She shook her head positively. "No, not I."

They had approached the outer edge of the Thousand Thieves section; now they turned back, and at the Cafe Pamphylia stopped for refreshment.

A mechanical doll brought two frosty glasses containing vermilion Sangre de Dios.

"This will refresh you," said Waylock. "You will forget your fatigue."

"But I am not tired."

He sighed. "I am."

The Jacynth leaned forward mischievously. "But you insist that the night has only just started."

"I will drink several of these." He lifted the goblet, tilted his mask, drank.

The Jacynth watched him speculatively. "You have not told me your name."

"That is the way of Carnevalle."

"Oh come now—your name!"

"My name is Gavin."

"I am Jacynth."

"A pleasant name."

"Gavin, take off your mask," said The Jacynth abruptly. "Let me see your face."

"At Carnevalle faces are best concealed."

"That is hardly fair, Gavin. The silver conceals nothing of me."

"Only a beautiful person, a vain one, would dare such a costume," said Waylock gravely. "For most of us, glamour lies in concealment. With this mask on, I'm the prince of your imagination. Remove the mask, and I am only my workaday self."

"My imagination refuses to supply a prince." She laid her hand on his arm. "Come," she wheedled, "off with your mask."

"Later, perhaps."

"Would you have me think you ugly?"

"No, of course not."

"Are you ugly, then?"

"I hope not."

The Jacynth laughed. "You're setting out to pique my curiosity!"

"Not at all. Consider me the victim of an obscure compulsion."

"A peculiarity you share with the ancient Tuaregs."

Waylock looked at her in surprise. "Amazing lore to find in a young glark girl."

"We are an amazing pair," said The Jacynth. "And what is your phyle?"

"Glark, like yourself."

"Ah." She nodded sagely. "Something you said made me wonder."

Waylock stiffened. "Something I said? What?"

"All in good time, Gavin." She rose to her feet. "And now, if you've had drink enough to overcome your fatigue, let us be away."

Waylock joined her. "Wherever you wish."

She put her hands on his shoulders, looked provocatively up at him. "Where I wish to go, you will not come."

Waylock laughed. "I'll go wherever you choose to lead."

"So you say."

"Try me."

"Very well. Come along." She led him back to the Concourse.

As they went up the avenue, a great gong sounded midnight. The air became heavier, the colors richer, the movements of the celebrants became meaningful and deliberate, invested with the ritualistic passion of a stately dance.

Waylock pressed close to The Jacynth, walked with his arm around her waist. "You are a miracle," he said huskily. "A fabulous flower, a legend of beauty."

"Ah, Gavin," she said reproachfully, "what a liar you are!"

"I speak the truth," he told her reproachfully.

"Truth? What is truth?"

"That no one knows."

She stopped short. "We will discover Truth—for here is the Temple of Truth."

Waylock hung back. "There's no Truth in there—only malicious fools exercising their wit."

She took his arm. "Come, Gavin, we will out-malign and out-fool them."

"Let's go on to—"

"Now, Gavin, you claimed you'd follow wherever I led."

Reluctantly Waylock let himself be taken through the portal.

The attendant asked, "The Naked Truth or the Decorous Truth?"

"The Naked Truth!" said The Jacynth.

Waylock protested; The Jacynth looked slantwise at him. "Did you not claim, Gavin—"

"Oh, very well. I have no more shame than you."

"To your left hand, if you please," said the attendant.

"Come, Gavin." She led him along the corridor. "Just think, you will know exactly my opinion of you."

"So you'll have me out of my mask, after all," muttered Waylock.

"Of course. Didn't you plan as much before the night was done? Or did you hope to embrace me while wearing your mask?"

The attendant conducted them each to a booth. "You may disrobe in here. Hang the numbered placard around your neck. You will carry this microphone with you, and to any comment, criticism, praise or disparagement of people you will meet, prefix the number of the person in question and speak privately into the microphone. As you leave you will receive a printed copy of comments made about you."

Five minutes later The Jacynth Martin came out into the central hall. Around her neck hung the number 202, and she carried a small microphone. She wore no garments.

The hall was carpeted with a deep rough pile, comfortable to the bare feet. Fifty nude men and women of all ages wandered here and there talking to each other.

Gavin Waylock appeared, wearing the number 98—a man rather taller than average, youthful-seeming, well-shaped, nervously muscular. His hair was dark and thick; his eyes pale gray; his face handsome, harsh, expressive.

He came forward, meeting her gaze squarely. "Why do you stare at me?" he asked in a brittle voice.

She abruptly turned away, and looked around the hall. "Now we must circulate, and allow ourselves to be evaluated."

"People will be oppressively frank," said Waylock. "However," and he eyed her from head to toe, "your appearance is beyond all criticism." Putting the microphone to his mouth, he spoke a few sentences. "My candid impressions are now on record."

For fifteen minutes they moved around the bright room, their bare feet comfortable on the heavy carpet, making small talk to people who seemed anxious to do the same in return. Then they returned to the booths, resumed their costumes. At the exit they were handed folded sheets of paper imprinted with the words THE NAKED TRUTH. Inside were collected the comments of those whom they had met within, generally the bluntest and most candid observations imaginable.

The Jacynth first frowned, then giggled, then blushed, then read on with eyebrows raised in amused vexation.

Waylock glanced at his sheet, at first almost negligently; then, bending his head sharply, he read with intense concentration:

Here is a face I recognize, but how and where I cannot be sure. A voice in my mind speaks a name—The Graven Warlock! But this dread Monster was tried, adjudged, and delivered to the assassins. Who, then, can this man be?

Waylock raised his eyes. The Jacynth was watching him. He carefully folded the report, tucked it into his pocket. "Are you ready?"

"Entirely."

"Then—let us go."

II

GAVIN WAYLOCK cursed himself for a shallow fool, a mooncalf. At the frivolous persuasion of a pretty face, he had nullified the vigilance of seven years.

The Jacynth could only guess at the emotions in Waylock's mind. The brass mask hid his face, but his hands clenched as he read the report, and his fingers trembled as he folded the paper, tucked it into his pocket.

"Has your vanity been wounded?" asked The Jacynth.

Waylock turned his head; his eyes glared through the slits of the mask. But when he spoke his voice was quiet. "I am easily wounded. Let's rest a few moments at the Pamphylia."

They crossed the street to the pleasant terrace-cafe planted with orchids, red mace, and jasmine. The spirit of careless flirtation had vanished; each was engrossed in his own throughts.

They seated themselves beside the balustrade, only an arm's-length from the passing crowd. An attendant brought tall thin vials of a pungent essence. They sipped a moment or two in silence.

The Jacynth covertly watched the brass mask, picturing the sardonic intelligence behind. Another vision came into her mind, unbidden, like a corollary: an image of the tall priests at Tonpengh, placed there by the proto-Jacynth and invested with all the proto-Jacynth's horror.

The Jacynth shuddered. Waylock looked up quickly.

The Jacynth said, "Did the Temple of Truth distress you?"

"I'm somewhat puzzled." Waylock displayed the report. "Listen to this." He read the paragraph which had caused him such emotion.

She listened without apparent interest. "Well?"

Waylock leaned back in his chair. "Strange that your memory serves you so far back, to a time when you could have been no more than a child."

"I?" exclaimed The Jacynth.

"You alone in the House knew my number. When I left you, I turned the face of the placard to my skin."

The Jacynth replied in a metallic voice, "I admit that I found your face familiar."

"Then you have deceived me," asid Waylock. "You cannot be glark, because seven years ago you wouldn't have been concerning yourself with scandal. For the same reason, you are not Brood. So you must be past the stage of your primary inoculations—Wedge or higher. A girl of eighteen or nineteen in Wedge is rare indeed; in fact, she is unique."

The Jacynth shrugged. "You build a magnificent edifice with your speculations."

"If you aren't glark; if you're neither Brood, Wedge, Third, nor Verge, then you'd be Amaranth. Your remarkable beauty confirms this idea: rarely do unmodified genes produce such perfection. May I ask your name?"

"I am The Jacynth Martin."

Waylock nodded. "I am correct in my deductions; you are partly right in yours. My face is indeed that of The Grayven Warlock. We are identities; I am his relict."

2

When an Amaranth had been admitted into the Society and had taken his final inoculations, he went into seclusion. Five cells were extracted from his body. After such modification of the genes as might be desired, they were immersed in a solution of nutrients, hormones and various special stimulants, where they rapidly evolved through the stages of embryo, infant, child and adolescent, to become five idealized simulacra of the original Amaranth. When invested with the prototype's memory-bank, they became the identity of the original: full-fledged surrogates.

During the development of the surrogates, the Amaranth was vulnerable to accident, and therefore guarded himself with a near-obsessive caution. After seclusion, however, he was safe from the hazards of life: should he be killed by violence, there was a replica of himself, equipped with his own personality, memories and continuity, ready to graduate into the world.

In spite of every precaution, there were occasions when an Amaranth was killed during seclusion. His un-empathized surrogates then became 'relicts.' Usually, by one means or another, they escaped into the world, to ply their own lives, differing from ordinary men and women only in the immortality from their prototype. Should they wish to make their own climb up phyle, they must register at the Actuarian like any other man or woman. Should they remain glarks, they might live indefinitely, always young, but usually obscure and anxious to avoid attention, because once identified, they were automatically listed as Brood.

Gavin Waylock claimed to be such a relict. The Jacynth Martin, on the other hand, was a surrogate with the personality and thought-processes of the original Jacynth Martin, who had extinguished herself as soon as complete empathy had been established.

3

"A relict," said The Jacynth thoughtfully. "Relict of The Grayven . . . seven years ago. . . . You seem very sophisticated for a relict of so few years."

"I'm highly adaptable," said Waylock gravely. "In a sense,

it's a handicap; nowadays it's the specialist who makes the steepest slope."

The Jacynth sipped her drink. "The Grayven Warlock fared well enough. What was his striving?"

"Journalism. He founded the *Clarges Direction*."

"I remember now. The Abel Mandeville of the *Clarion* was his rival."

"His enemy, too. They met one night, high in the Porphyry Tower. There were words, accusations; The Abel struck The Grayven. The Grayven struck back and The Abel fell a thousand feet into Charterhouse Square." A bitter note entered Waylock's voice. "The Grayven was branded a Monster; he was subjected to public scorn; he was delivered to the assassins, even before he had achieved full empathy with his surrogates." The eyes glittered behind the mask. "Among the Amaranth violence is not unknown. If transition does occur, it is nothing final. At most there's the inconvenience of a few weeks until the next surrogate comes forth. They made an example of The Grayven—because his act of violence couldn't be hushed up. The Grayven was given to the assassins, although he'd just become Amaranth."

"The Grayven Warlock shouldn't have left seclusion," said The Jacynth coolly. "It was a chance he took."

"The Grayven was impulsive, impatient; he couldn't isolate himself so long. He hadn't counted on the vindictiveness of his enemies!"

The Jacynth's voice rose in pitch; she spoke in a doctrinaire staccato: "There are the laws of the Reach. The fact that they are sometimes bypassed doesn't lessen their essential justice. Anyone who performs an obscene act of violence deserves nothing more than oblivion."

Waylock made no immediate response. He slumped a little into his chair, he toyed with his vial and watched her in quiet calculation. "What will you do now?"

The Jacynth sipped her liqueur. "I'm not happy in the possession of this knowledge. My instincts are to expose a Monster; I naturally shrink—"

Waylock interrupted. "There's no Monster to be exposed! The Grayven is seven years forgotten."

The Jacynth nodded. "Yes, of course."

A round face framed in black plumes pushed across the balustrade. "Here's old Gavin—good old Gavin Waylock!"

Basil Thinkoup stumbled into the terrace, seated himself with exaggerated care. His bird costume was disarranged. The black plumes drooped in sad disorder around his face.

Waylock rose to his feet. "You'll excuse us, Basil; we were on the point of leaving."

"Not so soon! Never do I see you except in front of your House!" He beckoned for more drink. "This man Gavin here," he told The Jacynth, "is my oldest friend."

"Indeed?" said The Jacynth. "How long have you known him?"

Waylock slowly sank back in his seat.

"Seven years ago we pulled Gavin Waylock out of the water. It was the barge *Amprodex*, Captain Hesper Wellsey in command. He went catto on the home trip. Remember that, Gavin, what a vicious sight?"

"I remember very well," said Waylock in a tight voice. He turned to The Jacynth. "Come, let's—"

She held up her hand. "I'm interested in your friend Basil. . . . So you pulled Gavin Waylock from the water."

"He fell asleep in his air car; it bore him out to sea, out beyond the power-broadcast."

"And seven years ago this occurred?" The Jacynth shot a side glance at Waylock.

"Seven years more or less. Gavin can tell you to the very hour; he has an exact mind."

"Gavin tells me very little about himself."

Basil Thinkoup nodded wisely. "Look at him now, like a statue behind his mask."

The two inspected Waylock carefully. Their faces swam in his vision; he felt peculiar immobility, as if he were anesthetized. By effort of will he reached out and drank from his vial; the pungent liquid cleared his brain.

Basil heaved himself to his feet. "Excuse me; I have an errand of the flesh; pray don't leave." He staggered across the terrace.

Waylock and The Jacynth observed each other across the table.

The Jacynth spoke in a soft voice. "Seven years ago The Grayven Warlock flees the assassins. Seven years ago Gavin Waylock is pulled from the sea. But no matter; the Monster has been destroyed."

Waylock made no comment.

Basil returned, sank heavily into his seat. "I've been urging Gavin to change his bootless occupation. I'm not without influence; I could start him out well . . ."

"Excuse me," said Waylock. He rose to his feet, and headed for the lavatory. Once out of range of vision, he turned into a public commu booth, tapped the buttons with trembling fingers.

The screen glowed, flooded blue-green as the connection was made. No face appeared in the screen, only a black circle.

"Who calls?" asked a voice, low and husky.

Waylock showed his face.

"Ah, Gavin Waylock."

"I must speak to Carleon."

"He is busy in his museum.' '

"Connect me with Carleon!"

A mumble, a mutter, the change was made.

A round white face appeared on the screen. Eyes like two agate pebbles inspected Waylock incuriously.

Waylock made known his desires; Carleon demurred. "I am conducting an exhibition."

Waylock's voice changed. "It must wait."

The lard-colored face made no quiver of expression. "Two thousand florins."

"One thousand is ample," said Waylock.

"You're a wealthy man, Waylock."

"Very well. Two thousand. But make haste!"

"There will be no delay."

Waylock returned to the table. Basil was speaking earnestly.

"You misunderstand; I hold no brief for itemistic methods. Each personality is a circle, rich and ripe as a plum. What can an outside mind find? A single point on the circumference, no more. There are many points on a circle, and as many valences to each human mind."

"It seems, then," said The Jacynth to Basil, with an appraising glance at Waylock, "that you tangle yourself even more resolutely. At least item-circuitry is an attempt at simplification."

"Ha ha! You fail to grasp the directness of my method. We all have favorite valences, at which we operate best. I try to find this valence and urge the patient into it, so he works at his optimum strength. But now I plan to bypass all this clumsy ex-

ternality. I have a new idea: if it works I'll strike directly at
the source of the trouble! It will be a tremendous step ahead, a
true achievement!" He paused self-consciously. "Excuse my
enthusiasm; it's out of place at Carnevalle."

"Not at all," said The Jacynth. She turned her head. "And
now what, Gavin Waylock?"

"Shall we leave?"

She smiled, shook her head, as Waylock knew she would.
"I'll wait here, Gavin. But I'm sure you're tired and sleepy. Go
home and have a good rest." Her smile quivered, almost became a laugh. "Basil Thinkoup will see me safe to my villa. Or
perhaps—" She looked into the crowd. "Albert! Denis!"

Two men in splendid costumes stopped, looked across the
balustrade. "The Jacynth! A delightful surprise!"

They came into the terrace; Waylock frowned, clenched
his fingers together.

The Jacynth made introductions. "The Albert Pondiferry,
The Denis Lestrange: this is Basil Thinkoup, and this is—
Gavin Waylock."

The Denis Lestrange was slender and elegant, and wore his
blond hair unfashionably short. The Albert Pondiferry was
hard and dark, with glittering black eyes and a careful terse
voice. They responded to the introduction with easy courtesy.

With a mischievous glance in Waylock's direction The
Jacynth said, "Truly, Albert and Denis, only at Carnevalle
does one meet interesting people."

"Indeed?" They inspected Basil and Waylock with dispas-
sionate curiosity.

"Basil Thinkoup strives as psychopathist at Balliasse Palliatory."

"We must share a number of mutual acquaintances," observed The Denis.

"And Gavin Waylock—you'll never guess!"

Waylock set his teeth.

"I'd never attempt it," said The Albert.

"Oh, I'll try," said The Denis, languidly eyeing Waylock.
"From that fine physique—a professional acrobat."

"No," said The Jacynth. "Try again."

The Denis threw up his hands. "You must help us with a
hint or two—what is his phyle?"

"If I told you," The Jacynth said wisely, "there would be
no more mystery."

Waylock sat rigid; the woman was intolerable.

"A pointless riddle," remarked The Albert. "I doubt if Waylock enjoys our speculations."

"I'm sure he does not," said The Jacynth. "But the riddle has a point of sorts. However, if you—"

There was a whisper of sound, so light and slight that only Waylock heard it. The Jacynth winced, put her hand to her shoulder; but the dart had been so swift, so sharp, so minute, that there was nothing to be felt, and she judged the sting no more than the sudden jump of a nerve.

Basil Thinkoup placed his hands flat on the table, looked from face to face. "I must say I've worked up a fearful hunger. Anyone for a go at some boiled crab?"

No one shared Basil's appetite; after a moment's indecision, he pulled himself to his feet. "I'll wander down to the esplanade and have a snack. It's time to be heading home, in any event. You lucky Amaranth, not to worry about tomorrow!"

The Albert and The Denis bade him a civil good evening; The Jacynth was swaying in her seat. She blinked in puzzlement; opened her mouth, gasped for breath.

Waylock rose to his feet. "I'll come with you, Basil. It's time I was finding my way on home."

The Jacynth was hanging her head, panting deep breaths. The Albert and The Denis looked at her with surprise.

"Is anything wrong?" asked Waylock.

The Jacynth made no reply.

"She seems indisposed," said The Albert. "Too much excitement, too much stimulant."

"She'll be all right," The Denis said lazily. "Allow her to relax."

The Jacynth slowly, gently, put her head down upon her arms; the pale hair spread loosely over the table.

Waylock asked doubtfully, "Are you sure she's well?"

"We'll take care of her," said The Albert. "Don't let us keep you from your meal."

Waylock shrugged. "Come, Basil."

As they left the cafe, he turned for a last look. The Jacynth had not moved. She lay completely inert. The Albert and The Denis were regarding her with growing concern.

Waylock heaved a great sigh. "Come, Basil. We're well out of it."

III

Waylock felt dull and exhausted. He took his leave of Basil in front of one of the river-front restaurants. "I'm not hungry; I'm just tired."

Basil clapped him on the shoulder. "Bear my advice in mind. We can always find a place for you at the palliatory!"

Waylock walked slowly along the esplanade. Dawn shimmered on the river, and with the first inkling of gray light Carnevalle faded. The colored lights lost their richness, the perfumes lay flat and stale on the air, the few remaining revelers walked with empty eyes and drawn faces.

Waylock's thoughts were bitter. Seven years ago he had struck too furious a blow; The Abel Mandeville had fallen a thousand feet. Tonight, to silence a woman who seemed intent on destroying him, he had instigated a second death. He was twice over a Monster.

A Monster. The word conveyed the ultimate in infamy and debasement inconceivable to one not native to the times. The word 'death' itself was an obscenity, a person who inflicted death was a creature of nightmare.

However, Waylock had extinguished the vitality of no one. The Abel Mandeville had resumed existence before a week had passed; a new Jacynth Martin would likewise emerge. If, seven years before, the assassins had managed to extinguish him, that would have been a desecration of life, for The Grayven had no surrogates in empathy. He had seized opportunity, had fled in an air car beyond the Reach. The assassins had cared little. It was considered certain death to leave the Reach; the Nomads held high festival when a man of Clarges fell into their hands.

Waylock, however, skirting the ultimate verge of the power field, had circled the Reach to the south, crossing Desert Skell, Lake Hush, Corbien and then the Southern Sea. In due course he spied the barge *Amprodex*, simulated a crash-landing, was taken aboard and signed into the crew to work his passage. Gavin Waylock had come into being.

If the assassins suspected that he had cheated them, they

would now act with decision and certitude. For several years Waylock had concealed himself, leaving Carnevalle no more than once a week, and then only with an Alter-Ego disguising his face.

He maintained lodgings in the Thousand Thieves section, but even in this place of outcasts no one saw him without his brass mask or his Alter-Ego. What stung him so bitterly was the fact that in a single month the law of Clarges would hold The Grayven Warlock legally defunct. Waylock could then make a career in his new identity, on his own terms.

Still, all was not lost. He had, so he hoped, repaired the effects of his folly. In a week or two the New Jacynth would appear, none the worse for her night at Carnevalle, and things would go as before.

Waylock made his way through the now-quiet avenues to his modest apartment and tumbled into bed.

2

After five or six hours of uneasy sleep, Waylock awoke, bathed, sat down to a reflective breakfast. He considered the night before, found it distasteful, and put it from his mind: only the future held meaning. His goal was clear. He must battle his way back up through the phyle; he must regain his place in the Amaranth Society. But how? The Grayven Warlock had succeeded in the field of journalism. He had founded the *Clarges Direction,* built it from a single flake into a great daily journal. But The Abel Mandeville must be reckoned his implacable enemy; journalism as a possible career could be discounted.

The most spectacular advances in phyle were achieved by creative artists: musicians, painters, aquefacts, pointellists, plaiters, writers, expressionists, mimes, chronotopes. In consequence, these occupations were seriously overcrowded. Space-exploration yielded automatic slope, but the mortality was high, and the proportion of spacemen reaching Amaranth was no greater than that in any other field.

During the first five years Waylock had codified systems for assimilating knowledge, acquiring skills and techniques, memorizing useful referents, ingratiating and impressing superiors. Then suddenly he had become victim to doubt. After all, wasn't he just plodding along a rut worn by ten generations before him? Excelling the field was the conventional approach to slope; thousands had won to Amaranth by adherence to this idea. Waylock would be falling in at the end of a long line, gradually inching forward, straining for the glitter at the horizon. If enough of those ahead wearied and staggered, blundered, became panicky, or collapsed into the palliatories, then Waylock might eventually regain his former status.

Surely there were short-cuts to the destination. Waylock would find these short-cuts. He would free himself from conformity, forgo conventional morality, put on a purposeful ruthlessness. Society had shown The Grayven Warlock no mercy, he had been sacrificed, almost frivolously, to mollify a popular emotion. Waylock would therefore use Society with remorseless self-interest.

To gear his mind to this new manner of thinking had required a year; to translate theory into a practical basis of action was a task he had not finally completed. Sitting in his apartment, he opened his notebook and considered the propositions:

Item 1:

   I.   Slope is slow, definite but minimal in the Vitality areas; i.e. institutions concerned with education (crêches, lyceums, colleges), psychopathics (the palliatories), the rise up-slope (the Actuarian), transition (the assassins). Application is more important than ability.

  II.   Slope in the fields of Art and Communication is a matter of vagary. Ability is not necessarily the key factor.

 III.   Slope is maximal only in the field of Space-travel. Space-travel is correspondingly dangerous.

 IV.   Slope is steady and favorable in the sciences, technical studies and applications. Innate ability is requisite.

  V.   Slope in Civic Services (members of the Prytaneon, the Tribunes, the Judiciary) is uncertain. Basis is public appraisal.
Ability is of less import than personal attitude, character and ostensible sincerity.

      a.   The office of Chancellor is an anachronism, purely honorary, and derives no slope whatever.

Item 2:

The most rigid institutions and areas of effort are the most brittle and most susceptible to attack. Most rigid institutions: the Actuarian; the College of Assassins.

Waylock put down the notebook. The words were familiar from much pondering. Seven years of planning were at their end. In one month—to the Actuarian! Gavin Waylock, glark, might live forever if he could just avoid public attention. But Grayven Warlock had made the climb; so should Gavin Waylock. The sooner he joined Brood, the sooner would he break through into Amaranth.

IV

THE MONTH passed without incident. Waylock worked his usual hours at the House of Life, made his weekly visits to the address in Clarges which no one but himself knew.

The month passed, and with it passed the seven years since The Grayven Warlock had departed the Reach. The Grayven Warlock was now legally dead.

Gavin Waylock, secure in his own identity, could once more walk the streets of Clarges, wearing neither brass mask nor Alter-Ego. The Grayven Warlock was dead. Only Gavin Waylock lived.

He took his leave of the House of Life, departed his lodgings in the Thousand Thieves, and took a bright apartment on Phariot Way in the Octagon, a few hundred yards south of the Mercery, as far north of Esterhazy Square and the Actuarian.

Early in the morning he boarded the slideway at Allemand Avenue, rode to Oliphant Street, walked three blocks directly into the shine of the morning sun, and so came to Esterhazy Square. A neat path led through the lawns, scattered plane trees, the flower beds, past the Cafe Dalmatia, and into the plaza before the Actuarian. Waylock stopped at the cafe for a mug of tea—a recognized diversion for those with leisure. There was always activity in the plaza, human drama at the "ooze-boxes" along the front of the Actuarian, where the men and women of Clarges came to learn the status of their careers.

Waylock felt a quiver of apprehension. His life the past seven years had been relatively untroubled. The act of registering in Brood would change all this: he would know the same tensions and anxieties which plagued the other inhabitants of Clarges.

Sitting in the warm morning sunlight, he found the idea uncomfortable. But when he finished his tea, he rose from the table, crossed the plaza, and entered the Actuarian.

2

Waylock went to a long counter marked "Information." The attendant, a pale young man with glowing eyes, a pinched mouth in blue-shadowed jaw, asked, "How may I help you, sir?"

"I want to register in Brood."

"Kindly activate this form."

Waylock took the form to a coding machine, pressed keys which recorded his statements in typescript, and at the same time deposited magnetic information-bits by which the form could be filed.

A middle-aged woman approached the counter. Her face was lined with worry and she could not meet the luminous stare of the clerk.

"How may I help you, madam?"

The woman tried several sentences, abandoning each, and finally blurted out, "It's about my husband. His name is Egan Fortam. I've been away three days at a seminar; today when I came home he was gone." Her voice blurred with worry. "I thought maybe someone here could help me."

The clerk's voice was sympathetic; he filled out the inquiry form with his own hand. "Your name, madam?"

"Gold Fortam."

"Your phyle?"

"I'm Wedge; I'm a schoolteacher."

"Your husband's name again?"

"Egan Fortam."

"And his phyle?"

"Brood."

"And his basic code?"

"IXD-995-AAC."

"Your address?"

"2244 Cleobury Court, Wibleside."

"Just a moment, Mrs. Fortam."

He dropped the card into a slot, and gave his attention to a serious lad of eighteen, fresh from the lyceum, who, like Waylock, wished to register in Brood.

A card popped up from the slot; the clerk inspected it gravely, and turned to the middle-aged woman.

"Mrs. Fortam, your husband, Egan Fortam, was visited by his assassin at 8:39 P.M. Monday last."

"Thank you," whispered Gold Fortam, and turned away.

The clerk bowed his head gravely, and took up Waylock's application. "Very good, sir; please press your right thumb here."

Waylock did so, and the clerk dropped the print into a slot. "Have to search the files," he told Waylock with a waggish cock of the head, "or some clever scoundrel could re-register when his lifeline closes in on the terminator."

Waylock rubbed his chin thoughtfully. Surely they would have removed his old card from the files seven years ago, on the presumption of his death. . . . He waited. The seconds ticked by. The clerk examined his fingernails.

A sharp buzz rang out. The clerk looked toward the sound in disbelief, then sharply at Waylock. "Duplication!"

Waylock gripped the edge of the counter. The clerk took the returned card, read the notation. " 'Identical to print of The Grayven Warlock, destemporized by assassins.' " He glanced at Waylock in astonishment, read the date. "Seven years ago."

"I am his relict," said Waylock huskily. "I've waited seven years, getting ready for the time when I might enter Brood."

"Oh," said the clerk. "I see, I see . . ." He blew his cheeks out. "Everything is in order then, inasmuch as the prints are not those of a living man. We seldom see relicts."

"There are few of us."

"True. Very well, then." The clerk handed Waylock a metal wafer. "Your basis code is KAO-321-JCR. When you wish to inquire regarding your lifeline, key this code on the buttons in one of the booths, press your thumb against the scanner."

Waylock nodded. "I understand."

"Now, if you'll kindly step into Room C, we'll record your alphas for the televector file."

In Room C, a girl took Waylock to a cubicle, seated him in

a straight metal chair. An operative in a white mask fitted a metal cap over Waylock's head, and the terminals of a hundred electrodes pressed into his scalp.

The girl wheeled up a black box, adjusted a pair of contacts the size of boxing gloves to Waylock's temples. "We'll have to anesthetize you, so your brain radiations will be nice and clear," she said cheerily. She put her hand on a switch. "This won't hurt; your mind is merely numbed a moment or two."

She pushed the switch; instantly Waylock's consciousness departed. He awoke with no awareness of time lapse.

The girl removed the metal cap, smiling with impersonal brightness. "Thank you very much, sir. The first door to the right."

"Is that all?"

"That's all. You're now in Brood."

Waylock left the Actuarian, returned across the plaza to the Cafe Dalmatia. He resumed his seat, ordered another mug of tea.

From the Actuarian hung a capsule woven of iron bars: the Cage of Shame. Within it there now crouched an old woman, who had apparently been put there during Waylock's absence. Presumably she had violated the rules of the Actuarian and now, by ancient custom, paid the penalty.

At the table next to Waylock two men, one fat with lank hair and round eyes, the other tall and thin, discussed the situation. "Quite a sight, isn't it?" observed the fat man. "The old crow must have tried to trick the Actuarian!"

"They come more often nowadays," his companion remarked. "When I was young, the Cage was used no more than once a year." He shook his head. "The world's changing, what with these Weirds and Whitherers and all the new styles."

The fat man rolled his eyes lewdly. "The Weirds will be out tonight."

"Before, there'd never be such a display." The thin man spat angrily. "The midnight walk was a retreat from shame. . . . Now with the Weirds, it's disgusting. Monsters, they make of themselves."

The fat man looked across the plaza with a smug secret smile. "No man's a Monster against one of them." He cocked his head at the woman in the Cage. "Stealing our lives, that's what she's doing."

His friend turned away in disgust. "You have no life to

steal. You're a glark; you'll never be anything else."

"You're another."

Waylock was distracted from the argument by a young woman, slender, clean-limbed, walking along the plaza with buoyant purpose. She wore a flowing gray cloak buttoned at the neck; bright hair blew loose behind her.

It was The Jacynth Martin.

She passed close in front of the cafe. Waylock started a motion as she passed, but restrained himself. What could he say to her? She glanced at him; her eyes flickered in a kind of puzzled recognition, but her mind was on other matters. With gray cloak fluttering at her calves, she disappeared beyond the end of the cafe.

Waylock gradually relaxed. It had been an odd experience. He was a stranger to this new Jacynth. She was no more to him than any other beautiful woman, and to her he was only a face remembered in a grim context from the past.

Waylock put her out of his mind. His future was of more immediate concern.

He considered Basil Thinkoup's proffer of employment at Balliasse Palliatory. Unpleasant idea. He would be exposing himself to stimuli of the most disturbing sort. Better a new field, or one muddled and mismanaged enough to discourage orthodox workers.

A rack of newspapers caught his eye. As in other eras, the journals of Clarges were principally concerned with tribulation, vice and misery, and so should stimulate his thinking.

He went to the rack, looked along the mastheads. He smiled as he reached for the *Clarion*. Poetic justice of a sort! Returning to his table, he began a slow study of the news.

In spite of the technical excellence of the Reach's industrial processes, there was still disorder at the human level. For example, sociologists were troubled by a wave of "self-induced transition." Waylock read further.

The Wedge contributes the greatest per capita number of these disappearances, followed closely by Third, then Brood. Verge and the glarks are least susceptible to this fantastic abuse. Amaranth are of course immune.

Waylock considered. A means to detect, apprehend and punish would-be self-killers would win slope. . . .

Waylock read on. Two Amaranth, The Blade Duckerman and The Fidelia Busbee, had been pelted with grapes at a wine-making festival in the little up-country town of Meynard. Apparently the whole town had joined the game, and had chivvied the two Amaranth through the town with shouts and hunting calls. Local authorities were appalled, but could attribute no cause to the disgraceful incident except drunken high spirits. They offered their apologies, which both The Blade and The Fidelia had accepted.

The Amaranth were probably swanking around, thought Gavin Waylock. No harm done. He wished he had been on hand. Could points be gained organizing parties of this nature? Hardly likely. . . . He scanned the columns. Condemnation of slums in Gosport, in preparation for a new six-level skyway. Points there for someone. An interview with Didactor Talbert Falcone, eminent psycho-pathologist, Verge. Didactor Falcone was

. . . dismayed by the ever-rising tide of mental illness. Ninety-two per cent of hospital occupancy is due to psychological trouble. One person out of every six is at some time committed to a palliatory. Clearly our techniques are in need of overhaul. But no one studies the problem; in a field so confused there is little hope for recognition or a steady access of career-points; there is no attraction for our best minds.

Waylock re-read the paragraph. Almost his own words! He read further.

Of the various irregularities, the manic-catatonic syndrome is the most widespread. There is no mystery as to its cause. A man or woman, intelligent, hard-working, foresighted, finds that his lifeline inexorably points toward the terminator. No effort, no investment of time and thought, is of value. Doom is a juggernaut over which he has no control. He gives up. He gives up with an utter finality. He lapses into a trancelike state more or less complete. At intervals, at the promptings of an unknown stimulus, he becomes a screaming maniac, and wreaks havoc until he is restrained, when once more he goes catatonic.
This is the characteristic trouble of our age. I am sorry to report that it is becoming ever more prevalent as advance

*up-phyle becomes more difficult. Is this not a great trage-
dy? We, who have probed the secrets of matter, traversed
interstellar space, built our towers into the clouds, and
destroyed age: we, who know so much and can achieve
so much, we stand helpless outside the portal of the
human mind!*

Waylock thoughtfully replaced the paper in the rack. Now
too restless to sit, he left the cafe, crossed Esterhazy Square,
walked slowly up Rambold Street into the Mercery.

Here was a field which exactly fitted his requirements—in
which Basil Thinkoup only last night had offered him a foot-
hold. He could hardly hope to start in any other capacity than
orderly. An unpleasant job, to be sure. He had no background;
it would be necessary to study, to learn the jargon, perhaps
even attend night school. But Basil Thinkoup had undertaken
these steps; and already Basil was anticipating breakthrough
into Third.

Waylock boarded the slideway, rode north. At the Pelagic
Industries Tower, a lift carried him up to the new Sunray
Skyway, a favorite promenade for sightseers. The view was
magnificent, embracing fifty miles of the River Chant; the
drab wastelands of Glade County; Carnevalle, sparkling like
a wad of crumpled Christmas paper; the Chant estuary and a
glimpse of the distant sea. Below were the deeps of the city,
roaring with a low sound; above was the sky. Waylock idled
along the slideway, letting the wind blow into his face.

He looked across the great city, and suddenly a great surge
of enthusiasm rose within him! He felt inspired. Clarges, the
Reach and the city, a glorious citadel in a savage world! He,
Gavin Waylock, had already gained the ultimate heights.

He could do it again.

V

NORTH OF the Mercery the river swung back and forth, round-
ing Semaphore Hill, swerving into that valley known as Angel's
Den, then out and around Vandoon Ridge, whose crest, Vandoon Highlands, was the best residential district in Clarges.

The northern slope of Vandoon Ridge was Balliasse, still an expensive district, but somewhat less exclusive. The residents were mainly Verge, with a few Third and a proportion of rich glarks, who compensated for lack of phyle by an extravagant mode of living.

The palliatory was situated low on the bluff, only a few hundred yards up from Riverside Road. Waylock left the tube at Balliasse Station, and arriving at the surface found himself on a concrete slab under a broad roof of green and blue glass. A sign reading "Balliasse Palliatory" pointed to a slideway. Stepping aboard, Waylock was carried up a slope, through a pleasant hillside park of trees, shrubs and creepers. The slideway dipped, passed through a short tunnel, then rose and discharged him into a reception lobby.

Waylock went to the desk, asked to see Basil Thinkoup, and was directed to Suite 303 on the third floor. He rode up on the escalator, and with some difficulty found Suite 303. The door bore a legend in flowing green slave-light script:

BASIL THINKOUP
Assistant to the Resident Psychopathist.

And below in smaller letters:

SETH CADDIGAN
Psychotherapist

Waylock slid back the door, entered.

At a desk sat a man working with an air of dedicated intensity, plotting curves with a chartograph. This was evidently Seth Caddigan. He was tall and lankly muscular, with a bony face, sparse reddish hair, a nose as unkindly short as his upper lip was long. He looked impatiently up at Waylock.

"I'd like to see Mr. Basil Thinkoup," said Waylock.

"Basil's in conference." Caddigan returned to his work. "Take a seat, he'll be out in a few minutes."

Waylock, however, went to look at the photographs on the wall. They were group pictures, evidently the staff at an annual outing. Caddigan watched from the corner of his eye. Suddenly he asked, "What do you wish to see Mr. Thinkoup about? Perhaps I can help you. Are you seeking admittance to the palliatory?"

Waylock laughed. "Do I look crazy?"

Caddigan studied him with a professional dispassion. " 'Crazy' is a word with unscientific implications. We don't often use it."

"I stand corrected," said Waylock. "You're a scientist, then?"

"I consider myself such."

On his desk lay a sheet of gray cardboard scrawled with red pencil. Waylock picked it up. "And an artist as well."

Caddigan took the drawing, inspected it down his nose, replaced it on the desk. "This drawing," he said evenly, "is the effort of a patient. It is used diagnostically."

"Well, well," said Waylock. "I thought it was your work."

"Why?" asked Caddigan.

"Oh, it has a certain flavor, a scientific quality, a—"

Caddigan bent to check the scrawl, then looked up at Waylock. "You really think so?"

"Yes, indeed."

"You must experience the same delusions as the poor wretch who drew this."

Waylock laughed. "Just what is it?"

"The patient was asked to draw a picture of his brain."

Waylock was interested. "Do you have many of these?"

"A large number."

"I suppose you have some means of classifying them?"

Caddigan indicated the chartograph. "That is a project I am currently at work upon."

"And after you've got them classified—then what?"

Caddigan seemed reluctant to answer. Finally he said, "You perhaps are aware—most informed persons are—that psychology has not advanced as swiftly as other sciences."

"I suppose," said Waylock thoughtfully, "that it attracts few first-rate men."

Caddigan's glance strayed briefly toward a door across the room. "The difficulty is the complexity of the human nervous system, together with its inaccessibility for study. There is a tremendous library of research and data—for instance, diagnosis by pictures." He flicked the cardboard sheet. "It's been done again and again. But I believe my approach may contribute some small originality."

"The field is static?"

"Anything but static. The science of psychology roams at will, to every quarter of the horizon. But it is always tethered to the core of its primary difficulty—the intricacy of the brain, the lack of precise methods. Oh, there's slope to be had, and some are Amaranth today through a restatement of Arboin or Sachewsky or Connell or Mellardson. The leaves get raked from one corner of the yard to the other, but today the palliatories are full and our treatments are hardly different from those of the days of Freud and Jung. All rule of thumb, as easy for eager students as didactors." He fixed Waylock with a piercing stare. "How would you like to become Amaranth?"

"Very much."

"Solve any one of the twenty basic problems of psychology. The way will be cleared." He bent over the scrawl with with an air of ending the discussion. Waylock smiled and shrugged and wandered around the room.

A sound penetrated the walls, a shrill, terrible screaming. Waylock looked at Seth Caddigan. "Good old manic-catatonic," said Caddigan. "Makes our living for us."

The door in the side wall slid back; Waylock glimpsed an inner office with a glass partition, a large chamber beyond. In the doorway stood Basil Thinkoup, in a severe gray uniform.

2

Late in the afternoon Gavin Waylock left the palliatory. Hailing an air cab, he flew back across town, while the sun sank in orange haze beyond the dreary wastes of Glade County. The towers of the Mercery caught the last light, burnt with a few moments of sad glory, then faded. Lights began to blink and glow; across the river Carnevalle flickered.

Waylock considered his new striving. Basil had been delighted to see him, and declared that Waylock was making the wisest of choices. "There's work to be done, Gavin—mountains of work! Work and slope!"

Caddigan had gnawed at his underlip, perhaps envisioning in Waylock the first of a series of dilettantes whose only recommendation to the field was ignorance.

It would be wise, thought Waylock, to gain at least a smattering of the jargon. But always must he remember his purpose—which was to avoid the ruts worn by a hundred thousand predecessors.

He must approach the subject critically, alert for contradictions, pedantry and vagueness.

He must reject in advance the work of classical as well as present-day authorities.

He must be able to recognize, but still stand aside from, the methods and doctrines which to date had achieved little.

But until opportunity for advancement presented itself—or until he created that opportunity—he must be able to make the sounds which commended one to one's superiors and the Board of Review. Up the slope! Devil take the hindmost!

The cab set him down on Floriander Deck, in the heart of the Octagon, only three minutes by drop and slideway from his apartment.

He stopped at a newsstand, which was also a branch of the Central Library, glanced through the index. He selected two general works on psychology and one on the organization and management of mental health institutions. He dialed the code numbers, dropped a florin in the slot, and in a minute received three flakes of microfilm in cellophane envelopes.

He rode the drop down to ground level, stepped on the Allemand slideway, and was conveyed to Phariot Way.

The exhilaration of the morning had worn off; he was tired and hungry. He prepared a platter of food, ate, then lay down on his couch and drowsed an hour or two.

He awoke, and the apartment seemed cheerless, small and drab. He collected his microbooks, a viewer, and went out into the night.

He walked moodily to Estherhazy Square and by force of habit turned into the Cafe Dalmatia. The plaza, dark and empty this time of night, seemed to echo with the footsteps of those who had passed during the day. The Cage of Shame still hung over the plaza; inside crouched the woman. At midnight she would be released.

He ordered tea, with gentian cakes, and applied himself to his studies.

When next he looked up, he was surprised to see the cafe almost full. The time was eleven o'clock. He returned to his books.

At quarter to twelve the tables were all occupied, by men and women who looked everywhere but into each other's face.

Waylock could study no longer. He sought through the shadows of Estherhazy Square. Nothing stirred. But everyone knew the Weirds were there.

Midnight. Voices in the cafe hushed.

The Cage of Shame swayed, descended. The woman within gripped the bars with both hands, peering out into the plaza.

The cage touched the terrace. Segments snapped up; the woman was free. Her formal punishment was at an end.

In the cafe everyone leaned a little forward, breathing deep.

The woman began to move tentatively along the face of the Actuarian, toward Bronze Street.

A stone clattered on the terrace beside her. Another and another. She was struck on the hip.

She ran, and the stones poured down out of the darkness. A stone the size of a fist hit her at the base of the neck. She stumbled, fell.

The stones jarred her as they struck.

Then she was on her feet, scuttling for Bronze Street, and disappeared.

"Mmph," came a mutter; "she escaped."

Another voice said, in a tone of heavy banter, "You regret it; you're as bad as the Weirds themselves."

"Did you notice the number of stones? Like hail!"

"They're increasing, these Weirds."

"Weirds and Witherers and all the other odd ones—I don't know. I don't know. . . ."

VI

THE NEXT morning Waylock arrived at the palliatory promptly on time; it gave him cause for bitter reflection: *Already like all the other ulcerated clamberers.*

Basil Thinkoup was occupied for the morning; Waylock reported to Seth Caddigan.

Caddigan pushed a printed form across the desk. "Fill this out, if you please."

Waylock, looking it over, frowned austerely. Caddigan laughed. "Fill out the form; it's your application for the position of orderly."

"But I'm already employed as orderly," said Waylock.

Caddigan spoke with strained patience, "Just fill out the form, there's a good chap."

Waylock scribbled a few words in the blanks, inserted dashes and question marks where he preferred not to respond, tossed the form across the desk. "There you are. My life history."

Caddigan glanced down the insertions. "Your life seems to be one long question mark."

"It's really of little consequence."

Caddigan shrugged his high shoulders. "You'll find that the guiding spirits around here are sticklers for regulation. This —" he indicated the application—"is like a red flag to a bull."

"Perhaps the guiding spirits need stimulation."

Caddigan gave him a hard stare. "Orderlies seldom are agents of stimulation without regretting it."

"I hope not to remain orderly long."

Caddigan smiled quietly. "I'm sure you won't."

There was a short silence. Then Waylock asked, "Were you an orderly?"

"No. I'm a graduate of Horsfroyd College of Psychiatrics. Worked two years as interne at Meadowbrook Home for the Criminal Insane. Therefore—" Caddigan turned out his lank hands— "I was able to bypass the menial jobs." He looked with sardonic expectancy at Waylock. "Eager to learn the nature of your duties?"

"Interested, at least."

"Very well. In all candor, it's not nice work. It sometimes is dangerous. If you injure one of the patients you lose career points. We're not allowed violence or emotion—unless of course we ourselves go manic." Caddigan's eyes gleamed. "Now if you'll come with me . . ."

2

"Here is our little empire," said Caddigan in an ironic voice. He motioned up the room which, by some obscure association, awoke in Waylock's mind the word "museum." Beds extended from both sides into the room. The walls were buff, the beds were white, the floors were covered with a checker of linoleum in brown and gray. Partitions of transparent plastic separated each bed from the next, creating a series of stalls along both walls. Although the plastic was very clear, the beds at the far end of the room were indistinct and clouded, an effect like the multiple images in mirrors held opposite. The patients lay on their backs, arms lax along their sides. The eyes of some were open; others were clenched shut. They were all male, men of late youth or early middle age. The beds were immaculately tended, the faces shone pinkly clean.

"Nice and tidy and quiet," said Caddigan. "These are all strong cattos; they hardly ever stir. But every once in a while —*click!* Something pops in their brain. You'll notice restless motions, their mouths work, they convulse. That's the manic stage."

"Then they're violent?"

"It depends on the individual. Sometimes they just lie there and writhe. Others leap to their feet and stride down the corridors like gods, destroying whatever they touch. Rather," he added with a grin, "they would if they were allowed. Notice," he pointed to the floor at the foot of the first bed, "those holes. As soon as weight leaves the bed, stress-tubes shoot up and block off the stall. The patient is unable to escape, and can only tear up the sheets. After considerable experimentation, we have developed sheets which tear with optimum sound and vibration. The patient works off much of his fury, and presently we enter the booth with a swaddle and bear him back to his bed." He paused, looked down the passage. "But these strong cattos aren't too bad. There are worse wards." He looked toward the ceiling. "Up there are the shriekers. They lie like statues, but every so often, like a clock striking, they cry out. It's hard on the orderlies. They are human, after all, and the human mind is sensitive to certain timbres of the voice." He paused and seemed to muse. Waylock looked dubiously along the row of rigid faces. "I have often thought," Caddigan went on, "that if one had an enemy, a sane and sensitive enemy, how exquisite a torture to confine him in the shrieker ward, where he could hear and not escape. He would join the shrieking in six hours."

"Don't you use sedatives?"

Caddigan shrugged. "For the strong manics, of necessity. Otherwise we operate by the theory—whim, if you prefer—of the psychiatrist in charge. In this ward it is—nominally—Didactor Alphonse Clou. But Didactor Clou is preparing a treatise: Synchrocephaleison among the Doppelgangers, or, if you prefer, the symbiotes, who need each others' presence to exist. He rejects the influence of telepathy, which to my mind is ridiculous; however, I am Brood and Didactor Clou may make Verge on the strength of his treatise. With Clou occupied, Basil Thinkoup is the man in authority; and this ward is his domain. Basil does not drug. His ideas are unconventional. He espouses the remarkable principle that whatever is established practice is incorrect, and in fact the diametric opposite of what should be done. If painstaking research suggests that mild massage is beneficial to victims of hysterical delusion, Basil either wraps in rigoroid or runs them violently around a course attached to a mechanical guide. Basil is an experimenter. He tries anything, without qualm or moderation."

"With what results?" asked Waylock.

Caddigan pushed out his lips in sour amusement. "The patients are none the worse. Some seem to benefit. . . . But of course Basil doesn't know what he's doing."

They walked along the central aisle. The faces, of all contours and casts, had one element in common: an expression of the most profound melancholy, dreariness without hope.

"Good heavens," muttered Waylock. "Those faces . . . Are they conscious? Do they think? Do they feel as they look?"

"They are alive. At some level their mind is functioning."

Waylock shook his head.

"Don't think of them as human beings," Caddigan declared. "If you do, you're lost. For our purposes they are only elements of the striving, to be manipulated in such a way as to win us career-points. . . . Come now, I'll show you what must be done."

3

Waylock found his duties altogether repellent. As orderly he was required to wash, air, force-feed and attend to the bodily evacuations of thirty-six comatose patients, any one of whom might suddenly be keyed into violent mania. In addition he was obliged to keep records, and to assist Caddigan or Basil Thinkoup in any special treatment or exercise.

Basil Thinkoup looked into the ward about lunchtime, and seemed in high good spirits. He clapped Waylock on the back. "Mind now, Gavin, don't let Seth put you off with his mockery; he's really a smart enough lad."

Caddigan pursed his lips and looked off across the room. "I think I'll be seeing to my lunch." He nodded curtly and sauntered loosely off. Basil took Gavin's arm. "Come along. I'll show you the cafeteria; we'll have a good meal and see what's to be done."

Waylock looked down the ward. "What about the patients?"

Basil's expression became quizzical. "What about them

indeed? Where can they go? What harm can befall them? They recline as if frozen; if they thaw or erupt—what then? The bars hold them; they tear up the sheets; they spend themselves and sleep once more."

"I suppose that's the practical attitude."

"*And* eminently sensible!"

The cafeteria occupied a half-hemisphere cantilevered out from the main structure, providing a view of sunny air and blue-gray river. Tables were arranged in concentric half-circles, with all the chairs turned outward. Basil led Waylock to a table at the far end of one of the inner circles—a self-effacing choice, made without apparent calculation. Others in the room seemed rather cool toward Basil.

As they seated themselves, Basil winked at Waylock. "Professional jealousy at work; did you notice?"

Waylock made a noncommittal response.

"They know I'm progressing," said Basil complacently. "Pulling a prize out from under their very noses, and it irks them."

"I imagine it would."

"This group," Basil made a sweep with the back of his hand, "is riddled with suspicion and jealousy. Since I seem to be advancing rapidly, they turn on me like small-town gossips. Seth Caddigan no doubt has been condemning my practices, right?"

Waylock laughed. "Not exactly. He says you are unconventional; and it disturbs him."

"He should be disturbed. He and I started on equal terms. Seth burdened his mind with hypotheses derived at fourth or fifth hand from classical case studies; I ignored the lot and played by ear, so to speak."

A menu wrought from slave-light fine as wire drifted down to each of them; Basil ordered lettuce, pickled shad and crackers, explaining that he felt better for light eating. "Seth frets and eats himself away with self-pity, and develops his wit instead of his psychiatry. Myself, hmm—perhaps I am boisterous. So they describe me. But I have no misgivings. Our society is the most stable structure in human history, and shows no tendency to change. This being the case, we can expect our typical ailment, the catatonic-manic syndrome, to continue its advance. We must attack it vigorously, with our gloves off." Waylock, busy with cutlet and watercress, nodded his understanding.

"They say I use the patients as guinea pigs," Basil complained. "Not so. I do try various systems of therapy as they occur to me. The waxers are expendable. They're of value to no one, not even themselves. Suppose I aggravate twenty of them, thirty, or a hundred? What then?"

"A detail," said Waylock.

"Correct." Basil stuffed his cheeks with lettuce. "The condemnation might be justified if my methods produced no results—but—ha, ha!" He spluttered with laughter, holding his hand over his mouth. "To the intense dismay of all, some of my patients improve! I have discharged several as cured, which increases the contempt in which I am held. Who is less popular than the lucky bungler?" He clapped Waylock on the arm. "I am pleased to have you here, Gavin! Who knows, we may make Amaranth together! Great sport, eh?"

After lunch, Basil took Waylock back to Ward 18 and left him to his duties. Waylock went unenthusiastically to work, touching each patient with a nozzle which puffed a dosage of vitamins and toners through the skin into the blood stream.

He considered the row of beds. Thirty-six men whose common denominator was a slack lifeline. There was no mystery as to the source of their psychosis. Here they would live out their years until finally the black-glassed limousine called to take them away.

Waylock strolled along the passage, pausing to look into the desolate faces. At each bed he asked himself. What stimulus, what therapy would I use?

He halted by a bed where a thin man, mild and soft, lay with eyes closed. He noted the man's name. Olaf Gerempsky, and his phyle, Wedge. There were other notations and code marks which he did not understand.

Waylock touched the man's cheek. "Olaf," said Waylock in a soft voice. "Olaf, wake up. You are well. Olaf, you are well. You can go home."

Waylock watched closely. Olaf Gerempsky's face, slack and pointed, like the face of a white rat, underwent no change. Evidently this was the wrong approach.

"Olaf Gerempsky," said Waylock in a stern voice, "your lifeline has broken through into Third. Congratulations, Olaf Gerempsky! You are now Third!"

The face was unchanged. The eyes never moved. But Waylock thought a small glow of personality quiver came timidly up from infinite melancholy. "Olaf Gerempsky, Third. Olaf Gerempsky, Third," said Waylock in the tone of voice he used from the booth before the House of Life. "Olaf Gerempsky, you are now of Third Phyle, Olaf Gerempsky, you are Third!" But the small blaze had sunk despondently back into the depths.

Waylock stood back, frowned at the mask. Then he bent close above the still face of Olaf Gerempsky.

"Life," he whispered. "Life! Life! Life eternal!"

The face persisted in its melancholy calm. From within came a sense of ineffable regret, the sadness of watching a sunset fade. The glimmer passed, the mind slowly became blank. Waylock bent closer. He drew back his lips.

"Death," he said huskily. "Death!" The vilest word in the language, the ultimate obscenity. "Death! Death! Death!"

Waylock watched the face. It remained still, but underneath something quickened. Waylock drew back an inch or two, staring in complete absorption.

The eyes of Olaf Gerempsky snapped open. They rolled right and left, then fixed on Waylock. They glared like campfires. The lips contracted, the upper curled up under the nose, the lower drawn down to show the locked teeth. A gurgle started up from the throat, the mouth opened; from Olaf Gerempsky's throat came an appalling scream. Without seeming to move his muscles, he rose from the couch. His hands plunged for Waylock's neck, but Waylock had jumped away. He felt a cool contact at his back: the bars of toroidal light had automatically sprung up from the floor.

Gerempsky was on Waylock; his hands were like tongs. Waylock made a hoarse sound, beat down at the arms; it was like beating at iron pipe. Waylock pushed Gerempsky in the face; Gerempsky toppled to the side.

Waylock tugged at the bright bars. "Help!" he shouted.

Gerempsky was at him again. Waylock tried to push him off, but the maniac caught his crisp new jacket. Waylock dropped to the floor, pulling Gerempsky on top of him, then heaved up on his hands and knees. Gerempsky clung to his back like a squid; Waylock threw himself over backward, tore himself loose. His jacket remained in Gerempsky's hands. Waylock scrambled around behind the bed, yelling for help. Gerempsky, cawing in wild laughter, jumped at him. Waylock ducked under the bed. Gerempsky paused to tear the jacket into shreds, then looked under the bed. Waylock proved out of reach; Gerempsky vaulted the bed, in order to reach in from the other side, but Waylock rolled away again.

The game went on for several minutes, Gerempsky leaping back and forth, Waylock rolling to the side opposite. Then Gerempsky stationed himself on the bed, and made no motion; Waylock, below, was trapped. He couldn't watch both sides at once; in the middle, he could be reached from either side.

He heard voices, the sound of steps. "Help!" he called. He saw the legs of Seth Caddigan. "I'm in here," he cried. The legs came to a halt; the feet pointed at him.

"This maniac will strangle me!" called Waylock. "I don't dare move!"

"Just hold on," said Caddigan in a solicitous voice. Behind appeared other legs. The bars of light vanished; Gerempsky roared, lunged for the corridor. He was caught in a voluminous swaddle, enfolded, forced back on the bed.

Waylock crawled from below and scrambled to his feet. He stood by, brushing his clothes, while Caddigan pushed a nozzle into Gerempsky's mouth and discharged a spray. Gerempsky flung his arms out to the side, lay limp. Caddigan turned away, glanced at Waylock, nodded with careful courtesy, stepped past and returned down the corridor.

Waylock stared after him, took a couple of long steps, then halted. He composed himself as well as possible, followed Caddigan into the anteroom which Caddigan used as an office. Caddigan was immersed in a pile of mimeographed papers, making notes and collecting references. Waylock sank into a chair, ran his hand through his hair.

"That was quite an experience."

Caddigan shrugged. "You're lucky Gerempsky is a weakling."

"Weakling! His hands were like iron! I've never seen such strength!"

Caddigan nodded, and a small tremulous smile twitched on his mouth. "The feats of an hysterical maniac are incredible. They contradict the basic engineering of the human body. But then, so do many other phenomena." His voice became a pedantic drone. "For instance, the fire-walking of many peoples, both ancient and modern, and the even more spectacular habits of the Czincin Mazdaists."

"Yes," Waylock said restively. "No doubt."

"I myself have seen the power of a man called Phosphor Magniotes. He controls the flight of birds, ordering them up, down, right or left, singly or in whole flocks. Do you believe that?"

Waylock shrugged. "Why not?"

Caddigan nodded. "One thing is clear: these individuals command a source of power which we cannot even identify. The Amaranth no doubt use this energy to achieve empathy with their surrogates, who knows?"

"Quite probable," said Waylock.

"This energy must be on call to the maniacs. Olaf Gercmpsky displayed six times his usual strength, but Olaf actually is a weakling. You should observe our strong ones: Maximilian Hertzog or Fido Vedelius. Either of these would have plunged a hand through the bed, and pulled you back up through the hole. Therefore—" Caddigan's grin came a trifle broader— "I must warn you, and this is what I have been leading up to, that it is perilous business trifling with a patient, no matter how placid he may seem."

Waylock held his tongue. Caddigan leaned back in his chair, pressed his fingers together.

"I will be blocking out your progress sheet. It goes without saying that I strive for absolute fairness. In this regard, I can't find it possible to rate your day's work highly. I don't know what you were up to. I don't want to know."

Waylock started to speak, but Caddigan held up his hand. "Perhaps you have adopted Basil Thinkoup as your model; perhaps you are seeking to emulate him and his successes. If so, I suggest that you plan more carefully, or else learn the source of his amazing luck."

Waylock restrained himself. "I think you misunderstand the situation."

"Perhaps I do," Caddigan exclaimed with mock heartiness. "I feared that you and Basil Thinkoup were the precursors of a whole new trend in psychiatric thought, to be known perhaps as the Hammer and Tongs School."

"I find your humor superfluous," Waylock said.

Basil Thinkoup had entered the room, stood looking from one to the other. "Is that rascal Caddigan after you already?" He came forward. "When I first came to Balliasse, it was my sole diet. I believe I went Wedge to escape Caddigan."

Caddigan made no comment. Basil turned to Waylock. "So you've had an adventure."

"A trivial matter," said Waylock. "I'll be on my guard next time."

"That's the spirit!" said Basil. "Just so."

Seth Caddigan rose to his feet. "If you'll excuse me, I'll be away. I have two classes tonight and I must make ready." He bowed his long head and left the room.

Basil shook his head, smiling indulgently. "Poor Seth, he's making slope the hard way, cramming himself with uselessness. Tonight—let me see—it will be The Behavior Patterns of Viruses and Absolute Zero Surgery. Tomorrow he studies Recapitulation, Social and Evolutionary, in the Developing Embryo. Next night it's something else."

"Quite a program," observed Waylock.

Basil seated himself with a puff and a blowing out of florid cheeks. "Well, the world's a big place; we can't all be alike." He rose to his feet. "Your shift is about over; you might as well go home. We have a big day tomorrow."

"Gladly," said Gavin. "I've got some studying of my own to do."

"Seriously making the drive, eh, Gavin?"

"I'll get to the top," said Waylock. "One way or another."

Basil grimaced. "Don't go at it so hard that you end up like—" He jerked his thumb toward the ward behind them.

"I don't intend to."

VII

WAYLOCK LET himself into his apartment, stood for a moment in the small foyer, looking left and right in dissatisfaction. The rooms were cramped, the furniture tasteless; and Waylock recalled The Grayven Warlock's airy manse in Temple Cloud with regret. His own property, but how could he claim it?

He felt vaguely hungry, but when he looked through the storage bank, nothing tempted him. Annoyed, he found his texts and his viewer, and departed.

He dined in a noisy over-sumptuous restaurant which

catered to glarks. As he ate, his mind wandered over the events of the last few days: he considered The Jacynth; saw her as she had appeared in the Temple of Truth, slender as a wand, supple as a kitten, unnaturally beautiful. A warm urgency awoke inside him. Suppose he called her on the commu —but what could he say to her? He could hardly mention that he was one of the last persons to see her former version alive. No telling what sort of investigation was going on, although he, Gavin Waylock, could hardly be involved. Neither the new Jacynth, The Denis nor The Albert knew his identity. It would be wise to let matters remain on this basis.

What should he do with himself, then? He considered and rejected public entertainments. He wanted human companionship, good-fellowship, conversation. The Cafe Dalmatia? No. Basil Thinkoup? No. Seth Caddigan? Not the most amiable person in the world certainly, and he had manifested small love for Waylock; still—why not?

Never one to resist an impulse, Waylock went to the commu booth, twisted the directory dial. The screen blurred as the names flowed past. A . . . B . . . C . . . Ca . . . Caddigan . . . Seth Caddigan. Waylock centered the name, pressed the call button.

Seth Caddigan's face appeared "Oh—Waylock."

"Hello, Caddigan. How did the classes go?"

"About as usual." Caddigan was terse, guarded.

Waylock improvised a pretext for the call. "Are you extremely busy? I have a problem, and you might be able to advise me."

Caddigan, not very graciously, invited Waylock to drop by his apartment, and Waylock set forth immediately. Caddigan lived in Vauconford, a suburb to the east, rather bohemian in character. His apartment walls were lively brown, melonred, black and mustard, embellished with none of the usual inlay or ormolu. The furnishings were period pieces, severe slabs of glass, metal, flat wood, and fabric; illumination came from three balloons of pale yellow slave-light, floating here and there about the room. Distortionist paintings hung on the wall, curious ceramic objects stood on the long low book-cases. Waylock found the total effect rather eccentric.

Further to Waylock's surprise, Caddigan had a wife, a woman as tall and homely as Caddigan, but possessed of high vivacity, charm and good will.

Caddigan introduced her as Pladge, and said sourly, "Pladge has beat me into Wedge. She's in stage design, and seems to be making a good thing of it."

"Stage design!" exclaimed Waylock. "That accounts for the—for the—"

Pladge Caddigan laughed. "For the antiques? Don't be embarrassed. Everyone thinks we're queer. But we just happen to like the simplicity, the feeling of material and mass in these old things. They're better designed than much of our present-day stuff."

"The room is distinctive enough," said Waylock.

"Yes, it does have style. But now if you'll excuse me, I've got my studying to do; I'm taking up kaleidochrome. It's fascinating, but complex as tritesimals."

Pladge took her odd angular self out of the room, and Caddigan's eyes followed her with somber pride. He turned back to Waylock, who was examining a section of the wall he had not noticed before. It was papered with slope reports from the Actuarian; the recurrence of lines, angles, curves, and printed statement made a pleasing pattern.

"There it is," came Caddigan's sardonic voice, "the record of our triumphs and defeats, naked and open for all to see. Our biography, the picture of our lives. Sometimes I think I'd prefer going glark. A short life and a merry one." His voice changed. "Well, here you are. What's your trouble?"

"I suppose I can rely on your discretion?" Waylock said.

Caddigan shook his head. "I'm not a discreet man. I'd be better off, no doubt, if I were."

"Well, can you regard what I tell you as confidential?"

"Frankly," said Caddigan, "I can't guarantee anything. I'm sorry if I appear churlish, but it's better that we risk no misunderstanding."

Waylock nodded. This was well enough, since he had no real problem. "I'd better keep my own counsel."

Caddigan nodded. "Wiser all around. Although it requires no very agile imagination to deduce what your problem might be."

"You're several steps ahead of me, Caddigan," said Waylock mildly.

"I intend to remain so. Do you want to hear how I construe your 'problem'?"

"Go ahead—construe."

"It clearly concerns Basil Thinkoup. There is no one else from whom you would have me withhold information. Now: what problem troubles you that you cannot take to Basil—a problem which concerns Basil, but which can be resolved not by Basil, but by someone close to him? You are an ambitious man, quite possibly ruthless."

"Today everyone is ruthless," said Waylock. Caddigan paid no heed.

"You must be asking yourself, how closely should I tie to Basil? Will he rise or fall? You'd rise with him, but you have no desire to share a fall. You want my estimate of Basil's future. When I propound this estimate, you will listen but reserve judgment, because you know that I represent a school opposed to Basil's energetic pragmatism. Nevertheless you consider me sufficiently honest and observant to make you a fair appraisal of Basil's prospects. Am I right?"

Waylock smilingly shook his head.

Caddigan's mouth took on a twist even wryer than usual. "Now," he said, "we have disposed of the superficialities; may I offer you a glass of tea?"

"Thank you, yes." Waylock leaned back. "Caddigan, apparently you've taken a dislike or at least a prejudice, to me. May I ask why?"

" 'Dislike' is the wrong word." Caddigan spoke with didactic precision. " 'Prejudice' is better, but still inexact. I feel that you are not a sincere psychiatrist. I feel that you have no concern for the advancement of knowledge, that you consider psychiatry a field where career-points are easy to pick up. I assure you," he said in his driest voice, "that they are not."

"How did Basil make Wedge so fast?"

"Luck."

Waylock pretended to think this over.

Presently Caddigan said, "Let me hint of a matter which I'm sure you don't apprehend."

"By all means."

"It's easy to be fooled by Basil. Now he exudes cheer and optimism. But you should have seen him before he made Wedge. He was teetering up and down into melancholia; he almost became one of the patients."

"I had no idea his case was that critical."

"One thing I'll say for Basil, he sincerely wants to improve the world." And Caddigan turned Waylock a sharp look. "He's discharged nine patients—not a bad record, all in all. But he has the ingenuous idea that if a little bit of his therapy discharges nine patients, a lot will discharge nine hundred. He's like an imbecile with a pepper shaker; a little makes his food taste good, therefore a lot will make it wonderful."

"Then you don't think he's going on up?"

"Nothing is impossible, naturally."

"What of this therapy he's been hinting about?"

Caddigan shrugged. "The imbecile with the pepper shaker."

Pladge Caddigan came jingling into the room, with a dozen bronze anklets and an equal number of bracelets. She wore a batik sari of red, gold, black and brown, a pair of absurd red sandals with green glass baubles.

"I thought," Caddigan remarked drily, "that you were studying your tectonics—or was it kaleidochrome?"

"Kaleidochrome. But I had this marvelous idea, and I had to get into costume to show it to myself."

"Grasshopper-thinking never slants lifeline," observed Caddigan.

"Oh, slope. Bah and nitchevo."

"You'll sing a different song, when I make Wedge and then Third."

Pladge rolled up her eyes. "Sometimes I'm sorry I'm Wedge. Who wants to be Amaranth?"

"Me," said Waylock with a grin. He approved of Pladge, and was amused to notice that Seth, realizing this, was annoyed.

"I do too," Seth said stiffly. "And so do you, if you'd only talk sense."

"I am talking sense. In the old days they feared extinction—"

"Pladge!" said Seth in a curt voice, with a side glance at Waylock.

Pladge flourished her jingling wrists. "Don't be such a silly prude. All of us are mortal—except the Amaranth."

"It's hardly a nice thing to talk about."

"I don't see why. Let's bring these things into the open, that's what I say."

"Don't mind me," said Waylock. "Bring them out as far as you like."

Pladge settled into one of the stark old chairs. "I have a theory. Want to hear it?"

"Of course."

"Pladge," Caddigan remonstrated, but Pladge ignored him.

"Latent in everyone, so I believe, is a dissolution urge. There might be fewer patients in the palliatories if we were open and forthright about it."

"Nonsense," said Seth. "I'm a trained psychiatrist. That urge to which you refer has little if any connection with the catatonics. They're victims of anxiety and melancholia."

"Perhaps so, but look how people act when they go to Carnevalle!"

Seth nodded at Waylock. "He's an authority on Carnevalle; he worked there seven years."

Pladge gave Waylock a look of delight and admiration. "How utterly lovely to live among all the color and lights, to meet people while they're off guard!"

"It was interesting enough," said Waylock.

"Tell me," said Pladge breathlessly, "there's a rumor about Carnevalle; I wonder if you can verify it."

"What's the rumor?"

"Well, Carnevalle is supposed to be outside the law, isn't it?"

Waylock shrugged. "More or less. People do things they'd get arrested for in Clarges."

"Or that they'd be ashamed to do," muttered Seth.

Pladge ignored him. "How deep does this lawlessness go? I mean—well, the rumor I heard was that in one of the Houses, in a very secret exclusive depraved House, people paid to see extinction! On young men and beautiful girls!"

"Pladge," Seth croaked, "what are you saying? Are you completely insane?"

"I've heard even," Pladge went on in a hoarse whisper, leaning forward, "that not only do they transite people for profit, but that if you have enough money—thousands and thousands of florins—you can buy a person, and despatch him or her yourself, in any way you want. . . ."

"Pladge!" Seth's hands kneaded the arms of his chair. "This kind of talk is absolutely vile!"

Pladge snapped, "Seth, I heard this rumor and I wonder what Mr. Waylock has to say. If he can verify it, I think something should be done!"

"I agree with you." Waylock thought of Carleon and his Museum, of Rubel and the Twisting Place, of Loriot and other Berbers. "I've met this rumor," he said," but I consider it just that—rumor. Or at least, I've never spoken to anyone with direct knowledge of such doings. As you know, visitors to Carnevalle do play at—at, well, transition: they throw darts at frogs, electrocute fish with probes; but I hardly think they consider what they're doing; it's a subconscious release."

Seth turned away in disgust. "Nonsense."

"Now, Seth, *you're* the nonsensical one. You're a scientist, but you ignore any ideas leading where you don't choose to look."

Seth paused a moment, then said in a mock-gallant voice. "I'm sure Mr. Waylock is deriving an entirely false impression of you."

"No, no," said Waylock. "I'm charmed, I'm interested."

"You see?" chirped Pladge. "I knew he was. Mr. Waylock has the look of a man without prejudices or preconceptions."

"Mr. Waylock," said Seth sourly, "is—shall I say—a predator. He is driving up-slope; how and whose feet he steps on he cares not a whit."

Waylock grinned and settled back into his chair.

"At least he's no hypocrite," Pladge declared. "I think he's nice."

"A handsome face, a good manner—"

"Seth," said Pladge, "aren't you afraid you'll offend Mr. Waylock?"

Seth smiled. "Waylock is a realist. He'll hardly be offended by the truth."

Inwardly uncomfortable, Waylock forced himself to sit easily. "You're half-right and half-wrong," he said. "I have certain ambitions—"

A musical note interrupted him; the commu screen over the radiator mantel lit up to depict the man who stood outside the door. He wore the formal black uniform of the assassins, complete with tall black hat.

"Good heavens," cried Pladge, "they've come for us! I knew I should have studied tonight!"

"Can't you ever be serious?" snapped Seth. "Go see what he wants."

Pladge opened the door; the assassin said courteously, "Mrs. Pladge Caddigan?"

"Yes."

"According to our records, you have never filed with us your formal declaration of Wedge status; I believe we've sent you several notifications."

"Oh," said Pladge with a fluttery laugh. "I guess I've just never got around to it. But you know I'm Wedge, don't you?"

"Of course."

"Then why do I need to notify you?"

The assassin's voice was cool. "Each of our regulations is designed to prevent some specific difficulty of misunderstanding, and you can make our work a great deal easier by co-operating with us."

Pladge said in a light voice, "Oh well, if you want to put it on a personal basis . . . Do you have the form with you?"

The assassin gave her an envelope; Pladge closed the door, flung the envelope to a table. "They make such a fuss about nothing. . . . Oh well, I suppose it's the way we live. It's two sides of the penny. If it weren't for the assassins, there'd be no Amaranth. And since all of us want to be Amaranth, we've got to help the assassins."

"Exactly," said Seth.

"A vicious circle; chasing ourselves like hoop-snakes. Whither, whither?"

Caddigan looked sidewise at Waylock. "Pladge has become a Whitherer, and now it's all I hear."

"A 'Whitherer'?"

"A person who asks 'Whither?' " said Pladge. "It's as simple as that. We've formed an association and we all ask 'Whither?' together. You must come to one of our meetings."

"I'd like to. Where do you hold them?"

"Oh, here, there, anywhere. Sometimes at Carnevalle in the Hall of Revelation."

"With the rest of the crackpots," muttered Caddigan.

Pladge took no offense. "It's convenient, and we're not conspicuous. We've had some excellent sessions."

There was a short pause; Waylock rose to his feet. "I think I'll be on my way home."

"You never did mention your problem," Seth remarked gravely.

"The problem will keep," said Waylock. "In fact I've worked it out just sitting here, listening and watching you." He turned to Pladge. "Good night."

"Good night, Mr. Waylock. I hope you'll call again!"

Waylock looked at the silent Seth. "I'd like to very much."

2

In the morning, when Waylock arrived at the palliatory, he found Seth Caddigan already at his desk. He acknowledged Waylock's arrival with no more than a nod, and Waylock set about his duties. Several times during the morning Caddigan came through the ward, looking right and left with a critical eye, but Waylock had been careful, and Caddigan had no fault to find.

Shortly before noon, Basil Thinkoup came hurrying by. He saw Waylock and stopped short. "Hard at work, eh?" He looked at his watch. "Time for lunch; come along, join me, I'll have Caddigan look after the ward."

In the cafeteria they seated themselves at the table where they had previously lunched. The view through the hemisphere was spectacular. A sudden storm had blown in from over the mountains; ragged clouds flew through the sky; black rain-brooms swept the River Chant; trees in the park jerked to sudden gusts of wind.

Basil glanced out, then turned his eyes away, as if the view distracted him from matters more important.

"Gavin," said Basil, "it's a hard thing to say—but you're the only man in the palliatory I have faith in. Everyone else considers me a lunatic." He laughed. "To be utterly blunt, I need your help."

"I'm flattered," said Waylock. "Also surprised. You need *my* help?"

"It's a simple process of elimination. Much as I admire you, I'd prefer to work with someone experienced in the field." He shook his head. "It won't do. Those above me consider me an 'empiricist'; those below me, who normally would owe me respect, such as Seth, become infected and consequently I'm on my own."

"Today everyone is on his own."

"You are right," said Basil, rather sententiously. He leaned toward Waylock, tapped him on the wrist. "Well, what do you say?"

"I'll be glad for the opportunity to help you."

"Good!" said Basil. "In a nutshell, I want to try a new therapy. On Maximilian Hertzog—one of our choicest specimens."

Waylock remembered that Seth Caddigan had mentioned his name.

"A case of exaggerated catatonia," said Basil. "As a waxer, he's immobile—like marble; as a wingding, he's awesome."

"How do you need me?" was Waylock's cautious question.

Basil looked right and left with great care before responding. "Gavin," he said huskily, "this time I've got the answer—a specific cure for the psychosis. Effective, so I believe, on eighty per cent of our patients."

"Hm." Waylock considered. "I wonder."

"You wonder what?"

"If we return the palliatory population to the world outside, we increase the concentration and competition there."

Basil's face pursed into a thoughtful expression. "You imply that we should make no effort to heal sick minds?"

"Not necessarily," said Waylock. "But it seems possible that increased competition will drive more participants into psychosis."

"Possibly," said Basil without enthusiasm.

"Curing the present palliatory population might return us a crop twice as large."

Basil pursed his lips, and said with impatient energy, "Why attempt any cure whatever, then? These patients are our responsibility; they might be ourselves; in fact, except for the intervention of—" Basil hesitated, and Waylock remembered Caddigan's remarks about Basil's own melancholia. "Well, in any event, it's not ours to judge our fellows; this is the function of the Actuarian. We can merely work at the tasks we have set ourselves to."

Waylock shrugged. "As you say, it's not our problem. Our responsibility is to cure, no more. The Prytaneon establishes public policy, the Actuarian weighs our lives, the assassins maintain equity; those are their functions."

"Correct," said Basil, blowing out his cheeks. "Now, as I say, I've made one or two tests with the therapy and I have achieved a certain success. Maximilian Hertzog is an advanced, I may say, an extreme example. I believe that if I can cure, or significantly help Maximilian Hertzog, I have proved my case." Basil sat back in his chair.

"It appears to me," said Waylock, "that you might very well make Third, if things go as well as you hope."

"Third, possibly Verge. This is a remarkable achievement!"

"If it works."

"Which is what we hope to prove," said Basil.

"May I inquire the nature of this therapy?"

Basil looked cautiously to the side. "I'm not quite ready to discuss it. I will say that in contradistinction to usual therapies, it is fast and violent—shock treatment. Naturally Hertzog's condition may be aggravated. In which case—" He smiled wistfully—"I will be in trouble. They will accuse me of terrible things—using human beings for guinea pigs. And I suppose it's true enough. But, I ask you, of what other use are these poor people? How can they better dedicate their miserable lives?" Now Basil became crisp. "I need your help. If I am successful, you will profit by association. By this token, you also run a risk."

"How so?"

Basil looked scornfully across the cafeteria. "The authorities have small sympathy with my ideas."

"I'll help you," said Waylock.

3

Basil Thinkoup led Waylock through the palliatory. Through ward after ward they walked, past interminable rows of beds, each with its blank white face, and at last came to a door of ribbed magnesium studded with stinger cells. Basil spoke into a mesh and the door slid aside.

They passed through a short white-tiled tunnel into Ward 101. It was a wide pentagonal chamber, with plastic stalls around the periphery. The patients lay on white canvas disks supported by metal hoops. Over each patient hung a second hoop, webbed with elastic bands, ready to be dropped upon the patient the instant he evinced signs of the manic phase. The patients wore no more than a basket of perforated metal around their loins; the purpose of which, so Basil explained, was to prevent the patient from maiming himself in his frenzy.

"The strength and desperation of these people is incredible. You see the swaddle-disk above the bed?"

"It looks efficient," Waylock said.

"It is. Each band of webbing is tested for tensile strength of fourteen hundred pounds. Ample, wouldn't you say?"

"Ample, certainly."

"Roy Altwenn, in his fury, burst three of them. Maximilian

Hertzog has burst two on three different occasions!"

Waylock shook his head in wonder. "And which is Hertzog?"

Basil pointed through the capsules, where the patients lay like insects metamorphosing in great glass eggs. Hertzog, not a tall man, was exceedingly wide and thick, with muscles knotted like tamarack roots.

"Amazing," Basil declared reverently, "the physical tone these fellows maintain! One would expect a general atrophy—but they maintain the physique of circus athletes!"

"A subject for research, possibly," Waylock remarked. "Could the catatonic mind secrete a hormone, a muscle builder, something of the sort?"

Basil pursed his lips. "It's certainly possible . . ." He frowned and nodded. "Yes, I must look into that. An interesting conjecture. . . . More likely, the muscular tone results from the constant strain and tension; notice the expression of the faces. They're quite unlike other cattos."

Waylock saw that this was true; each face was a mask of haggard despair, each set of teeth was clenched, each nose appeared pinched and bloodless, like carved bone. Maximilian Hertzog's face was the wildest and most desperate of all. "And you think you can cure him?"

"Yes, yes. First—we take him to my office."

Waylock considered the thick body of Maximilian Hertzog, which, clenched and intense, seemed like a boiler under tremendous pressure. He spoke in a hushed voice. "Is it safe?"

Basil laughed. "Naturally, we take every precaution. Such as half a grain of meioral. He'll be meek as a mouse."

He entered Hertzog's capsule, pushed the head of a hypospray against Hertzog's neck. There was a hiss as the sedative was blasted into Hertzog's bloodstream. Basil backed out of the capsule, signalled.

Two attendants brought a carrier, edged it into the capsule, passed straps under Hertzog's shoulders, hips, and knees. One of the attendants produced a form which Basil signed, and this was the only formality. They powered the carrier, it lifted, and they towed it, swaying under Hertzog's weight, to the special lift-tunnel, which ran under the floor of the ward.

"Now we can go," said Basil. "Hertzog will be delivered to my private workroom."

4

Basil and Waylock passed through the outer office, where
Seth Caddigan sat at his files and charts. He glanced up, returned to his work. They entered Basil's office, crossed to a
door in the far wall. Basil played a code on four buttons; the
door slid back, they entered Basil's laboratory.

It was a small room, modestly equipped. To one side was a
pallet, upholstered in white saniflex; to the other was a counter,
with various instruments, screens, measuring and recording
equipment, and a cabinet, stocked with bottles, cartons, flasks
and books.

Basil crossed the room, slid back a panel; there, suspended
from the pale tube of slave-light was the relaxed body of
Maximilian Hertzog.

Basil rubbed his hands. "Here he is, the instrument by which
we shall project ourselves up-slope. And in the process, poor
Hertzog will be cured, we hope."

They swung Hertzog out and laid him on the pallet. Basil
loosed the straps, Waylock pulled them free. "Now," said
Basil, "here is the procedure. In a certain sense it is—" He
paused—"Well, perhaps it is best defined as attacking the
source of the trouble."

He straightened Maximilian Hertzog's heavy frame, arranged the arms and legs. Stupefied by the sedative, Hertzog's
face showed less evidence of internal strain. Basil went to an
instrument panel, flipped several switches, returned to Hertzog,
pressed a metal cylinder to the great chest. Spots of light
flickered on a screen; at the bottom a number appeared: 38.

"Pulse is a little slow," said Basil. "We'll wait just a few
minutes. Meioral wears off quite rapidly."

"Then what?" asked Waylock. "Will he be catto or manic?"

"Probably catto. Sit down, Gavin, and I'll try to explain the
procedure."

Waylock seated himself on a stool; Basil leaned back against
the pallet. The pulse-counter rested on Hertzog's chest; the
screen made its intermittent report, and the number now read
41.

"In the schizoid mind," Basil began, "the circuits are disturbed or disarranged to a greater or less extent. The catto's

mind is different. It corresponds to a stalled motor; it has been halted by an apparently inexorable obstacle."

Waylock nodded his comprehension. The pulses on the screen were coming slightly faster; the number was now 46.

"Naturally," said Basil, "there have been endless theories and practices. They all can be classified under one or another fundamental variety: analysis, which is applicable only to the milder troubles and where communication is still open; hypnosis or suggestion, which constitutes a superimposition upon the basically unsound foundation; drugs, very useful aids to the above processes, and of a certain usefulness in themselves. Their action, however, is merely a numbing of the malfunctioning parts, and is by no means permanent. Then there is shock, by chemical, glandular, electrical, mechanical or spiritual methods. Under certain circumstances shock produces surprising results; more often the shock is traumatic in itself.

"There is surgery, which is actual excision of the disturbed section; there is electro-staging, which is the blurring or erasing of all circuits. There is likewise the vortex principle, or addling of the entire brain. And lastly there is the system proposed by Gostwald Pevishevsky, identical to the process by which the Amaranth produce their surrogates: the development of a new individual from a cultured cell, a process which hardly can be described as therapy, although such is the eventual effect. Naturally I considered all of these processes, but I was dissatisfied. None of them appeared to attack the source of the catto's trouble—which is merely his frustration and melancholia. To cure the catto we must either remove the obstacle—which is to say, change our entire system of life, manifestly impractical—or we must arrange the catto mind so that the obstacle no longer appears insuperable."

Waylock nodded. "All this I follow."

Basil smiled almost bitterly. "It seems simple, you think? Correct—but it is astonishing how few of the proposed therapies take account of these basic principles. How to remove this sense of frustration from the catto mind? Suggestion or hypnosis are obviously too weak; surgery is too extreme, since the catto has no organic difficulty. Shock and vorticizing are of no application, since the catto circuits are all in good order. Electro-staging or drugs seem rather more hopeful, since they erase or numb; the problem is to make them selective."

Waylock's eye went to the screen. Hertzog's pulse was 54.

"I located a basic clue in the work of Helmut and Gerard, of the Neuro-Chemical Institute," said Basil. "I refer, of course, to their studies of synaptical chemistry—in short, what happens when an impulse travels from nerve to nerve, which is the basic process of thought. Their findings are vastly interesting. When a stimulus is passed from one nerve to another, no less than twenty-one consecutive chemical reactions occur at the synapse. If any of these reactions is halted, the stimulus fails to pass the synapse."

Waylock said, "I think I see where you're leading."

"Here we have a suggestion on a means to control the thought processes of our catto. What we would like to do is to extirpate memory of his obstacle or problem. How to be selective? The obvious way is to attack one of the compounds, or its catalyst, at one or more synapses of the particular thought track. In order to be selective we choose a compound which is fugitive and which appears only during the process of thought transfer. I settled upon the substance Helmut and Gerard label heptant, because it has a highly definite chemical identity. The problem now is merely the formulation of a chelate which will weld to heptant, and remove it permanently from operative function. I farmed out the problem to Didactor Vauxine Tudderstell of the Maxart Bio-Chemical Clinic." Basil went to the cabinet, brought forth an orange bottle. "Here it is—anti-heptant. Water-soluble, non-toxic, highly effective. When it is present in the cerebral blood supply, it acts like the eraser button of a recorder, canceling whatever circuits are active, but inactive toward those not in use."

"Basil," Waylock declared in complete sincerity, "this has the ring of true genius."

"One serious problem remained," said Basil, smiling. "We wouldn't want to cancel any portion of our patient's vocabulary, which would seem an inevitable by-product of the treatment. By sheer luck, the anti-heptant bypasses the vocabulary. Why this should be, I don't know, and at the present time don't care; I only rejoice."

"You've tested this anti-heptant?"

"In a limited sense, upon a patient whose trouble was only minor. Maximilian Hertzog will be the crucial subject."

"His pulse rate is approaching normal," said Waylock. "If we're not careful, he'll—"

Basil made an easy gesture. "No cause for worry; we can

always drop the swaddle." He indicated a harness suspended above the pallet. "In fact, our aim is to stimulate him to mania."

Waylock raised his eyebrows. "I should think our greatest concern would be to prevent it."

Basil shook his head. "We want nothing in his mind except his obstacle and his troubles. Then we administer anti-heptant. Whisk! The heptant of the malevolent thought processes is completely extirpated; the circuit is broken and with it goes the obstacle itself. The man is sane."

"As simple as that!"

"Simple and elegant." Basil peered down into Hertzog's face. "He's returning to normal. Now Gavin, you handle the swaddle and meter the anti-heptant."

"How do I proceed?"

"First we arrange a gauge to keep us informed as to the concentration of anti-heptant in Hertzog's brain. If we administer too much, we blank out too much of his mind: the process continues too long." Basil brought a contact calipers from the cabinet, fitted it to Hertzog's head. "The anti-heptant is faintly radioactive; we can easily measure its coming and going. . . . First we standardize our instrument." Basil led a wire to the console of his screen, plugged it into a socket. A small area glowed purple. Basil twisted a dial, the spot of light became magenta, red, vermilion, back to red, and, as Basil adjusted the dial, remained red. "This is our gauge. We want a sufficient concentration of anti-heptant to color the light yellow, but not enough to tinge it green. Follow me?"

"Perfectly."

"Good." Basil now prepared a seep hypodermic, and without ceremony thrust it into Hertzog's carotid artery. Hertzog twitched. His pulse rose to 70.

Basil connected the tube to a reservoir. "Now, Gavin, notice this button. Each time you touch it you release a milligram of anti-heptant into Hertzog's head. Here is the trigger to the swaddle. When I give the word, drop it. Be careful not to catch me underneath it. When I signal, tap the anti-heptant button. Understand?"

Waylock said he did.

Basil consulted the screen. "I'll treat him with a stimulant, restore him to normal catatonia." Selecting a hypospray from his cabinet, he blasted a drug into Hertzog's blood.

Hertzog's chest heaved; his breath came deep and heavy; the expression of his face pinched into its characteristic intensity. Waylock noticed him quiver, and saw his fingers flexing. "Careful, he's ready to go winging."

"Good," said Basil, "that's what we want." He surveyed the arrangements. "Be quick on the swaddle, if necessary."

Waylock nodded. "I'm ready."

"Good." Basil bent over the massive body. "Hertzog. Maximilian Hertzog!"

Hertzog seemed to take a slow breath.

"Hertzog!" cried Basil in a hectoring voice. "Maximilian Hertzog! Wake up!"

Hertzog twitched.

"Hertzog. You must wake up. I have news for you. Good news. Maximilian Hertzog!" Hertzog's eyelashes flickered. Basil said to Waylock, "Anti-heptant."

Waylock tapped the button. The tube to the needle pulsed, and chemical seeped into Hertzog's neck. After a slight pause the red light became orange and brightened to orange-yellow. Basil watched the color, nodded.

"Hertzog! Wake up. Good news!"

Hertzog's eyes opened a slit. The yellow began to deepen to red. "Anti-heptant," said Basil. Waylock tapped the button; the light became yellow.

"Hertzog," said Basil in a low urgent voice, "you are a failure. You won't make Third—*anti-heptant, Gavin*—Hertzog, you tried hard, but you made mistakes. You have only yourself to blame. You've thrown away life, Hertzog."

A low sound like a rising wind came from Hertzog's throat. Basil beckoned for anti-heptant. "Maximilian Hertzog," he said in a hurried voice, "you are inferior. Other people can make Third—but not you. You have failed. You wasted your time. You studied the wrong techniques."

Veins appeared on Hertzog's forehead. The sound rasped loud in his throat. "Anti-heptant, Gavin, anti-heptant."

Waylock tapped the button, the light glowed yellow. Basil returned to the quivering form. "Hertzog—remember how you threw life away? Remember the chances you missed? The people who are no wiser than you but who are Third and Verge? And you have nothing before you except a ride in the high black car!"

Maximilian Hertzog slowly sat up on the pallet. He looked at Basil, he turned his head and fixed his stare on Waylock.

No one spoke. Basil crouched; Waylock was unable to move or shift his stance. The light on the screen was once more red.

Waylock finally asked, "More anti-heptant?"

"No," said Basil in a nervous voice, "not just yet. . . . We don't want to blot out too much."

"Blot out too much what?" asked Maximilian Hertzog. He reached to his head, felt the caliper contacts, the dangling tube stuck into his neck. "What is all *this?*"

"Please," said Basil, making a quick restraining gesture. "Do not touch them; they are a necessary part of the treatment."

"Treatment?" Hertzog was puzzled. "Am I ill? I feel fine." He rubbed his forehead. "I've never felt better. Are you sure you've got the right man? I'm—" He frowned. "My name is . . ."

Basil glanced significantly at Waylock. Anti-heptant had erased Hertzog's recollection of his name.

"Your name," said Basil, "is Maximilian Hertzog."

"Ah. Yes—that's it." Hertzog looked around the room. "Where am I?"

"You are in the hospital," said Basil soothingly. "We are taking care of you."

Maximilian Hertzog shot him a keen hard glance. Basil continued. "I think it would be better if you just lay back, relaxed. In a few days you'll be well and off about your business."

Hertzog sank back on the pallet, looking suspiciously from Basil to Waylock. "Just where am I? What's wrong with me? I still haven't any notion." He caught sight of the swaddle hanging above him. "What—?" He shot a swift glance at Waylock; his eyes focused on the right chest of Waylock's uniform, where the words *Balliasse Palliatory* were embroidered.

"Balliasse Palliatory," croaked Hertzog. "Is that what's wrong? I'm a waxer?" His throat corded, his voice came hoarse. "Let me out of here, there's nothing wrong with me; I'm as sane as anyone!" He ripped off the cerebral contacts, the tube of the seep-needle.

Basil anxiously interposed. "No, no, you must lie quiet!"

Hertzog swung Basil aside with a sweep of his arm and started to climb to his feet.

Waylock released the swaddle; the harness bore Hertzog back to the pallet. He began to roar and froth, and lapsed into a screaming frenzy, his arms thrust up through the holes of the harness, grasping and groping like the legs of an upturned beetle.

Basil dodged close with the hypospray, and presently Hertzog was silent again.

Waylock released his pent breath. "Phew!" Basil sat down heavily. "Well, Gavin, what do you think?"

"For a short while he was rational," said Waylock carefully. "The process certainly shows promise."

" 'Promise'!" exclaimed Basil. "Gavin, there's never been a technique to show such spectacular results!"

They removed the swaddle from the recumbent hulk, straightened him on the pallet, returned him to the tube.

"Tomorrow," said Basil, "we'll probe rather deeper into the cross-connections. We'll not only have to root out the immediate stimuli; we'll have to clean out the subsidiary elements."

When they returned through Basil's office, they found Seth Caddigan putting away his work. "Well, gentlemen," he asked, "how did the investigations proceed?"

Basil's reply was casual. "Well enough."

Caddigan gave him a skeptical side glance, started to speak, but shrugged and turned away.

Basil and Waylock crossed Riverside Road to one of the ancient taverns. They took a seat in a booth built of waxy dark wood and ordered beer.

Waylock toasted Basil's achievements; Basil replied with a hope for Waylock's future.

"Certainly," said Basil, "you are well shed of Carnevalle. By the way, the Amaranth woman, The Jacynth Martin, called me on the commu last night."

Waylock stared at him.

"I can't imagine what she wanted," said Basil, swirling the beer in his stein. "We chatted a few moments, then she thanked me and dimmed out. A fascinating creature." Basil tilted his stein high, set it down with a thump. "Well, it's home for me, Gavin Waylock."

Outside the tavern the two men parted company. Basil took the tube to his modest apartment on Semaphore Hill; Waylock walked thoughtfully along Riverside Road.

The Jacynth was curious as to the manner of her passing. Well, there was little that could be learned from Basil, and nothing from himself, unless he chose to speak.

A Monster. Waylock smiled hollowly. So would the people of Clarges describe him. A man of dread who plundered vitality.

In the case of The Jacynth Martin the crime had been concealed—most often the case where an Amaranth was concerned. Waylock recalled with bitterness the passing of The Abel Mandeville, seven years before.

He came to another of the old river taverns, the Tusitala, standing on piles out over the dark stream. He entered, drank another mug of beer and ate a pastry cornucopia full of golden seafood.

The wall screen displayed the face of a new commentator. Waylock absorbed the news of the day with his dinner—affairs of only topical importance. The Commission of Natural Resources had authorized the reclamation of Lost Lake Swamp, in the south of Glade County, opening a hundred thousand new acres for cultivation. On the strength of this expectation, a population increase of one hundred and twenty-three thousand persons would be allowed, enlarging the scope of every phyle. The originator of the scheme, Guy Laisle, was shown receiving congratulations on the decision. The commentator predicted that Laisle would almost certainly make Amaranth by virtue of his success.

In the next item, Chancellor Claude Imish performed his age-old ritual of calling the Prytaneon into session. Imish was a big loose-featured man with a smile full of conscious charm. He had no particular talents; few were required for conduct of his now archaic office.

"Home from outer space," said the commentator, "is the ship *Star Enterprise!* The intrepid voyagers visited the Pleiades, explored the Dog Star and the ten Dog-planets, brought home a cargo of curios not yet made public."

Next the commentator presented a two-minute interview with Caspar Jarvis, Director-General of the Assassins, a tall heavy man with a pale face, thick black eyebrows, burning black eyes. Jarvis spoke of the alarming activity of the Weirds and the Berbers, who infested the darker areas of Carnevalle. Unless conditions showed a turn for the better, it would be necessary to post a Special Force in Carnevalle. Unspeakable deeds had lately been reported at Carnevalle. The people of Clarges demanded a return to decency.

The commentator finished with his Vitalistics report—gossip of those who had broken into the higher phyle, inside hints, new twists and shortcuts to aid the listeners in the race up-slope.

When Waylock departed the Tusitala, night had fallen over Clarges. The sky glowed with reflected lights. Standing on the sidewalk he could feel the sub-audible hiss of the city, the quiver of ten million minds.

A few miles further south lay Elgenburg and the spaceport. Waylock resisted an impulse to visit the *Star Enterprise*. He rode the Riverside Road slideway downstream, past the wharves and docks, past the dark warehouses of Wibleside, into the Marbone District. At Marbone Station, he descended to the tube terminus, entered a capsule and dialed for Ester-hazy Station. He returned to the surface almost beside the Cafe Dalmatia.

He took a seat at his favorite table and presently was joined by an acquaintance, who introduced him to Odin Laszlo, a weedy, owl-eyed young man who strove as mathematician in the Actuarian. Laszlo was making a secondary career of choreography. Learning that Waylock strove at Balliasse Pallia-tory, Laszlo became excited.

"Tell me about it! I've had in mind a ballet, unique if rather macabre: a day in the life of a catto. I show dawn and the catto brain like a clear crystal. Then the slow building of tension, the culmination of the wingding; the restraint and the pitiful anguish. Then night and the dark desolation, and the slow waning into the early hours."

It made Waylock uncomfortable. "You're taking me back to work, and I came here to escape it," he complained.

He drank his customary glass of tea, bade good evening to his acquaintances and returned up Allemand Avenue to Phariot Way, and so to his apartment.

He opened the door. The Jacynth Martin sat quietly on his couch.

VIII

THE JACYNTH rose to her feet. "I hope you will excuse me. The door was open, so I made free to enter."

Waylock knew the door had been locked. "I am glad you did." He took a long step forward, put his arms about her, and kissed her warmly. "I've been waiting for you."

The Jacynth extricated herself, looked at Waylock uncertainly. She wore a pale blue leotard with white tunic, white sandals, a dark blue cloak lined with white. Her hair hung in a loose golden flow, her pupils had dilated, her eyes seemed large and dark.

"You are extraordinary," said Waylock. "If you would register, you would win to Amaranth on your beauty alone."

He put out his arms once more, but she stepped back.

"Let me disabuse you," she said coldly. "Whatever your relationship to the previous Jacynth, it does not extend to me. I am the new Jacynth!"

"The new Jacynth? But your name is not Jacynth!"

"I am the best judge of that." She moved a step farther back, looked him over from head to toe. "You are—Gavin Waylock?"

"Of course."

"You greatly resemble another—a man named Grayven Warlock."

"The Grayven Warlock is no longer alive. I am his relict." The Jacynth raised her eyebrows. "Indeed?"

"Indeed. But I don't understand why you are here."

"I will explain," she said crisply. "I am The Jacynth Martin. A month ago my previous version was destemporized at Carnevalle. It seems that you escorted me during a certain part of the evening. We arrived at the Pamphylia together, and were joined by Basil Thinkoup, and then The Albert Pondiferry and The Denis Lestrange. Immediately prior to my passing, you and Basil Thinkoup departed. Is this all correct?"

"I must arrange my thoughts," said Waylock. "Evidently your name is not Mira Martin and you are not glark?"

"I am The Jacynth Martin."

"And you were fatally taken?"

"Did you not realize this?"

"We saw you relax upon the table. Apparently you were overcome by intoxicants. The Albert and The Denis were attending you. We departed." He waved a hand toward his couch. "Sit down; let me serve you wine."

"No. I came here tonight only for information."

"Very well then. What do you want to know?"

Her eyes blazed. "The manner of my passing! Someone evil robbed me of life. I would know his name, and bring his depravity home to him."

"Depravity is hardly the word," Waylock pointed out gently. "You still have your life. You stand before me, you breathe, your blood flows, you radiate life and beauty."

"That is how a Monster might justify his crime."

"You suggest that I am a Monster, that I took your vitality?"

"I made no such accusation; I commented on the style of your thinking."

"Then I shall refrain from thinking," said Waylock. "Anyway, I should prefer to spend the time in a pleasanter form of activity." He reached for her again.

She took a step back, flushing in anger and embarrassment. "Whatever your relationship with my predecessor was, it is now canceled; you are a stranger to me."

"I will gladly begin at the beginning," said Waylock. "Come, won't you drink a glass of good wine?"

"I don't want a drink, I want knowledge! I must know how I was transited." She clenched her fists. "I must know and I will know! Tell me!"

Waylock shrugged. "There is little to tell."

"You and I met—where did we meet? When? Did you not work at Carnevalle, before the House of Life?"

"I see you have had a good gossip with Basil Thinkoup."

"Yes. One month ago you strove at Carnevalle. Suddenly you gave over this occupation of seven years, you registered in Brood, you changed your life. Why?"

Waylock advanced on her. She fell back until the wall halted her. He put his hands on her shoulders. "Your questions are impertinent."

"So!" she said in a low voice. "How simple it was to find you, how clear the guilt on your face."

"You have made up your mind; you insist on thinking evil of me."

She put her hands on his wrists, pushed them up and away from her shoulders. "I won't have your hands on me."

"Then there is no object in your presence here."

"You will not answer my questions freely and willingly?"

"No—not under the pressure of your assumptions."

"Then you will answer against your will. Mind-search is the means to truth, and that is how it will be." She marched past him, and to the door. Here she paused, looked at him once more, and departed.

2

Waylock listened to the sound of her retreating footsteps. For several minutes he stood motionless, deep in thought. If there had been any trace of suspicion in her mind, how had she dared to visit him alone, so late at night?

A thought struck him, he looked around the apartment, then began a swift search. Under the couch he found the transmitter, a box smaller than half his hand. Someone evidently had listened to the conversation, alert for any sound of struggle. This, then, explained her boldness.

Waylock ground the transmitter under his heel and threw the wreckage into the disposal chute.

He broke a bulb of wine from the stem, slumped back on the couch, and tried to arrange his thoughts.

The Jacynth Martin need only sign a warrant of complaint. The assassins would conduct him to a cell of inquiry. Three tribunes would be on hand to guard him against irrelevant probing, but any information pertinent to the charge would emerge from his mind.

If he demonstrated himself innocent, The Jacynth became liable for damages. If he were guilty, he would find short shrift; the world would know no more of Gavin Waylock.

Waylock morosely considered his apartment. His own mind would betray him; there was no way to defeat mind-search. . . . He jumped to his feet. Mind-search! Let them search his mind! They would learn nothing! Being a Monster obviously lubricated his mental machinery. The taboo was like a dike pressing back a wild sea; break the dike and the whole sea flowed in.

He paced the floor, thinking furiously. Half an hour passed. Then he seated himself by his recorder and dictated two lengthy statements. The first he packed in a carton; the second he left on the recorder, together with a brief note of explanation addressed to himself.

Then, setting an alarm to call him at seven o'clock, he sought his couch.

3

Waylock arrived early at the palliatory, passing the nurses and orderlies coming off night shift.

A reception clerk demanded identification. Waylock satisfied him, rode the lift to the third floor.

On Basil's desk the recorder signal was blinking; Waylock pressed the button to learn the message.

"From Superintendant Benberry's office," spoke a female voice. "Attention Basil Thinkoup." Then came Benberry's reedy voice. "Basil, please check with me at once. I am seriously disturbed. We must formulate some policy to render your research less disturbing to the Board. These undisciplined efforts must proceed no further. See me before you proceed with your work."

Waylock went through the office and into the workshop. There he selected a hypospray, and charged it from the orange bottle of anti-heptant. There was very little left. But Basil Thinkoup would have no more need for anti-heptant. On an occasion such as this one it might prove invaluable.

He transferred the contents into another bottle, replenished the orange bottle with water. Returning into Basil's office, he seated himself at the desk, fitted the first of his reels into the recorder.

He raised the hypospray, and placed the nozzle to his neck. Then he hesitated, put down the hypospray, and wrote a note which he laid on the desk. Once again he took up the hypospray, set it in position and pressed the trigger.

He waited, concentrating on the task. *Keep mind blank.* Every thought, every idea must be erased. *Think of nothing. Think of nothing.* His brain was like a bruise, sensitive as sunburn. . . . *My name is Gavin Waylock.* . . .

He only thought it once; after that he knew nothing of his name. Exuding tiny beads of sweat, he blanked his consciousness. *Nothing, nothing, nothing.* The recorder began to speak. He heard his voice describing the death of The Jacynth Martin, and the preceding events.

The recording ended. Waylock closed his eyes, lay back, warm, lethargic, relaxed. The anti-heptant dissipated itself. Waylock's brain began to function; thoughts moved and wavered, indistinct, like shapes in heavy fog. . . . He sat up in the chair. The note he had written caught his eye. He picked it up and read.

> *I have just removed the memory of an experience from my mind. Perhaps I have forgotten other things. My name is Gavin Waylock. I am the relict of The Grayven Warlock, if anyone should ask. My address is 414 Phariot Way, Apartment 820."*

There was other information and memoranda, ending with:

> *. . . Other lapses in memory to be expected. Do not wonder about subject erased. It is possible that the Special Squad may call; there may be a mind-search in connection with the violent passing of The Jacynth Martin, of which I know nothing.*
> NOTE: *Erase the final fifteen minutes on the recorder. Do not listen to it, as this will defeat purpose of memory-blotting. Be sure to erase recorder.*

Waylock read the note twice, then thoughtfully erased the recording. So his name was Gavin Waylock: it had a familiar sound. . . .

He returned the hypospray to the workroom, then removed all traces of his visit.

Seth Caddigan arrived a few moments later; he glanced at Waylock in surprise. "What brings you here so early?"

"Diligence," said Waylock. "Conscientiousness."

"Astonishing." Caddigan went to his desk, sorted out his papers. "Nothing seems to be missing."

Waylock ignored him. A moment later Caddigan said, "There's a rumor going around the palliatory. Basil's hours here are numbered. He's to be discharged on grounds of professional incompetence. You will fare no better, obviously. If I were you, I would consider another striving."

"Thank you," said Waylock. "Frankly, Caddigan, I find your candid dislike refreshing. I prefer it to a synthetic camaraderie."

Caddigan smiled grimly, and returned to his work.

Presently Basil Thinkoup's steps were heard. He bounced cheerfully into the room. "Good morning, Seth; good morning, Gavin! Another busy day! So let's to business. The clock moves forward; wasted time is life defeated!"

"My word, how brisk!" Caddigan gibed.

Basil waved a minatory finger at him. "You'll think of old Basil's advice when the assassin knocks. Gavin, let's go to work."

Waylock reluctantly followed Basil into the inner office, and stood awkwardly while Basil heard Benberry's orders on the recorder. Basil stood limp and flabby a moment; then seemed to draw a deep breath. "Bah!" He turned his back on the recorder, marched across the room. "I didn't hear that. You heard no orders of Benberry's, did you, Gavin?"

Waylock hesitated. The orange bottle now contained not anti-heptant, but water. Basil said, "We can't stop now! We're on the verge of a great advance! If we let ourselves be harassed by trifles we're lost."

"Perhaps it might be better—" Waylock began. Basil interrupted brusquely. "You must do as you think best, Gavin. I intend to see the experiment through. I can manage alone if you prefer to be elsewhere."

Waylock choked on his words. He cared nothing for Benberry's orders; but he could scarcely explain his use of the anti-heptant.

Basil had already gone to the intercom; he was ordering Maximilian Hertzog to be brought to his laboratory.

Waylock followed on reluctant feet. An injection of water would do little to Hertzog; it was possible that he might not even arouse from trance. And if he did—well, there was always the swaddle.

He made a last lame effort to delay the experiment; but Basil was impervious to suggestion. "If you'd rather be elsewhere, Gavin, go, and my good wishes go with you. But I must see this through. It means a great deal; I'll show up these do-nothings; I'll post their inefficiency for all to see! Benberry—that ridiculous ape!"

A chime sounded; the tube door swung open; the great body of Maximilian Hertzog floated into the laboratory.

Basil made his preparations. Waylock stood stiffly in the center of the room. If he confessed purloining the anti-heptant he would have to explain his motive. His memory was now blank on this score; but there had been an ominous hint in the note he had written to himself.

Basil took his presence for tacit cooperation. "You remember your duties?"

"Yes," muttered Waylock. The swaddle suddenly seemed very frail. He opened the door into the storeroom.

"Why do you do that?" asked Basil.

"Just in case the swaddle doesn't hold."

"Mmmf," said Basil. "Today we won't need the swaddle. And now if you are prepared—anti-heptant!"

Waylock touched the release; a few grams of water flowed into Hertzog's blood.

Basil watched the radioactive indicator. "More, more." He inspected the seep-needle. "What the devil's wrong with the setup!"

"The wrong type of radio-actant, or perhaps it's old."

"I can't understand. It was accurate yesterday." Basil examined the orange bottle. "This is the identical solution. . . . Well, we must do our best." He bent over the inert figure. "Maximilian Hertzog! Awake! Maximilian Hertzog—today we discharge you from the palliatory. Awake!"

Hertzog sat up on the pallet so suddenly that Basil fell backward, bumping into Waylock. Hertzog flung aside the cerebral-contacts, the seep-needle. A guttural sound came from his throat, he sprang to his feet and stood swaying in the middle of the room, eyes glaring.

"The swaddle!" Basil called.

Hertzog bent forward, snatched at him; Basil scuttled aside like a crab. Waylock threw a table in front of Hertzog, seized Basil's arm, dragged him tripping into the storeroom.

Hertzog kicked the table aside, and came at them. The door slid shut in his face. He put his shoulder to the door; Basil and Waylock felt the wall bulge.

"We can't stay in here, we've got to overpower him," Basil said.

"How?"

"I don't know—but we've got to! Else I'm ruined!"

From outside came a faint jangle, sound of steps that were at once heavy but curiously resilient. They became inaudible. Then came a muffled roar, a cry of terror: Seth Caddigan's voice.

Waylock felt sick. The cry became a whimper, cut off. There was a thud, a crash, a peal of laughter, a great windy voice: "I am Hertzog! Hertzog the killer! Maximilian Hertzog!"

Basil had collapsed to his knees. Waylock looked down at him, knowing that he himself should be the shamed one. He opened the door, went cautiously through the office into the study.

Seth Caddigan was dead. Waylock stared down at the broken body. He felt himself truly the Monster of popular lore. Tears came to his eyes.

Basil Thinkoup tottered into the room. He glimpsed Caddigan, turned away with his face in his hands. From the hall came a shrill wavering screech, a hoarse yell, then a sound like a dog worrying something alive.

Waylock ran into the laboratory, loaded a hypospray with the anesthetic called "Instant-Out." When he had finished he had only a small metal tube, ineffective as an egg-whisk. Waylock seized a four-foot length of plastic tubing, taped the hypospray to the end, tied a pull-string to the trigger. Now he was armed.

He ran out into the office, through the reception room, detoured Basil, jumped over Caddigan. He looked cautiously into the corridor.

A woman's voice, quavery and broken, indicated Hertzog's whereabouts. Waylock ran down the corridor, looked through a door which had been smashed open. Hertzog was standing on the body of a dead man.

Against the wall a matron stood, glassy-eyed and rigid. Hertzog had one hand in her hair, was playfully twitching her head back and forth, as if preparing to tear it off with a single jerk. Through a crystal pane horrified faces gazed, open mouths like carnations.

Waylock faltered in the doorway, starring at the face of the dead man. It was Didactor Benberry.

He took a deep breath, ran forward, thrust the hypospray into the nape of Hertzog's neck, yanked the string; the hypospray spat out its charge.

Hertzog dropped the matron's head, wheeled. He clapped a hand to his neck, looked at Waylock with an expressionless face, jumped forward. Waylock poked at his face with the spray, feinted and fenced.

"You can't scare me that way," Hertzog growled. "Let me get my hands on you, I'll tear you apart. I'll kill the whole mortal world, beginning with you."

Waylock backed away, brandishing the rod. "Why don't you cooperate? Then you'd be set free!"

Hertzog danced forward, caught the tube, snatched it out

of Waylock's hands. "You may cooperate," said Hertzog, "by voiding up your life." He staggered and sagged as Instant-Out paralyzed his brain.

Waylock picked up the tube and waited till the orderlies arrived. With them came Didactor Sam Yudill, Assistant Superintendent of the palliatory. They stopped in the doorway, staring in awe at the bodies.

Waylock leaned against the wall. The babble of voices seemed to recede; he heard only the thumping of his heart. Seth Caddigan and Didactor Rufus Benberry: both transited. . . .

"There'll be a devil of a shake-up over this," someone said. "I'd hate to be in Thinkoup's shoes."

4

Caddigan's body had been removed. Basil stood by the window kneading his palms. "Poor Caddigan. . . ." He turned and faced Waylock, who sat glumly to the side. "What could have gone wrong? Gavin, what *could* have gone wrong?"

"A flaw somewhere along the line," Waylock said hollowly.

Basil came to a halt, stared at Waylock, and for an instant, a glimmer of speculation shone behind his eyes. But it dimmed; he turned away, knitting his fingers, kneading his palms.

Waylock had another thought. "I suppose someone has called Caddigan's wife?"

"Eh?" Basil frowned. "Yudill must have notified her." He winced. "I suppose it's my place to offer condolences and learn her new address." It was a custom, when one member of a family died for the survivors to change residence.

Waylock said, "I'll call, if you want me to. I know her slightly."

Basil agreed with relief.

Waylock called Pladge Caddigan on the screen. She had already been notified of the tragedy, and one of the palliatory physicians had despatched her a packet of anti-grief pills—"Non-Sobs"—of which she had evidently made good use. Her long face was flushed; her eyes were bright; her voice was high-pitched and agitated.

Waylock recited the optimistic predictions which in this era took the place of condolences, Pladge dutifully told him her plans for an active career, and the call was terminated.

Basil and Waylock sat in silence for a few minutes. Then a call came through for Basil. It was Didactor Sam Yudill, now acting Superintendent of the palliatory.

"Thinkoup, the Board of Investigation is here; we want to make a preliminary inquiry. Meet us in the Superintendent's Office."

"Certainly," said Basil. "I'll be there at once."

The commu clicked off; Basil rose to his feet. "Here I go," he said heavily. Then, noting Waylock's somber face, he added with false cheerfulness, "Don't worry about me, Gavin; I'll wriggle out of it." He clapped Waylock wearily on the shoulder and departed.

Waylock went into the laboratory. The room was in disorder. He found the orange bottle, poured its contents into the sink, destroyed the bottle. Then he returned to the reception room and seated himself at Caddigan's desk.

He felt steeped in tragedy and foreboding, from the events of the morning, from some other affair. The Jacynth Martin? What of her? They had made the rounds at Carnevalle. . . . He knew nothing more.

He walked back and forth, trying to throw off his despondency. Why should he feel guilt? he asked himself. Life in Clarges was dog-eat-dog. When a person achieved Wedge, he diminished the existence of everyone else in Brood by a certain number of seconds. Gavin Waylock saw life for the hard game it was; he played by his own competitive rules. This was his right, he told himself: society owed him at least so much. The Grayven Warlock had already traversed the road; Amaranth status was rightfully his; he was justified in using any means to regain it.

There was a step at the door. Basil Thinkoup trudged into the room, shoulders sagging. "I've been discharged," he said. "No longer connected with the Balliasse Palliatory. They say I'm lucky to escape the assassin."

5

The violent transitions of Didactor Rufus Benberry and Seth Caddigan aroused a sensation in Clarges. Gavin Waylock was acclaimed for his ingenuity and his "unexampled bravery." Basil Thinkoup was labeled a "stolid mechanist," who "used the unfortunate cattos entrusted to his mercy as stepping-stones up-phyle."

When Basil finally said farewell to Gavin Waylock, he was a forlorn man. His cheeks hung pendulous, his eyes were bright with repressed tears; he was bewildered. "What could have gone wrong?" he cried time after time. There must have been a fundamental flaw in his reasoning, he decided. "Perhaps it's not fated, Gavin. Perhaps the Great Good Principle intended us to suffer the manic-catatonic syndrome as a trammel on our pride." He smiled wanly.

"What do you propose to do?" Waylock inquired.

"I will find another occupation; quite possibly psychotherapy was not my best field. I have another employment under consideration, and if I make good, then perhaps—" He stopped short. "But that is for the future."

"I wish you the best of luck," said Waylock.

"And I you, Gavin."

IX

THE NEW Superintendent of Balliasse Palliatory was Didactor Leon Gradella, a stranger to Balliasse, drafted from one of the up-country institutions. He was an ill-proportioned man, with a heavy torso, spindly legs and arms. His head was huge and well-groomed; his eyes were shrewd and hot.

Gradella announced that he would interview each member of the staff, with an eye to possible reassignment. He started at once with the resident psychiatrists.

No one came smiling from these interviews, and there was no disposition to report what had happened. On the second day, late in the afternoon, Gavin Waylock was summoned by Gradella. He entered the office and Gradella motioned him to a seat. Without words, he dropped the strip of film, which was Waylock's dossier, into a viewer.

"*Gavin Waylock, Brood.*" Gradella read on, then looked up. The little mahogany eyes studied Waylock's face. "You've been here a very short time, Waylock."

"True."

"You are employed as orderly."

"True."

"Why did you not properly complete your application?"

"I intended that my work should speak for itself."

Gradella was not impressed. "Sometimes a man is able to bluff his way up-slope. There will be none of that here. Your stated qualifications are utterly inadequate."

"I disagree."

Gradella leaned back in his chair. "No doubt—but can you convince me?"

"What is psychiatry?" Waylock challenged. "It is the study of mental illness and the curing of this illness. When you use the word 'qualifications,' you evidently refer to formal training in the field. Those with formal training, or 'qualifications,' are generally unsuccessful in palliating or curing mental illness. Therefore your 'qualifications' are illusory. True qualifications would consist of proved ability to cure psychoses. Do you yourself possess these qualifications?"

Gradella's smile was almost jovial. "No, not by your definition. Hence I suppose you feel that I should be orderly and you superintendent?"

"Why not? I am agreeable."

"No, you may keep your position. You will be carefully watched and rated."

Waylock bowed and departed.

2

Early the same evening, the entry buzzer disturbed Waylock at his studies. A tall man in black stood outside the door.

"You are known as Gavin Waylock, Brood?"

Waylock looked the speaker up and down before responding. The man's face was long, exaggerated; the chin dwindled to a point, the forehead was a pale knob covered with dingy brown wool. The shapeless black garments actually were a uniform; in his lapel the man displayed the insignia of the Assassin Special Squad.

"I am Waylock. What do you want?"

"I am an assassin. You may inspect my credentials if you wish. I respectfully request that you accompany me to the District Cell for a short interrogation. If the present time is inconvenient, I will be glad to arrange a more suitable time."

"Interrogation as to what?"

"We are investigating the leave-taking by violence of The Jacynth Martin, a heinous crime. An information has been placed against you. We want to determine your connection, if any, with the affair."

"May I ask who lodged the information?"

"Our sources are confidential. I advise you to come with me now. The matter, however, is at your option."

Waylock rose to his feet. "I have nothing to hide."

"If you will follow me, an official car will take us."

They drove to the heavy old district agency in Parmenter Place, climbed narrow stone steps to the second floor. In a narrow room with whitewashed walls the assassin relinquished Waylock to a young preceptress with shoe-button eyes. She seated him in a high-backed chair, proffered a choice of spirits or mineral water.

Waylock refused both. "The tribunes," he demanded, "where are they? I want no prying into my thoughts without tribunes at hand."

"Three tribunes are here, sir. You may call for any further representation you think necessary."

"Who are the tribunes?"

She named them. Waylock was satisfied; each bore a reputation for zeal and integrity.

"They will be with us in a moment; we are just completing another examination."

Five minutes passed; the door slid back; three tribunes entered, followed by the inquisitor, a tall hollow-cheeked man, his great slash of a mouth trembling in a wistful smile.

The inquisitor made his formal statement: "Gavin Waylock, you are to be questioned regarding the passing of The Jacynth Martin and your activities during the period in which her passing occurred. Do you have any objection?"

Waylock considered. "You say 'during the period in which her passing occurred.' I think this is too vague. It might include a second, an hour, a day, or a month. You may question me as to my activities at the exact time the passing occurred; this I believe, is sufficient for your purposes."

"The time is not exactly established, sir. We must be allowed a certain degree of leeway."

"If I am guilty," Waylock pointed out, "I will know the exact instant of the crime. If I am innocent it will serve no purpose to intrude upon my privacy."

"But sir," the inquisitor said, smiling, "we are public servants, sworn to discretion. Surely there is nothing in your life you would have concealed?"

Waylock turned to the tribunes. "You have heard my stipulation. Will you protect me accordingly?"

The tribunes upheld him. One of them said: "We will allow only questions bearing upon the three minutes preceding the time of the passing of The Jacynth Martin, and the three minutes following. This is the usual lat.tude."

"Very well," said Waylock. "You may proceed." He settled back into the chair; the preceptress at once brought a pair of padded head-contacts, pressed them to the sides of his head. There was a hiss, a moist tingle at the nape of his neck, where the woman had touched him with a hypo spray.

There was silence in the room. The inquisitor walked fretfully back and forth; the tribunes sat in a line, stolidly watchful.

Two minutes passed; the inquisitor touched a button. The head contacts buzzed and pulsed; patterns of light formed on a screen before Waylock's eyes; they coalesced, spiralled, seemed to clench ever closer into the center.

"Watch the lights," said the inquisitor. "Relax . . . that's all there is to it. Merely relax . . . it will soon be over."

The lights twisted into a hard bright knot, receded to a tiny white spot. Waylock's consciousness went out with it, out into the depicted distances, and there rested. He was aware of a mumble, of voices coming and going, of small movements at the edge of his vision. The light gave a little jerk, expanded, unwound, burst back into the large pattern, releasing Waylock's mind.

He was conscious. The inquisitor stood to the side, inspecting him with a glum face. It was evident that the mind-search had been unproductive. The tribunes looked off into distance, secure in the knowledge that uncompromising rectitude gained them slope. Behind the tribunes stood The Jacynth Martin.

Waylock half-rose from his chair. He pointed an angry finger. "Why has this woman been allowed in here? You have done me a serious wrong; I shall apply for redress! None of you will escape!"

The Chief Tribune, John Foster, wearily held up his hand. "The presence of this woman is irregular; it is in poor taste. However, it is not illegal."

"Why not conduct mind-search out in the street?" Waylock

asked bitterly. "Then all who pass can satisfy their curiosity."

"You misunderstand. The Jacynth is present because she is so entitled. She herself is an assassin. A recent enrollee, I may add."

Waylock turned to stare. The Jacynth nodded, smiling a cold smile. "Yes," she said. "I am investigating my own transition. Some horrible creature did his worst upon me; I am curious to learn who he may be."

Waylock turned away. "Your preoccupation seems morbid and unnatural, if I may say so."

"Perhaps, but I do not plan to give it up."

"Have you made any progress?"

"So I believed—until we encountered your peculiarly porous memory."

The inquisitor cleared his throat. "You have no conscious information to volunteer?"

"How could I?" Waylock demanded. "I know nothing about the crime."

The inquisitor nodded. "We have established that. Your mind is void of incident during the critical period."

"Well then?"

"There seem to be hints of peripheral association."

"I'm afraid I don't know what you're talking about," said Waylock.

"No," the inquisitor replied. "I expect you wouldn't." He stood back; the tribunes rose to their feet. "Thank you, Mr. Waylock. You have been very helpful."

Waylock bowed to the tribunes. "Thank you for your help."

"It is our duty, Mr Waylock."

Waylock turned one burning glance toward The Jacynth, stalked from the room, and down the corridor toward the reception room. Behind came the pound of quick footsteps; it was The Jacynth. Waylock turned and waited. She came up to him with a tentative and not very convincing smile. "I must talk with you, Gavin Waylock."

"What about?"

"You hardly need ask."

"I can tell you no more than what you learned by mind-search."

The Jacynth bit her lips. "But you were with me during that evening—for how long I do not know! This part of the evening is blank. It must contain a clue!"

Waylock made a noncommittal gesture.

She took a step forward, looking earnestly into his eyes. "Gavin Waylock, will you talk with me?"

"If you like."

3

They found a quiet table at the Blue Bobolink, an ancient cellar-tavern, paneled with wood black with age. On the wall hung a collection of ancient photographs—sports heroes in characteristic costumes. A waiter brought small salty pastries, cheese, anchovies and beer, departed without a word.

"Now, Gavin Waylock," said The Jacynth, "tell me what occurred that evening."

"There is little to tell. I spoke to you; we were mutually attracted, or so it seemed. We went to various Houses and amusements, and at last to the Pamphylia. The rest you know through your friends."

"Where did we go before the Pamphylia?"

So far as he recalled, Waylock described their activities. He reached the area which had been deleted from his memory, hesitated, then recounted the events immediately prior to the departure of himself and Basil Thinkoup.

The Jacynth protested. "Here you omit much—there is an evident lapse!"

Waylock frowned. "I don't remember. Perhaps I was intoxicated."

"No," said The Jacynth. "The Denis and The Albert agree that you were completely alert."

Waylock shrugged. "Apparently nothing occurred to impress me."

"Another thing," said The Jacynth, "you neglect to mention that we visited the House of Truth."

"Did I? Another matter which has fled my recollection."

"Odd. The attendant remembers distinctly."

Waylock agreed that it was odd.

"Would you care to hear my theory?" The Jacynth asked in a gentle voice.

"If you care to reveal it."

"I believe that sometime during the evening, probably at the House of Truth, I acquired information you could not bear to have known. To erase this knowledge it became necessary to erase me. What do you say to that?"

"Nothing."

"You had nothing to say during mind-search." Her voice was bitter. "Significantly, these particular matters are the only ones which have fled your mind. How you have contrived it, I don't know. In any event, I intend to learn the truth. In the meantime I will see that you derive no benefit from your crime."

"Exactly what do you mean?"

"I will say no more."

"You are a strange creature," said Waylock.

"I am an ordinary person with strong feelings."

"I likewise have strong feelings," said Waylock.

The Jacynth sat very still. "What do you intend to imply?"

"Only that a contest between us might bring ill consequences."

The Jacynth laughed. "You are more vulnerable than I."

"And correspondingly more reckless."

The Jacynth rose to her feet. "I must go now. But I do not think you will forget me." She ran quickly up the stairs and out of Waylock's sight.

The next morning Waylock reported for work at the Palliatory. Before an hour had passed he was summoned to the office of Didactor Gradella.

Gradella was terse, cold and forthright. "I have reconsidered your case. You have no proper credentials for the position you hold, and you are hereby discharged."

X

BASIL THINKOUP called Waylock on the commu the day after Waylock's discharge from the palliatory. "Ah, Gavin! I was afraid I wouldn't find you home."

"You needn't have worried. I'm no longer connected with Balliasse Palliatory."

Basils' pink face pursed up like a baby's. "Too bad, Gavin! What a misfortune!"

Waylock shrugged. "The work wasn't particularly congenial. Perhaps I'm better suited to other strivings."

Basil shook his head dolefully. "I wish I could say the same."

"You have no plans then?"

Basil sighed. "In my youth I did creditably at glass-blowing. I might formulate one or two refinements. Or I might return to the barges. I am still unsettled and uncertain."

"Don't dive headlong into the first vacant cranny," Waylock said.

"Of course not. But I've got my slope to consider, and I hang a long way below Third."

Waylock poured himself a fresh cup of tea. "Let's give this matter some thought."

Basil made a deprecatory motion. "You mustn't concern yourself; I always land on my feet. Still, I am at a low ebb."

"Well, let us consider . . . You have shown that the palliatories stand in need of original thinking."

Basil shook his head wearily. "But where was the profit?"

"Another similar institution," said Waylock, "is the Actuarian. Is it possible we take its operation too much for granted?"

Basil rubbed his nose doubtfully. "A peculiar notion. You have a flexible mind."

"There's nothing sacrosanct about the Actuarian."

"It's merely the keystone of our entire life!"

"Exactly. Let us consider it. The basic operation was established three hundred years ago. Many changes have taken place. But the Actuarian is geared to the same equations, the same phyle ratios, the same birthrate."

Basil was dubious. "What value could come of change?"

"Well—merely to hypothecate—our population limit was based on estimated maximum productivity of the Reach. Increased productivity might allow a higher proportion of Verge and Amaranth. A man who could verify such a proposition would gain slope."

Basil sat looking blankly at a spot above the sending lens. "Surely these matters are controlled by persons in authority?"

"Was Didactor Benberry anxious to help you cure the cattos?"

Basil shook his head. "Poor old Benberry."

"Something else," said Waylock. "The Cage of Shame."

"Distasteful," muttered Basil.

"A cruel punishment, even before the Weirds appeared on the scene."

Basil smiled. "A man could gain slope by ridding Clarges of the Weirds."

Waylock nodded. "Undoubtedly. But the man who took the initiative in abolishing the Cage of Shame would win a great deal of approval and considerable slope."

Basil shook his head. "I'm not so sure. Who protests when the Cage of Shame is swung out? No one. And when the culprit takes his midnight walk, respectable people come to watch."

"Or to mingle with the Weirds."

Basil drew a deep breath. "Perhaps you've set me on the trail of something important." He fixed eyes on Waylock. "It's decent of you to take all this trouble."

"Not at all, the discussion helps us both."

"What will you do then?"

"I have an inkling of an idea: a clinical study of the Weirds, research as to their psychology, motives, and habits; their phyle distribution, their total number."

"Interesting! Rather a forbidding topic, however."

Waylock smiled faintly. "And one which would command a large readership."

"But where would you obtain your material? No one admits to Weirdity. You'd need endless patience, stealth, bravado . . ."

"I was a resident of Thousand Thieves for seven years. I command the services of a hundred Berbers, so long as I pay well."

"The money, then! Thousands of florins!"

"My least concern."

Basil was impressed but unconvinced. "Well, we must both busy ourselves. I'll keep in touch with you."

The commu dimmed. Waylock went to his desk and prepared a rough outline of the study he had in mind. Research would require six months, the writing another three. The result might well lift him into Wedge.

He made an appointment at one of the better-known publishing houses, and later in the day presented himself with his outline.

The interview went as he had hoped. Verret Hoskins, the editor to whom he spoke, put forward the same difficulties that

Basil had, and Waylock countered them in the same way. Hoskins was won over. The study, he declared, would throw valuable illumination upon a matter heretofore shrouded in half-truth and salacious rumor. The contract would be ready for signature on the next day.

Waylock returned to his apartment in elation. This was the work to which he was suited! Why had he ever let himself get involved at the palliatory? Seven years of stagnation evidently had stifled his imagination; now he was back in the harness, and nothing would stop him—he'd break open a new field of sociological study; he'd shock and astonish the preoccupied people of Clarges. . . .

Verret Hoskins called Waylock on the commu later in the afternoon. His manner was subdued; he couldn't meet Waylock's gaze.

"It seems I acted precipitously, Mr. Waylock. Apparently we aren't in a position to publish a work of this nature after all."

"What!" exclaimed Waylock. "Whatever has gone wrong?"

"Well—certain matters have arisen, and my superiors have vetoed this particular undertaking."

Waylock snapped off the commu in cold fury. The next day he approached several other publishing houses. None of these would so much as give him a hearing.

Returning to his apartment, he paced the floor. Finally he seated himself by his commu, located The Jacynth Martin in the directory, put through a call.

The screen burst into The Jacynth's identification medallion: black and red spangling on a blue field. Then The Jacynth appeared, cool and beautiful.

Waylock wasted no words. "You have been interfering in my affairs."

She looked at him a few seconds, smiling faintly. "I have no time to talk to you now, Gavin Waylock."

"You'd do well to hear what I have to say."

"Consult me some other time."

"Very well. When?"

She considered. Suddenly an idea seemed to amuse her. "Tonight I shall be at the Pan-Arts Union. You may tell me whatever you wish." She added softly, "Perhaps I may have something to tell you."

The screen glowed with her personal blazon once more, then went dull. Waylock sat back, thinking. . . .

Assassins had traced his movements, the Amaranth Society had forestalled his success: so much was evident. The favorable prospects of the day before were an illusion. He felt a melancholy so deep and dreary that further struggle seemed insupportable. How sweet it would be to rest, to sink into a blessed numbness.. . . .

Waylock blinked. He took a deep breath. How could he think of submitting, even for a moment?

He rose to his feet, slowly changed into evening wear of dark blue and gray. He'd go to the Pan-Arts Union, meet his opponent on her own ground.

Halfway through the process he paused. The Jacynth's last words—had they conveyed something sinister? He grunted, continued to dress, but his uneasiness persisted.

After checking the room for any spy cell which might have been planted in his absence, he brought out his old Alter-Ego and drew it over his head. His face now appeared heavier and longer; his mouth was red and loose, his complexion tinged with pink, his hair a coarse brown mat. Then he pulled a mustard-colored jacket over his conservative evening dress and arranged a pretentious three-clawed silver hair-clasp on his head.

2

Phariot Way was quiet and dim. A few dark shapes moved along the sidewalks, loitering aimlessly. Waylock watched them from his window for several minutes. Mere apprentices practicing regulation stealth, they could easily be evaded. Serious surveillance involved air-car observation and an elaborate communications system. This arrangement could also be frustrated, but with greater difficulty. A bulb of slave-light with a spy cell might be hovering near by; a deft operative might seek to spray his clothes with some telltale radiant, or tag him with the minute device known as a "leech." All these devices could be circumvented through the use of appropriate ingenuity. Televection could trace him infallibly, but this method was denied to the Special Squad by law.

Waylock wanted to avoid observation entirely, in order to

maintain the worth of his disguise. The critical area lay in the hall, immediately outside his apartment. He slid the door open a crack, examined the vicinity as carefully as possible. He saw nothing, but a spy cell at the far end of the corridor would be invisible.

Waylock returned within, removed his Alter-Ego and his jacket, made a neat bundle, and carrying it under his arm, left the apartment.

He walked down Phariot Way to the Allemand Avenue Station, dropped to the tube depot, and making sure that no one jostled him or approached closely enough to apply a tracer to his person, entered a capsule and switched himself to a random destination: Garstang. The capsule slid away, and Waylock once more invested himself with the identity of his Alter-Ego. He diverted the capsule to Floriander Deck, and arrived feeling secure that he had frustrated any pursuit.

At a kiosk he bought a tube of assorted Stimmos*, and after a moment's reflection, swallowed the yellow, the green and the purple.

Ahead rose the glowing shoulders of successive hills: far ahead Temple Cloud, then the Vandoon Highlands, with Balliasse and the palliatory down by Riverside Road; and closer, Semaphore Hill overlooking the Angel's Den, where Basil kept his apartment. On the crest of Semaphore Hill, overlooking all the city, was the Pan-Arts Union.

He rode up to the flight deck and boarded one of the waiting cabs. They rose through the steaming traffic levels and flitted through the towers of the Mercery. Lights by the thousands blinked above, below, to all sides. Carnevalle, burning across the black flow of the Chant, cast a colored shimmer on the water.

---

*Stimmos: pills which worked upon the brain to build synthetic moods. Orange Stimmos brought cheer and gaiety; red, amativeness; green, concentration and heightened imagination; yellow, courage and resolution; purple, wit and social ease. Dark blue Stimmos (the "Weepers") predisposed to sentimentality and intensity of emotion; light blue Stimmos firmed the muscular reflexes and were useful to precision workers, operators of calculating machines, musical instruments and the like. Black Stimmos ("Dreamers") encouraged weird visual fantasies; white Stimmos ("Non-Sobs") minimized emotional response. It was possible to take combinations of up to three pills with a vast number of compound effects. A dosage of more than three Stimmos or too frequent use diminished the effect.

XI

THE AIR CAB set Waylock down on a plat crowded with private fliers, glossy toys which only Amaranth and glarks could find time to enjoy. A broad dull path, like a strip of black carpet, led to the hall. Waylock stepped upon the path; microscopic fibers, vibrating too rapidly to be felt, slid him up the slope. He was carried through a gold and glass portal, into a vestibule.

A poster read:

TONIGHT
THE AQUEFACTS
of
REINHOLD BIEBURSSON

A large, languid woman sat at a small table, where a card read: *Donation gratefully accepted*. The woman appeared bored, and crocheted an intricate ribbon from metallic thread. Waylock put a florin on the table; she said, "Thank you" in a hoarse voice without breaking the rhythm of her work. Waylock stepped through portieres of wine-colored velvet into the reception hall.

The aquefacts of Reinhold Bieburssen, intricate constructions of congealed water, occupied pedestals around the walls. On cursory inspection, Waylock found them strange and bleak, and turned his attention to the guests.

There were two hundred persons present. They stood in groups making conversation, or circulated past the glistening aquefacts. Reinhold Bieburssen himself stood near the door, a great gaunt man seven feet tall. He seemed not so much the guest of honor as a martyr reconciled to suffering. This exhibition must have represented something to him—triumph, vindication, perhaps only a financial transaction—but for all the expression on his face, Bieburssen might have been walking in solitude through a lonely forest. Only when someone spoke directly to him did he lower his eyes from their brooding search of the air, and then his expression became attentive and kind.

95

The Jacynth stood across the hall conversing with a young woman in a dramatic gray-green leotard. She wore a sheath of a gown the exact color of her hair, which tonight was dressed in the style of the Aquitani street-dancers, combed straight up into the shape of a candle flame. Her eyes brushed Waylock as he came through the portieres, but passed on with no glint of recognition.

Waylock drifted with the slow stream of people around the room. The Jacynth took no heed of him, but maintained her watch on the door. Her companion, a small alluringly shaped woman, seemed to share her vigilance. Her face, piquant, narrow at the jaw, wide at the cheekbones, with great dark eyes and a tousle of dark hair, awoke a sense of vague familiarity in Waylock; somewhere he had seen this face.

He passed behind the two, and paused, so close that fragments of their conversation came to his ears.

"Will he come, will he come?" The Jacynth asked in a petulant staccato.

"Of course," the dark-haired girl replied. "The ridiculous creature dotes on me."

Waylock raised his eyebrows. The watch, then, was not for him. He felt a bit deflated.

The Jacynth laughed nervously. "Even to the extent of—well, even to this extent?"

"Vincent would distribute uplift pamphlets among the Nomads if I so ordered. . . . Here he is now."

Waylock followed their gaze to the man who had just entered the room. He was in his late youth, with the look of middle-phyle about him. His clothes were faintly precious; he carried himself with self-consciousness. Small clay-colored eyes, a long and very sharp nose, a small cleft chin, contributed to give him an expression didactic, inquisitive and minatory.

The Jacynth turned half-around. "Probably he should not see us together."

The dark-haired girl shrugged. "As you wish . . ."

Waylock, now in The Jacynth's line of vision, thought it best to move on, and heard no more. The dark-haired girl, turning to leave, bumped into two older men approaching The Jacynth. She made a charming apology, skipped away, to be intercepted by still another young man who had something to tell her; she became absorbed in his words. The two older men joined The Jacynth and engaged her in conversation.

Waylock continued around the room. The man named Vincent seemed to be involved in The Jacynth's schemes:-it might be wise to make his acquaintance.

Vincent had started toward the dark-haired girl, but seeing her occupied came to a halt with evident annoyance. He saw Reinhold Bieburrson talking with a sharp-faced young man.

Waylock strolled close.

"I am ashamed," the young man declared, "to say that I am not completely familiar with your work."

"Few people are." Biebursson's voice was guttural and labored.

"One thing puzzles me, Mr. Biebursson—and I am a technical man myself—the use of congealed water, this vitreous quartzlike substance. How do you form the water into these patterns, these compound curves, and hold it so while you concrete it with the mesongun?"

Biebursson smiled. "No problem, with the natural advantages that are mine. I am a spaceman—I work where the forces of gravity have no effect, where the whole of time is mine for contemplation."

"Marvelous!" exclaimed the young man. "But I should think the vastness of space would daze rather than stimulate you."

Biebursson smiled his grave smile. "The void is a mouth crying to be filled, a blank mind aching for thought, a cavity desperate for shape. What is not implies what is."

Waylock asked, "Where did your last voyage take you, Mr. Biebursson?"

"Sirius and the Dog-Planets."

"Ah," said the sharp young man. "Then you were aboard the *Star Endeavor!*"

"I am Master-Navigator," said Biebursson.

A stocky middle-aged man joined the conversation. He had a look of waggish good-humor. "Allow me to introduce myself," he said. "My name is Jacob Nile."

It seemed to Waylock as if the sharp-faced young man stiffened somewhat. "My name is Vincent Rodenave," he said.

Waylock said nothing; Biebursson regarded the three with quiet detachment.

Jacob Nile said to Biebursson, "I've never spoken with a spaceman before; would you think ill if I asked a few questions?"

"Certainly not."

"From what I read, it appears that worlds without number exist through the void."

Bieburrson nodded. "Worlds without number."

"Surely there are worlds where men may walk abroad and live."

"I have seen such worlds."

"Do you explore these worlds when opportunity offers?"

Bieburrson smiled. "Not often. I'm no more than the pilot of an air cab, who flies at the wish of his customer."

"But surely," Nile protested, "you can tell us more than that!"

Bieburrson nodded. "There is a world I seldom speak of. Fresh and beautiful, a primeval garden. It is mine. No one else claims it. This virgin earth with its ice-caps, continents and oceans, its forests, deserts, rivers, beaches and mountains—mine. I stood on a savannah sloping down to a river. To right and left were blue forests; far ahead a great mountain range rose. All this—mine. No other man within fifteen light-years."

"You are wealthy," observed Nile. "A man to be envied."

Bieburrson shook his head. "This world I chanced upon once, as a man might see a beloved face in a crowd. I have lost it. Perhaps I will never find it again."

"There are other worlds," said Nile. "Perhaps one for each of us, if only we would go forth to seek it."

Bieburrson nodded indifferently.

"It is a life I should have chosen," said Waylock.

Jacob Nile laughed. "We of the Reach are not spacemen by instinct. Reinhold Bieburrson is not one of us. He is a man of the past—or of the future."

Bieburrson inspected Nile with melancholy interest, and said nothing.

"We live in a fortress," said Nile. "We hold back the Nomads with barriers; we are an island in a savage sea, and the situation suits us. Slope! slope! slope!—that's all to be heard in Clarges." Nile held up his hands in sardonic emphasis, and went his way through the crowd.

Rodenave moved on likewise, around the line of aquefacts. Waylock waited a moment or two, then joined him. They fell into conversation.

"What puzzles me," said Rodenave fretfully, indicating one of the aquefacts, "is how, even in conditions of no gravity, the exact shapes are maintained. The surface tension of water would quickly draw a shape like this into a sphere."

Waylock frowned. "Perhaps he uses a detensifier—or perhaps a surface film of air-hardening mucilage—or molds."

Vincent Rodenave agreed without conviction. They passed near The Jacynth, still in the company of the two distinguished elderly gentlemen.

"There's The Jacynth Martin," said Waylock casually. "Are you acquainted with her?"

Rodenave inspected Waylock sharply. "Only by reputation. Do you know her?"

"Slightly," said Waylock.

"Personally, I am here at the express invitation of The Anastasia de Fancourt," said Rodenave with a self-conscious tremble in his voice.

"I am not acquainted with her. Here was the source of the dark-haired girl's familiarity The Anastasia de Fancourt, the famous mime!

Rodenave shot Waylock a look of calculation. "She is a great friend of The Jacynth."

Waylock laughed. "There is no friendship among the Amaranth. The Amaranth are too self-sufficient to need friends."

"You evidently have made a serious study of Amaranth psychology," Rodenave observed with a trace of rancor.

Waylock shrugged. "Nothing very profound." He looked across the room. "Reinhold Biebursson: is he not high phyle?"

"Verge. Good reliable space-travel. No study, no strain—"

"Only a high mortality rate."

Rodenave presently divulged his own status, which was Third. He worked as technical supervisor at the Actuarian. Waylock asked what functions he performed.

"General research and trouble-shooting. For the last year my particular project has been a simplification of the televector system. Previously the operator had to interpret a code, then transfer the coordinates to a master map. Now the information is printed directly on a flake of film which is a section of the map itself. An improvement which took me into Third, incidentally."

"Congratulations," said Waylock. "A friend of mine is transferring to the Actuarian; he'll be pleased to hear that opportunity for advancement still exists."

Rodenave seemed to disapprove. "In what capacity?"

"Probably something to do with public relations."

"He'll make no slope there," sniffed Rodenave.

Waylock said, "Isn't there always scope for refinement? I've been thinking I might transfer to the Actuarian myself."

Rodenave looked bewildered. "Why this wholesale migration to the Actuarian? We're a prosaic lot; we face no challenges, no personnel difficulties, no turnover—in short, no significant scope for slant.'

"You seem to have done well enough," Waylock observed.

"The technical field is something apart," said Rodenave. "If a man has a logical mind, an exact memory, a penchant for perfection, he possibly will succeed—although I must admit I broke through into Wedge on an invention."

Waylock searched through the shifting crowd; The Jacynth still stood with the two elderly men. "Interesting. What did you invent?"

"Nothing of consequence. But its commercial popularity was such—well, you've probably warmed yourself before a Hearth-O-Matic."

"Of course!" said Waylock. The Hearth-O-Matic was a screen built into the wall, usually under a mantel. A turn of a switch projected the image of a fire upon the screen, anything from a crackling conflagration to a somber bed of coals, while infrared projections radiated a corresponding degree of heat. "You must have done well financially, along with your slope."

Rodenave snorted. "Who cares for money when time is so short? Right now I should be at home studying logarithms."

Waylock was puzzled. "Why study logarithms?"

"I should have said memorize. I am committing to memory the logarithms for every natural constant, and all the whole numbers to a hundred."

Waylock smiled incredulously. "What's the log of 42?"

"To base e or base 10? I have either."

"Base 10."

"62325."

"85?"

Rodenave shook his head. "I've only reached 71."

"71, then."

"85126."

"How do you do it?" said Waylock.

Rodenave made an offhand gesture. "Naturally I use a mnemonic system. I treat each digit as a part of speech. 1 is proper noun; 2 is noun, animal; 3 is noun, vegetable; 4 is noun, mineral; 5 is verb; 6 is adjective or adverb of emotion or thought; 7 of color; 8 of direction; 9 of size; null is negativity.

"I devise a code sentence for every number. It is as simple as that. 'Careful bear, grass and fish eats.' That's 62325, log of 42 base 10."

"Remarkable!"

"Tonight," Rodenave sighed fretfully, "I might have progressed to 74, or even 75. If it were not for The Anastasia—" He stopped short. "Here she is now." He seemed entranced.

The Anastasia came forward almost at a trot, ingenuous as a kitten.

"Good evening, Vincent," she called out in a clear fresh voice. She turned Waylock a quick side glance. Rodenave had forgotten him.

"I have that for which you asked; I secured it at no small risk."

"Excellent, Vincent!" The Anastasia laid her hand on Rodenave's arm, leaned forward with a quick intimacy that caused him to stiffen and grow pale. "Come to my dressing room after the performance."

Rodenave stammered assent. The Anastasia gave him another brief smile, turned Waylock another appraising side glance, then slipped away. The two men watched the supple form retreating. "Marvelous creature," muttered Rodenave.

The Anastasia stopped beside The Jacynth, who plied her with an eager question. The Anastasia made a small motion toward Vincent Rodenave. The Jacynth turned her head, saw Rodenave and Waylock standing together.

Her eyes widened in puzzlement. She frowned, turned away. Waylock wondered if she had penetrated his disguise.

Vincent Rodenave likewise had noted the interplay. He looked curiously sidewise at Waylock. "You have not told me your name."

"I am Gavin Waylock," said Waylock with brutal bluntness.

Rodenave's eyebrows snapped up, his mouth sagged open. "Did you say—Gavin Waylock?"

"Yes."

Rodenave's eyes darted back and forth, then focused. "Here comes Jacob Nile. I think I'll move on."

"What's wrong with Nile?" asked Waylock.

Rodenave gave him a quick look. "Haven't you heard of the Whitherers?"

"I've heard they hold caucuses at the Hall of Revelation."

Rodenave nodded shortly. "I have no wish to listen to Nile's vapidities. He's a glark to boot!"

Rodenave hurried away. Waylock looked toward The Jacynth; she was still occupied with the two elderly gentlemen.

Jacob Nile came up beside Waylock, and looked after Rodenave with a quizzical grin. "One would think young Rodenave wished to avoid me."

"He seems to fear your philosophy—whatever it is."

Jacob Nile started to speak, but Waylock excused himself and hurried after Rodenave, who now stood by one of the aquefacts. Rodenave saw him coming, and quickly turned his back.

Waylock touched him on the shoulder; Rodenave looked around with a surly expression.

"I want a word with you, Rodenave."

"I'm sorry," Rodenave stammered. "Just now——"

"Perhaps we'd be less conspicuous if we went outside."

Rodenave said, "I Have no wish to go outside."

"Then come into this side room; it is just possible that we can adjust the matter." He took Rodenave's arm, guided him into an alcove to the side of the hall.

Waylock held out his hand. "Give it to me."

"What?"

"You carry something intended for The Anastasia which concerns me. I want to see it."

"You are mistaken." Rodenave made as if to leave; Waylock grasped his arm roughly. "Give it to me, I said."

Rodenave began to bluster; Waylock cut him short by pulling open his jacket. In the breast pocket was an envelope. Waylock took it; Rodenave made an ineffective grab, then fell back in frustrated anger.

Waylock forced open the envelope. Within it were three small squares of film. He took one out, held it to the light. The detail was too minute to see, but an attached label read: The Grayven Warlock.

"Ah," said Waylock. "I begin to understand." Rodenave stood defeated and morose, the picture of angry guilt.

The second bit of film was labeled: Gavin Waylock; the third: The Anastasia.

"These appear to be televector films," said Waylock. "Suppose you tell me the——"

"I'll tell you nothing," Rodenave interrupted, anger shining in his eyes.

Waylock regarded him curiously. "Do you realize what can happen to you if I choose to lay charges?"

"A harmless incident, no more! A joke, a matter of curiosity."

"Harmless? A joke? When you interfere with my life? When even the assassins may not use televection?"

"You exaggerate the seriousness of the matter," Rodenave muttered.

"*You* exaggerate your distance from the Cage of Shame."

Rodenave defiantly held out his hand. "If you are done, give them to me."

Waylock looked at him incredulously. "Are you mad?"

Rodenave tried to minimize his role. "After all, I obtained these only at the behest of The Anastasia."

"What did she want with them?"

"I don't know."

"I believe she intended to give them to The Jacynth."

Rodenave shrugged sullenly. "No affair of mine."

"Do you intend to get others for her?" Waylock asked gently.

Rodenave met Waylock's eye, looked away. "No."

"Please make certain that you do not."

Rodenave looked toward the envelope. "What will you do with them?"

"Nothing which concerns you. Be thankful you have escaped as easily as you have."

Rodenave turned on his heel and left the alcove.

Waylock stood thinking a moment. He removed the Alter-Ego and his mustard-colored jacket, tossed them into a corner, and stepped out into the hall.

The Jacynth saw him almost at once. Their eyes met and the air between them tingled with the challenge. Waylock started across the floor. The Jacynth awaited him with a cool half-smile.

2

"Haldeman actually saw the ruins in the Bay of Biscay," one of The Jacynth's companions was saying. "A wall, a bronze stele, a trifle of mosaic, and more's the wonder, a pane of blue glass!" -

The other man slapped his hands together in enthusiasm. "Do you know, there's such a wonder of exciting things going on! If it weren't for my office, by the Sun! I'd join you on this expedition!"

The Jacynth put her hand on Waylock's arm. "Here's a man for high adventure! Any recklessness whatever!" She introduced him to her friends. "Mr. Sisdon Cam—" an erect man with a weatherbeaten face "—and his Honor, Chancellor of the Prytaneon, Claude Imish "—a well-fed, white-haired oldster.

Waylock made the formal responses; The Jacynth, perhaps sensing Waylock's inward seethe, prattled easily on. "We're just discussing Mr. Cam's striving. He's a submarine archaeologist."

Chancellor Imish chuckled, gazing around the hall at Biebursson's aquefacts. "He's come to the right place tonight! What are those if not bits of primordial sea-stone, relicts of the ice age?"

"Isn't it amazing, Gavin Waylock?" said The Jacynth. "Ruined cities under the sea!"

"Tremendously exciting," Chancellor Imish declared.

"What could be the identity of this city?" The Jacynth inquired.

Cam shook his head. "Who knows? Our next set of dives will tell us more, and we'll have a suction dredge."

"Are you not troubled by Nomad pirates?" asked Imish.

"To a certain extent. But they've learned caution."

Waylock could restrain his impatience no longer. He spoke to The Jacynth. "May I have a few words with you?"

"Certainly." She excused herself from Cam and Imish, stepped a little to the side. "Well, Gavin Waylock, how goes it?"

"Why did you have me come here tonight?" Waylock demanded.

She feigned surprise. "Didn't you want to speak with me?"

"I have this to say: If you interfere in my life I will interfere in yours."

"That sounds very like a threat, Gavin."

"No," said Waylock. "I would not threaten you—not under the eye and ear of that." He nodded to her recording button, a device occasionally worn by the Amaranth to simplify transference of sights and sounds to their surrogates.

"If only I had worn it that night at Carnevalle, when I was devitalized!" sighed The Jacynth. She looked past Waylock;

he saw her pupils dilate in excitement. "Here is someone you must meet: The Anastasia's current lover; one of them, at least."

Waylock turned; behind him stood The Abel Mandeville. The two men stared at each other.

"The Grayven Warlock!" exclaimed The Abel.

Waylock spoke with cold civility. "My name is Gavin Waylock."

"Gavin claims to be the relict of The Grayven," said The Jacynth.

"Well, I'm sorry if . . ." The Abel's eyes narrowed. "Relict? Not surrogate?"

"Relict," said Waylock.

The Abel was staring at Waylock, absorbing his every movement, each flicker of expression. "Possible. Possible indeed. But you are no relict. You are The Grayven, and the fact that you escaped your just deserts is an outrage." He turned to The Jacynth. "Cannot something be done, another Monster be brought to bay?"

"Perhaps," The Jacynth replied thoughtfully.

"Why do you hobnob with the man?" The Abel blazed.

"I admit he—interests me. And perhaps he is a surrogate—"

The Abel chopped the air with his big red hand. "Somewhere there is basic error; when the assassins take a man they should extirpate all of him, remove his taint from the Reach!"

"Abel," said The Jacynth, with a sly side glance at Waylock, "why delve into past wrongs? Aren't there present ones a-plenty?"

The Abel said in a hoarse voice, "Monsterism seems to have become respectable!" He turned on his heel and swung off.

The Jacynth and Waylock watched him hurrying across the floor. "He is more irascible than usual tonight," said The Jacynth. "The Anastasia is wayward; jealousy eats him like an ulcer."

Waylock asked, "Did you invite me here tonight to meet The Abel?"

"You are perceptive," she replied. "Yes, I wanted to witness the meeting. I was puzzled as to your possible motives for extinguishing me. I thought to recognize you as The Grayven."

"But my name is Gavin Waylock."

She brushed aside the remark. "I could not be certain. The

proto-Jacynth had no large interest in you; we had only sketchy inculcation into the Waylock-Mandeville case."

"Even if you were right, why should I seek to harm you?"

"Seven years have passed; The Grayven Warlock is legally a vacant name. A man professing to be his relict can walk abroad without danger. At Carnevalle I recognized you; you feared I would report you to the assassins."

"And—supposing these fictitious circumstances to be truth —would you have done so?"

"Certainly! You were guilty of an unspeakable crime, and you duplicated it at Carnevalle."

"You are obsessed," muttered Waylock. "The mind-search refuted your belief and still you cling to it."

"I am not a simpleton, Gavin Waylock."

"Even if I were guilty—which I will never admit—where is the heinousness of the crime? Neither you nor The Abel suffered more than inconvenience."

"The crime," said The Jacynth softly, "is abstract and fundamental: the innate depravity of extinguishing life."

Waylock looked uncomfortably around the room. Men and women talked, strolled beside the aquefacts, postured, gestured, laughed. His conversation with The Jacynth seemed unreal. "Now is hardly the time to argue this matter," he said. "However, I may point out that if extinguishing life is a crime, it is a crime everyone except the glarks are guilty of."

The Jacynth whispered in mock horror, "You appall me! Describe my crime—supply the grisly details."

Waylock nodded. "One Amaranth per two thousand population is the allowed ratio. When you were received into the Amaranth Society, an element of information entered the Actuarian. Two thousand black wagons went forth on their missions; two thousand doors opened; two thousand despairing creatures left their homes, climbed the three steps; two thousand times—"

The Jacynth's voice was harsh as the rasp of an untuned violin. "This is no guilt of mine; everyone strives alike."

"It is simple dog-eat-dog," said Waylock. "It's basic battle for survival, fiercer and more brutal than ever before in the history of man. You have blinded yourself; you subscribe to false theories; you are permeated with your obsession—not only you but all of us. If we faced the facts of existence, our palliatories would be less crowded."

"Bravo!" exclaimed Chancellor Imish, who had come up behind. "An unorthodox view, a fallacious premise developed with great vigor and conviction!"

Waylock bowed. "Thank you." He inclined his head to The Jacynth, and departed into the crowd.

3

Waylock seated himself in a quiet corner. The Jacynth had brought him here to establish his identity: if not through The Abel Mandeville, then by comparison of the televector flakes which she had prevailed upon The Anastasia to secure for her through her admirer, Vincent Rodenave.

Waylock brought forth the flakes, inspected them as well as he could without a viewer. Each was confused, as if two segments of the master map had been superimposed. There were two red crosses on each flake, one bright and distant, the other more diffuse. The congruence of the Gavin Waylock flake and that of The Grayven Warlock seemed to be absolute. Waylock smiled and tore the two flakes to shreds.

He examined The Anastasia's flake once more. Like his own, it presented an apparent superimposition. Why should this be, Waylock wondered. Surely there was no flaw in the televection machinery. It was almost as if the chart of two persons had been printed together. But this was hardly possible; the alpha-patterns of each brain were unique.

A possible solution suggested itself and with it, almost simultaneously, came the inkling of a tremendous idea—a concept so enormous that at first it struck him as unconscious humorous fantasy. . . .

But if my conjecture regarding the flakes is correct, where is the flaw?

Excitement gripped him. Details suggested themselves; in a few moments the entire plan lay clear before him.

A fanfare of cornets broke into his thoughts. The murmur of conversation died, the lights went dim.

4

A section of wall slid aside to reveal a stage hung with a black curtain. A personable young man appeared.

"Friends of art, fellow patrons! Tonight the most delightful

mime of all history has agreed to entertain us. I refer of
course to The Anastasia de Fancourt.

"Tonight she takes us behind the façade of the Apparent and
unveils the Actual. The program is necessarily short, and she
has asked me to apologize for the impromptu nature of the
performance; but this I refuse to do. Assisting will be the painstaking but essentially heavy-handed novice, Adrian Boss—
which is to say, myself."

He bowed and retired; the hall went dark.

The black curtain trembled, a spotlight focused. But no one
came forth.

A fragile white figure, a pierrette, came out of dark wings,
looked blinking into the light. She went hesitantly to the curtain
where the light had focused, drew it apart in curiosity. Something large and indefinable jerked violently; the pierrette
dropped the curtain, jumped back. She started to leave the
stage. The spotlight followed, caught her in the glare. She
turned to face the audience. Her face was chalk-white, her lips
black. A white cap was pulled smooth over her hair, a black
pompom dangled by a soft cord from the scalp. She wore a
loose white blouse and pantaloons, with small black pompoms
down the front. Her eyes were wide and black, her brows,
whitened like the rest of her face, cast a startled inquiring
shadow. She was half-clown, half-specter.

She walked to the far left of the stage, faced the curtain,
waited, and presently a section lifted and folded back.

So began the pantomime. It continued for fifteen minutes,
through three episodes, celebrating the triumph of vagary over
plan, affirming the wisdom of folly. Each episode was disarm-
ingly simple, a simplicity obscured by the weird charm of the
pierrette, her drooping black mouth, her eyes large and black,
like clamshells full of ink. Each episode proceeded at a definite
rhythm and was accompanied by a progression of chords, resolving at the denouément.

The first episode took place in a workroom of the Mozam-
bique Perfume Company. The pierrette slipped on a black rub-
ber apron, to become a laboratory technician. She set to work,
mixing syrups, oils and essences: bergamot, jasmine, myrcia,
bayberry; but producing only the most fetid vapors, which
blew out over the hall. She threw up her hands in vexation
and consulted a large book. Then she found a beaker, dropped
in first a fish head, then a handful of rose petals. The beaker

flickered with green flame. The pierrette was entranced. She judiciously dropped in her handkerchief, the beaker threw up a magnificent fountain of colored sparks, a pyrotechnical delight, and this was the resolving of the chord.

In the second episode, the pierrette cultivated a garden. The ground was barren and rocky. She dug holes with a metal spike, and in each hole tenderly planted a flower: a rose, a sunflower, a white lily. One after another the flowers sprouted into weeds; rank, unkempt, unlovely. The pierrette performed a jig of frustration. She kicked away the flowers and, as a final gesture of annoyance, plunged the metal spike into the ground —which at once put forth branches from which hung green leaves, golden apples, and red pomegranates.

In the third episode, the set was dark. There was visible only a high clock face which had two hands of green slavelight and a luminous red mark at the twelve position. The pierrette came on the set, looked a moment at the sky, then began to build a house. She piled together the most unlikely materials: broken boards, scraps of metal, fragments of glass. By some miracle the unlikely bits and pieces began to form a structure. The pierrette watched the sky, worked with ever greater urgency, while the clock hands moved closer toward the red mark.

The structure was finished; the pierrette was delighted. She found another nozzle, pointed it; and it sucked the paint away from the pile of trash, and the scraps rose by themselves into their previous form. The pierrette prepared to enter, but could not. She looked through the door, pulled out and warned off a vagrant ruffian, who was Adrian Boss, shooed out a flight of birds, and while she was so occupied the clock hands met the red line.

The pierrette froze in her tracks, then moved stiffly as if the air had congealed. She looked up at the clock; the hands moved backward, away from the red line; the pierrette laughed. The hands advanced once more with the finality of doom. There was a dazzle of purple light, a clap of thunder, an image of blazing white surf advancing to overcome the world. A roar, a rumble, a triumphant scream. And in the echoes, the resolution of the chord.

The room lights came on, the black curtain was quiet; the wall slid slowly back into place.

5

The Anastasia de Fancourt returned to her dressing room, slid the door shut. She felt exhilarated fatigue, like that of a person returning to a sunny beach after a plunge into ice-cold breakers. The production had gone over well, though there had been rough spots. Perhaps a fourth sequence might be included. . . .

The Anastasia stiffened. Someone was in the room, someone unfamiliar. She peered around the angle of wall into the little reception room. A man sat there, a big man, knees drawn up under his great head.

The Anastasia came forward, pulling away the skull cap, freeing her tousle of dark curls. "Mr. Reinhold Biebursson. I'm honored."

Biebursson slowly shook his head. "No. The honor—the presumption, perhaps I should say—is mine. I will not apologize. A spaceman feels that he is above convention."

The Anastasia laughed. "I might agree if I knew what convention you had in mind."

Biebursson turned his grave eyes away. The Anastasia went to the dressing table, picked up a towel. Wiping the white paste from her face, she came back to where Biebursson sat.

"I am not a man who speaks well," he said. "My thoughts come in images I cannot translate. For days, for weeks and months, I keep watch. I maintain the ship while the scientists and star-explorers sleep in the cells. It is better this way."

The Anastasia slid into a chair. "It must be very lonely."

"I have my work. I have my sculpture. And I have music. Tonight I watch you. I am surprised. Because only in my music do I find the eloquence, the subtlety . . ."

"That is to be expected. My craft is much like music. I and the musician both use symbols abstracted from reality."

Biebursson nodded. "I understand completely."

The Anastasia went close to Biebursson, peered into his face. "You are a strange man, a magnificent man. Why are you here?"

"I have come to ask you to go with me," said Biebursson with majestic simplicity. "Into space. The *Star Enterprise* is taking on stores and fuel; soon we shall leave for Achernar; I would have you with me, to live in the black and star-colored sky."

The Anastasia smiled her wry smile. "I am as craven as the rest."

"I find this hard to believe."

"It's true." She stood before him, her hands on his shoulders. "I could not leave my surrogates; our empathy would fail; our souls would diverge; there would be no identification, no continuity. I would not dare take them along, there is too much risk of total termination. So——" She made a wan gesture—"I am fettered by my own freedom."

Behind them came a clatter, a thud of feet, a harsh voice. "I must say, this is a pretty scene."

The Abel Mandeville stood in the doorway, surveying the room. He came forward. "Hobnobbing with this bearded scarecrow—embracing him!"

The Anastasia was vexed. "Abel, at last you overreach yourself!"

"Bah! My bluntness is less nauseating than your nymphiasis."

Biebursson rose from the chair. "I'm afraid I have brought dissension to your evening," he said sadly.

Mandeville barked a short sharp laugh. "Don't inflate yourself. You and everyone else of the gender."

A third male voice spoke. Vincent Rodenave looked through the door. "If I might have a word with you, Anastasia."

The Abel said, "Another one?"

Vincent Rodenave stiffened; his sharp face twitched. "You are offensive, sir."

"No matter. What do you do here?"

"I can see no basis for your interest."

The Abel strode forward; Vincent Rodenave, half his size, stood staunchly in place. The Anastasia thrust herself between them. "You cockerels! This must stop! Abel, will you go?"

The Abel was outraged. "Me, go! Me?"

"Yes."

"Then I will go after them. I want a word with you." He waved at Rodenave and Biebursson. "Go, you dancing-tom; go, spaceman!"

"All of you!" cried The Anastasia. "Leave me!"

Reinhold Biebursson bowed with a kind of gaunt grace and departed.

Vincent Rodenave frowned. "Perhaps I could see you later? I must explain——"

The Anastasia came forward, her face twisted in a wry

expression. "Not tonight, Vincent. I desperately want rest."

Rodenave hesitated, then reluctantly withdrew.

The Anastasia turned to The Abel Mandeville. "Now Abel, please. I must dress."

The Abel stood like a bull. "I want words with you."

"I want none with you!" Her voice rose suddenly into contempt. "Do you understand me, Abel? I am finished with you —finally, completely. Now—leave me!"

The Anastasia turned on her heel, went to her dressing table, began wiping off the last of her make-up.

Behind her came the pad of a heavy foot. The room sounded to a gasp, a groan, and then a steady drip, drip that soon stopped.

XII

THE DAY following the exhibition was a Sunday. Waylock awoke to a mood of gloom and pessimism. He dressed slowly, descended to the street, walked south in the shadow of the towers, to Esterhazy Square and Pearl Pavilion beside the lake. Selecting a table overlooking both mall and water, he ordered strong tea in a black glass, rolls and quince preserve.

The square was brilliant with sunshine and more than usually crowded. Near by a dozen noisy children played "Who's-a-Glark." On a bench below Waylock three young men sat in a sly huddle, exchanging obscene stories—anecdotes tweaking the prime taboo: "Did you hear about the horse-trainer who broke his leg? The horses thought he'd have to be *killed*." And, "This apprentice assassin drove the struggle-buggy to the wrong address. It was where Director-General Jarvis himself lived. They hauled him down and boosted him in . . ."

Waylock's gloom deepened. The three young men on the bench below snickered at their jokes; Waylock joined them in a sour grin. He should put his head over the parapet and say, "Look at me! I am a Monster. I have killed, not once, but twice. I am considering a course of action which may bring death to many others." Their eyes would stare, their mouths would fall open, their lewd laughter would choke back down their throats.

The sun warmed Waylock; he began to feel more cheerful. The horrible event of last night, after all, tended to vindicate him, as even The Jacynth must admit. If she would cease her persecution of him, he could forget the monstrous scheme which had formed in his mind. And yet—the idea stirred him by reason of its own intrinsic interest.

He reached in his pocket, brought out Rodenave's envelope. With a viewer he inspected The Anastasia's flake.

It should not be too difficult, he thought, to separate the two images. It was necessary only to identify some conspicuous landmark, which would provide a key to one of the superimposed charts. This could then be subtracted by photological techniques, or an application of phase analysis, leaving the second chart clear and distinct.

He replaced the flake in the envelope, returned it to his pocket. Rodenave had dared greatly for The Anastasia. If apprehended, he would suffer severely—certainly expulsion from his position and possibly the Cage of Shame. He had dared once without reward. It remained to be seen if he would dare a second time for higher stakes.

He looked across the sunny square, where children played games presaging their future; where men and women walked briskly toward the Actuarian and came away sagging with spent emotion. He picked up his newspaper. The Anastasia's picture stared from a box, fragile and fine as the face of a sylph: her passing was big news. The paper was the *Clarion*, The Abel's own.

He glanced through the other news of the day. A millionaire glark had sought to trade half his wealth for Amaranth inoculations, and had been severely rebuked. There was an article on Balliasse Palliatory, endorsing the new superintendent, Didactor Leon Gradella. The League for Civic Morality was up in arms against what they termed "indecent games and recreations" at Carnevalle, where living animals received "disgusting treatment" at the "hands of perverts."

Waylock yawned, put down the paper. Across the mall came an odd couple: a tall solemn young man and a woman equally tall, with lank red hair and a face long as a violin. She flaunted an arsenic-green smock, a sulphur-yellow skirt, and jangled a dozen brass bracelets on her arm.

Waylock recognized the woman: Pladge Caddigan. She met his gaze. "Gavin Waylock!" she cried, and waved her long arm till the bracelets clashed. She took the young man's arm and steered him through the pavilion to Waylock's table.

"Roger Buisly, Gavin Waylock," she said by way of introduction. "May we join you?"

"Of course," said Waylock. Any grief Pladge might have felt at the loss of Seth was clearly under control.

Pladge seated herself and the young man followed suit.

"I've great hopes, Roger," said Pladge, "of making Gavin Waylock one of us."

"One of what?" asked Waylock.

"A Whitherer, of course. Everyone of consequence is a Whitherer nowadays."

"I've never got it quite straight: exactly what is a Whitherer?"

Pladge rolled up her eyes despairingly. "There are as many definitions as there are Whitherers. Basically, we're people in a state of protest. We've made some attempt to form a coalition, to set up a central council."

"Why?"

Pladge looked surprised. "So we can organize function as a force, do something about our government!"

"What, specifically?"

Pladge performed one of her more extravagant gestures. "If we were agreed, the rest of it would be simple. Present conditions are intolerable; we all want a change—all, that is, except Roger Buisly."

Buisly smiled complacently. "This is an imperfect world. I believe that our present system is as good as can be hoped for. It holds up a standard, offers a goal, fulfills the dearest hopes of the human race; and it can be tampered with only to our great disadvantage."

Pladge grimaced wryly. "You can see how conservative our Roger becomes."

Waylock considered Buisly. "Why is he a Whitherer then?"

Buisly answered. "Why not? I am a Whitherer of Whitherers. They demand of each other, 'Whither the world?' I expand the question to: 'Whither the world, if these crackpots have their way?' "

"He has nothing constructive to offer," Pladge told Waylock. "He obstructs and carps."

Buisly protested. "Not at all! I have a sound position; it is so simple that Pladge and her abstruse friends are oppressed.

I reason in three stages. Step one: everyone wants eternal life. Step two: we can't permit it to everyone, or we'd have another Age of Chaos. Step three: the obvious answer is—give life to those who have earned it. This is our present system."

"But what of the human cost?" said Pladge. "What of the strain, the grief, the terror, the turmoil? What of the poor devils crowding the palliatories? Twenty-five per cent of all those participating!"

Buisly shrugged. "This is an imperfect world. There always have been grief and terror. We all want to minimize it. I believe that's what has been done."

"Oh Roger! You can't really believe that!"

"In the absence of proof to the contrary, yes." He turned to Waylock. "In any event, those are my views. I am detested, of course, but I afford these people a convenient butt for their sarcasm."

"It's probably a necessary function," Waylock told him. "I met a Whitherer last night. His name is Jacob Nile—"

"Jacob Nile!" Pladge prodded Buisly with her finger tips. "Roger, you must call Jacob on the commu; he lives so close by; see if he will join us."

Roger Buisly demurred, and when Pladge insisted made plaintive sounds.

"Very well," said Pladge in grand hauteur, "I'll call him myself."

She rose from the table, marched to the public commu.

"A very headstrong woman," Buisly observed.

"Evidently."

Pladge returned in triumph. "He was just leaving his apartment and he'll be right over."

A few minutes later Jacob Nile appeared, and was introduced to Waylock. He knit his brows. "Somehow you seem familiar. Have we met?"

"I believe I saw you at the Pan-Arts Union last night."

"Oh?" Nile frowned. "Perhaps. I don't recall your face. . . . A terrible affair."

"Terrible indeed."

"Eh? What's this?" asked Pladge and would not rest till she had heard all the details. The talk then returned to the Whitherers. Nile dwelt upon the decay and degeneracy which attacks a static society. Waylock moved in his seat, looked across the lake.

Roger Buisly expostulated: "Jacob, you speak with your head in the clouds! In order to go somewhere, we must have somewhere to go!"

"If we faced up to the challenge, we might find that someplace!"

"Challenge?"

"The challenge of life! Humanity has vanquished its final enemy; we have won the secret of eternal life; it should be at the option of everyone!"

"Ha, ha," Buisly laughed. "In the guise of kindness, you urge the cruelest doctrine of all. Clarges populated by Amaranth, breeding and multiplying. Then, oh, world, *sauve qui peut!*"

Waylock said thoughtfully, "The progression seems inevitable. We overcrowd the Reach, we seek to expand our borders. The Nomads declare a jehad; we take their lives, drive them back. Our population swells. We irrigate deserts, raise dikes against the ocean, clear the taiga, and all the while we are involved in wars and guerrilla battles."

"An empire," murmured Roger Buisly, "a structure of human bone, cemented with blood, landscaped with human souls."

"And in the end, what?" continued Waylock. "The Reach encompasses the world. After a century, eternal men will stand crowded shoulder to shoulder, wherever solid ground supports them, while millions more float on rafts."

Jacob Nile sighed, "This is what I mean by stagnation. We acknowledge the problem, we babble a set of inept solutions, and then we throw up our hands and return to live with the situation, comfortable in the thought that at least we have talked." His voice was bitter. "A healthier catharsis is bought at Carnevalle."

There was a pause.

"I think I will become a Weird," said Pladge.

"It is no less fashionable than Whithering," said Waylock.

Jacob Nile spoke. "Even had I the power, I would not shape the future to my own ideas. An urge must be felt by everyone; it must run irresistibly through the population; we must move with spontaneous feeling."

"But Jacob," said Pladge, "this is the dilemma! Everyone is troubled, everyone is ripe to move, everyone is looking for a place to go!"

Jacob Nile shrugged. "I know the direction I would go—but would others go with me? This is what I do not presume to dictate."

Roger Buisly suggested urbanely, "Perhaps you will indicate this direction?"

Nile smiled, and waved his hand at the sky. "There is our challenge, among the stars. The universe awaits us."

There was a silence, almost of embarrassment. Jacob Nile looked from face to face, smiling. "You think me a visionary? Perhaps I am. Forgive me for pressing my obsession."

"No, no!" Pledge protested.

"What you propose may well be a solution," said Buisly earnestly. "But not for us of Clarges. We have our careers, our customs; we are secure in the Reach—"

"The citadel complex," said Nile wearily. He pointed to the long façade of the Actuarian. "And there—the ultimate citadel, the heart of Clarges."

Pledge sighed. "Which reminds me, I must check my slope. I haven't looked for two weeks. Anyone for the ooze-boxes?"

Buisly agreed to accompany her; the group rose from the table, departed the pavilion and went their various ways. Waylock bought an afternoon newsstrip. There was an item of news which brought him to a halt.

The Abel Mandeville had committed a second abominable act—self-termination. It was hinted that the passing of the former Anastasia might have been a factor in his going. Chief of Assassins Aubrey Hervat had witnessed the act, had sought to prevent it, desiring to question The Abel, but to no avail.

We hope and strongly urge, went the text in an editorial box, *that those who may have dealings with the new Abel Mandeville, will be large-hearted, tolerant and forbearing. Knowledge of his prototype's act naturally cannot be kept from him, but it is not necessary to regard the new Abel as a man of potential depravity. Let us all give him a chance to rebuild his life, and try to treat him as a person no different from the rest of us.*

2

Early the next morning Waylock presented himself to the Personnel Office of the Actuarian, and made application for employment.

The brisk young woman who interviewed him was not disposed to be encouraging. "Naturally it is your right to strive where you will, but I suggest you reconsider. For each of the high-slope jobs, a dozen excellent men compete. An ambitious man would do better elsewhere."

Waylock refused to be discouraged; the woman processed his application, sent him to a side chamber where he underwent a set of aptitude tests. Returning to the Personnel Office, he found the young woman already examining and coding the results of the examination.

She observed him with a new interest. "Your overall score is Bracket A Code D—very good. But still I don't have much to offer you. Your technical background is inadequate for a laboratory or design post. . . . I believe we might work you into Public Relations, and I believe one of the Traveling Inspectors is almost due to be—retired. I'll make inquiries."

Waylock seated himself on a bench; the girl left the room. Minutes passed—ten, twenty, a half-hour. Waylock began to feel restless. Another ten minutes went by, and the girl returned. Her step was slow, and she kept her eyes averted from Waylock's face.

He went up to the counter. "Well?"

She said in a hurried voice, "I'm sorry, Mr. Waylock; but I find that I was mistaken. The place I mentioned is not open. I can offer you a choice of three positions: apprentice maintenance mechanic, assistant timekeeper in the salvage department and custodian trainee. The remunerations are roughly equivalent."

Observing the expression on Waylock's face she said with forced cheerfulness, "And perhaps in time you may qualify for a position with greater scope."

Waylock stared at her. "This is a peculiar situation," he said at last. "To whom did you speak?"

"The situation is as I have explained it, sir."

"Who instructed you to explain it?"

She turned away. "You must excuse me; I have other work."

Waylock leaned forward. She could not evade his eyes, and stopped, fascinated. "Answer me—whom did you consult?"

"I made a routine check with the supervisor."

"And then?"

"He felt that you were not suited to the first positions I mentioned."

"Take me to your supervisor."

"Just as you wish, sir," she said with relief.

The supervisor was Cleran Tiswold, Wedge, a chunky little man with a coarse red face and a bristle of sandy hair. At the sight of Waylock his eyes narrowed to slits.

The discussion lasted fifteen minutes. From first to last Tiswold denied the existence of outside influence, but his voice rang over-brassy; he rejected Waylock's challenge of mind-search with scornful amusement. He had to agree that Waylock had scored extremely high on the aptitude tests and that normally such a score would entitle an applicant to a responsible post. "However," said Tiswold, "I am the interpreter of these tests, and I weigh the score according to my evaluation of the applicant."

"How did you evaluate me without seeing me?"

Tiswold said, "I have no more time to spare. Will you accept the position offered you, or not?"

"Yes," said Waylock, "I accept." He rose to his feet. "I will report for work tomorrow. I go now to place a charge against you with the tribunes. I hope you spend a pleasant afternoon. It may be your last."

Waylock left the Actuarian with a slow tread. The sky was harsh and dismal. A gust of wind laden with cold rain struck him, and he drew back into the Actuarian.

For twenty minutes he stood by the tall glass panes, and his thoughts were dark as the rain clouds.

The issue had become simple and ominous. If The Jacynth Martin and others of the Amaranth Society did not desist from their persecution, Waylock would be driven to stringent counter-measures.

He must explain to The Jacynth where vindictive policy was leading.

Waylock went to the public commu, dialed The Jacynth's home.

Her blazon appeared on the screen; she spoke but did not release her image.

"Gavin Waylock! How grim you appear!" Her voice was mocking.

"I must speak with you."

"There is nothing I care to hear. If you wish to speak, go to Caspar Jarvis, confess to him how you violated my life, explain how you were able to negate the mind-search. That is what you must do."

"You are frivolous; you will not heed . . ." He stopped; the blazon had pulsed and died. The Jacynth had broken the connection.

He felt bleak and depressed. Who would intercede for him? Who had influence with The Jacynth? Surely, The Roland Zygmont, President of the Amaranth Society. He searched the directory; put a call to the home of The Roland.

The Roland's blazon appeared. A voice spoke. "The residence of The Roland Zygmont; who is calling and what are your wishes?"

"This is Gavin Waylock; I wish to speak to The Roland on a matter concerning The Jacynth Martin."

"Just a moment, if you please."

The screen presently snapped into focus; The Roland looked forth at Waylock—a man with a thin keen face, a speculative gaze, and expression devoid of emotion. "I recognize a face from the past," said The Roland. "That of The Grayven Warlock!"

"Be that as it may," said Waylock, "it is not relevant to what I wish to tell you."

The Roland held up his hand. "I am acquainted with the matter."

"Then you must restrain her!"

The Roland appeared surprised. "A Monster destemporized The Jacynth. We do not tolerate the violation of Amaranth lives; this must be made utterly clear."

"Is this persecution of me, then, the official policy of the Amaranth Society?"

"By no means. Our sole official policy is the pursuit of rigorous justice. I advise you to submit yourself to the law of the land. Your career will hold no promise otherwise."

"You reject the evidence secured by mind-search?"

"It was not legitimate mind-search. I heard a transcript of your case. It is clear that you have discovered some means to block out your memory. This knowledge is a threat to our society: one more reason why you must be brought to justice."

Without another word Waylock broke off the connection. Ignoring the rain which now hissed into the plaza, he walked through Esterhazy Square to the slideway, returned to his apartment.

He stepped out of his drenched clothes, showered, aired himself dry, slumped upon the couch. He dozed, fell into a restless slumber, to grimace and mutter in his sleep.

When he awoke it was late afternoon. The rain had stopped; the clouds had torn open into a great welter of black, gray and gold.

Waylock brewed himself coffee and drank it without enjoyment. He must talk to The Jacynth, explain himself; surely an adjustment of the difficulty could be arranged.

He dressed in a new suit of dark blue cloth, and set forth into the evening.

3

The Jacynth lived on a rocky promontory of Vandoon Heights, facing full to a vast view over Clarges. Her house was small but elegant. Tall cypress built a classical pattern behind; before were a few careful banks of flowers.

Waylock touched the door-plate; The Jacynth herself slid back the door. Her expression of welcome became one of surprise. "Why are you here?"

Waylock moved forward. "May I come in?"

She stood in his way for a moment. Then, "Very well," she said abruptly, and turning, led him into a sitting room, furnished in fretted ormolu, decorated with exotic objects from the outer lands; pottery of the Altamir Nomads, peacock fetishes from Khotan, carved glass of the Dodecanese.

The Jacynth looked her best. She wore a fragile gown; her sun-blond hair hung loose; her eyes shone bright with intelligence. She regarded him speculatively. "Well then, why have you come here?"

Waylock found it difficult not to be distracted by her physical appeal. She smiled frostily. "My guests will be arriving shortly. If you plan a violent destemporization, you could hardly hope to flee undetected; and there is hardly leisure for the amorous dalliance your expression suggests."

"I planned neither," said Waylock mildly. "Although your conduct calls for the one as much as your appearance urges the other."

The Jacynth laughed. "Will you have a seat, since you are disposed to be amusing?"

Waylock seated himself on the low couch beside the window. "I came to talk with you—to remonstrate—to plead, if that is necessary." He paused, but The Jacynth merely stood before him, alert and intent.

Waylock continued. "At least three times in the past two weeks you have thwarted me in my basic right to a career."

The Jacynth started to speak, then stopped.

Waylock ignored the quasi-interruption. "You suspect me of depravity. If you are mistaken, then you are doing me a great wrong. If you are right, then I am a desperate and resourceful man who will not accept your acts passively."

"Ah," said The Jacynth in a low voice. "You threaten me?"

"I make no threats. If you give up your efforts to harm me, each of us will find satisfaction in our future lives. But if you persist, there will be antagonism distasteful to me, distasteful and worse to you."

The Jacynth glanced up through the window, to a moth-blue Celestin settling upon the landing plat above the house. "Here are my friends."

Two men and a woman alighted from the air car and came toward the house. Waylock rose to his feet; The Jacynth spoke suddenly: "Stay and join us, for an hour or two we shall call a truce."

"I'd gladly make the truce permanent. An even closer relationship would be more acceptable yet."

"Well!" exclaimed The Jacynth. "He's as dexterous at lechery as at Monsterism. The victims must be watchful in all directions!"

Before Waylock could retort, the door chime sounded, and The Jacynth went to admit the first of her guests.

These were the composer Rory McClachern, Mahlon Kermanetz, who repaired and rejuvenated antique musical instruments, and a red-haired sprite of a glark girl known only as Fimfinella. A number of other guests presently arrived, including Chancellor Claude Imish and his secretary, a surly dark-visaged young man named Rolf Aversham.

The Jacynth served a pleasant dinner. The conversation was light and gay. Why, Waylock asked himself, couldn't it be like this always? He looked up to find The Jacynth's eyes on him. His spirits rose; he drank more wine than he might have otherwise, and contributed to the conversation with good effect.

During the evening, Rory McClachern played his new composition: a suite of seven parts, inspired by the fabulous olden times. It was the first hearing of the suite; the draft which

McClachern inserted into the reproducer still showed changes and erasures among the colored lines which controlled the orchestration. He laughed nervously as the sonophone hissed and buzzed. "Dirt and thumbprints. Not part of the composition."

Chancellor Imish presently became bored with the music. He and Waylock sat somewhat apart from the others and the Chancellor's undertone intruded only slightly into the music. "We have met somewhere recently, but the occasion escapes me."

Waylock reminded him of the circumstances.

"Yes, of course," said Imish. "I find it hard to separate all the people I meet; there are so many of them."

"Naturally; yours is a distinguished office," said Waylock.

The Chancellor laughed. "I lay cornerstones, congratulate new Amaranth, read addresses to the Prytaneon." He waved his hand contemptuously. "So much triviality. However, the full extent of my constitutional authority—if I choose to wield it—is actually rather remarkable."

Waylock politely agreed, knowing that twenty-four hours after the Chancellor exercised the least of his prerogatives, the Prytaneon would impeach him by unanimous vote. The office was an anachronism, no more than the symbol of executive potentiality, a survival from times when emergencies were daily occurrences.

"Make a careful reading of the Great Charter. The Chancellor was intended as a super-tribune, a public watchdog. It's in my power—in fact, it's my duty—to make inspections of public property and institutions. I summon the Prytaneon to emergency sessions and order recesses; I am supreme superintendent of the assassins." Imish chuckled hoarsely. "There's only one thing wrong with the job. There's no slope." His gaze fell on the dark, rather hunched young man who had arrived in his company. Imish scowled. "That young jackanapes is a second drawback to my position. A thorn in the side."

"Who is he?"

"My secretary, subaltern, potboy and scapegoat. His title is Vice-Chancellor and his job is even more of a sinecure than my own." Imish gazed at his assistant with dislike. "Rolf, however, insists on considering himself indispensable." He shrugged. "What is your striving, Waylock?"

"I strive at the Actuarian."

"Ah, indeed?" Imish was interested. "Remarkable place. Perhaps I'll make a tour of inspection one of these days."

The music ended; the audience burst out into congratulatory comment. McClachern tried to hide his pleasure with rueful little headshakes of dissatisfaction. There was general conversation.

At midnight the first guests began to depart. Waylock settled himself unobtrusively on a settee, and at last he and The Jacynth were alone.

4

The Jacynth joined him on the settee, facing him with one leg curled beneath her, her arms over the back.

She regarded Waylock with a quizzical expression. "Now then—you are to plead and remonstrate with me, remember?"

"I wonder if I would achieve anything?"

"I hardly think so."

"Why are you so relentless?"

The Jacynth abruptly shifted her position. "You have never seen what I have seen—or you might feel as I do." She turned him a quick side glance as if to verify a mental image. "Sometimes I return to Tonpengh in Gondwana. Everyday at the Grand Stupa there would be a great white fire, and the priests would dance. Every day there would be a dreadful act . . ." The Jacynth winced at the memory.

"Ah," said Waylock, "this may explain the fervor of your persecution."

"If demons exist," whispered The Jacynth, "they are all gathered at Tonpengh—" She focused her eyes on Waylock— "with one exception."

Waylock chose to ignore the personal allusion. "You exaggerate the evil of these men; you judge them too harshly. Remember that they live in their cultural context, not ours. They perform indecent sacrifices—but the history of man is a compendium of such evil. We are an evolutionary product, descendants of predators. A few synthetic foods aside, every morsel eaten by man is taken from another living thing. We are intended for murder; we kill to exist!"

The Jacynth grew pale at the terrible words but he paid

no heed. "We have no instinctive aversion to these acts; it is a product of our times."

"Exactly!" cried The Jacynth. "Don't you understand that here is the transcendent function of the Reach? We must perfect ourselves. Whenever we tolerate a Monster, we sin against the children of tomorrow."

"And you have marked me as one to be purged from the race."

She turned on him an exalted gaze but did not reply.

After a moment Waylock asked, "What of the Weirds? What of The Abel Mandeville? He not only destemporized The Anastasia, but also himself."

"If I had my way," she said between clenched teeth, "any and every Monster, of any and every phyle, would be totally expunged."

"Since this is not within your capability, why harass me?"

She leaned toward him, suddenly anxious for understanding. "I can't stop, I can't relent, I can't be faithless to my ideal."

Their eyes met, held in mutual fascination.

"Gavin Waylock," she said hoarsely, "if only you had trusted me at Carnevalle! Now you are my personal Monster, and I cannot ignore that."

Waylock took her hand. "How much better love is than hate," he said gently.

"And how much better life is than non-life," she responded drily.

"I want you to understand my position thoroughly," he said, his voice tense. "I will fight, I will survive. I will show a ruthlessness beyond your understanding."

Her hand became rigid. "You mean you would never submit to justice!" She snatched away her hand. "You are a rogue-wolf—your strain must be erased, before it corrupts a a thousand others!"

"Reconsider, I beg you," said Waylock. "I do not wish this struggle."

"What is there to consider?" she asked icily. "I am not the judge; I have presented your case to the Amaranth Council and they have made the decision."

Waylock rose to his feet. "Then you are determined?"

She stood up and her beautiful face glowed with vitality. "Of course."

Waylock spoke in a troubled voice. "Whatever happens may involve your fate, as well as my own."

The Jacynth's eyes moved doubtfully. Then she said, "Gavin Waylock, leave my house. I have nothing further to say."

XIII

On Monday morning Waylock reported for work at the Actuarian. He was given a subcutaneous identification imprint, and was then introduced to his superior, Technician Ben Reeve, a short, dark-skinned man with the placid gaze of a ruminant. Reeve welcomed Waylock absently, then stood back and considered. "I'll have to start you low. But naturally you expected nothing better to begin with."

Waylock spoke the usual formula, "I'm here for slope. All I want is a chance to do my best."

"That's the spirit," said Reeve mildly. "You'll get your chance. Well, let's see what we can do for you."

He took Waylock through a series of rooms, corridors, up and down ramps and man-lifts. With surprise and awe, Waylock observed the humming banks of machinery, the glass consoles, the computers and memory banks. They passed through rooms roaring to the flow of power, where the relays clicked and chattered like gossiping women; they skirted hundred-yard-long tanks of liquid air in which bands of silicon floated. They followed a white-marked path through the referential towers, in which long coils of slave-light maintained a fascinating movement, crossed the great hall where sixteen correlative spheres humped out of the floor, each singing its own weird song*.

Three times the black-uniformed guards challenged them, examined their badges, waved them forward after a word of explanation from Reeve. The precautions impressed Waylock; he had expected nothing quite so stringent.

"As you see, security is thorough," Reeve told him. "Don't go wandering out of your zone or you'll wind up in trouble."

---

*A number of musical compositions owed their themes to the plaintive sixteen-voice polyphony of the correlative spheres—so many, indeed, that at this time it was considered trite and mechanistic to compose in such a manner.

Their destination was far to the front of the building: a catwalk directly above the ooze-boxes. Reeve explained the nature of Waylock's duties. He must supply blank forms to the hoppers of the fifty-six printograms. Twice during the shift he must check certain dials, lubricate a half-dozen bearings which were divorced from the central lubrication system. He must maintain order in the corridor and keep it free of dirt and litter. It was a job for a lad from vocational school.

Waylock swallowed his annoyance and went to work. Reeve watched a few moments, and Waylock thought he detected quiet amusement in the man's face. "I know I'm not very efficient at this job," said Waylock, "but after I practice awhile, I'm sure I can handle it."

Reeve grinned openly. "Everybody's got to start," he said, "and this is it for you. If you want to get ahead, you should study—" and he named a series of technical courses available at improvement classes. Presently he left Waylock to his duties.

Waylock worked without enthusiasm, and after the day's shift, returned to his apartment with slow step. His interview with The Jacynth now seemed unreal and grotesque. . . . He cast a quick look behind him. Surely someone was trailing him—or did a spy-lume ride the air over his head? He must be cautious during his transactions; best if they were all conducted within the Actuarian where spy-mechanisms could not penetrate.

The next day he tried to arrange an interview with Vincent Rodenave, but Rodenave was off duty; instead he met Basil Thinkoup for lunch in the cellar restaurant.

"How are you doing in your new niche?" Waylock asked.

"Very well indeed." Basil's eyes glowed. "I've already been promised a promotion, and we're testing one of my ideas next week."

"Which is this?"

"I've always felt that life-charts issued the public were cold and, well, dehumanized. I think they can be improved. There's ample room on each of the charts for some kind of message, an inspirational motto, topical advice, possibly a bit of cheerful verse."

"The particular message might be keyed to the individual's progress," suggested Waylock. "Exhortation, jubilation, or solace, as the case demands."

"A clever refinement!" cried Basil. "We want the public to know the Actuarian as a human institution, dedicated to the welfare of all. These little messages will start the ball rolling." He looked at Waylock fondly. "I'm delighted—"

Suddenly the air was drenched with the sound of gongs and horns. Everyone in the cafeteria froze, faces white and slack, as if the alarm had surprised inner guilt in themselves.

Waylock called a question to Basil; it was lost in the noise. A man slipped into the cafeteria. He was slight, hollow-cheeked, with hair like taffy puff; his breathing was quick as that of a frightened bird. Everyone saw him, and everyone averted his eyes.

He sat and seemed to melt, to withdraw into himself like a snail into its shell. He put his forearms on the table and bent his head, his eyes closed, his mouth opening and shutting.

Three black-uniformed men burst into the cafeteria. They gazed to right and left, then strode across the room and grasped the fugitive. They lifted him to his feet, hustled him out.

The alarms cut off. The silence was numbing. There was no voice or motion in the room. Then a few tentative movements were made, and a mutter of conversation began.

"Poor devil," said Basil.

"Do they take him direct to the cage?" Waylock asked.

Basil shrugged. "Perhaps they beat him first. Who knows? The man is treated not as a criminal but as one guilty of blasphemy."

"Yes," mused Waylock; "the Actuarian is the sacred place of Clarges."

"It's a great mistake, "declared Basil hotly, "personalizing, or rather, deifying, a machine!"

Twenty minutes later Alvar Witherspoke, who worked in Basil's office, stopped by the table. His face was palpitant with excitement.

"What do you think of so bold a rascal?" He looked from Waylock to Basil. "Every day we must be more vigilant."

"We know nothing about the case," said Basil.

"He used to work here, in the mixistaging room. His trick was simple, ingenious. He caught his work report before it went into the tank and tried to drop a dot of magnetiscon behind the decimal."

"Clever," said Basil thoughtfully.

"It's been tried before. Everything's been tried. But nothing works. The alarms go off, then it's quickstep to the bird-cage."

"The alarms go off only when someone blunders," Waylock pointed out. "The successful tricksters don't ring the alarms."

Witherspoke looked down his long nose at Waylock, then turned back to Basil. "Anyway, the house assassins are questioning him, and it'll be the Cage of Shame and the midnight walk. There won't be much sport. He's too frightened, too spindly and poor to make a good run for it."

"I won't be there," said Basil in an even voice.

"Nor I, of course," said Witherspoke, rising to go.

They watched him stop by another table with the news.

Late in the afternoon, just before the end of the day's work, Waylock once more called Vincent Rodenave, and this time was successful. Rodenave greeted him without enthusiasm, and tried to hedge when Waylock asked for an interview. "I'm afraid I don't have the time tonight."

"What I have to say is urgent," said Waylock.

"I'm sorry, but—"

"Call me to your office for an interview."

"No, that's impossible."

Waylock said, "Do you recall an object which you procured for the deceased Anastasia?"

Rodenave looked at him, his face twisted, and slowly sank back into his seat. "Very well," he said in a tense voice. "I will send for you."

Waylock waited by the commu booth; a merry-eyed messenger girl presently came up to him. "Gavin Waylock, Apprentice Technician?"

"Correct."

"Will you come with me, please?"

She delivered Waylock to Rodenave's office. Rodenave touched the platen she extended, taking responsibility for Waylock's presence in the Purple Zone.

Waylock seated himself. "Is this room safe to talk in?"

"Yes." Rodenave looked at him as a housewife might regard a dead rat on the rug. "I have personally spy-proofed it; you may consider it sealed."

"And you are not recording our conversation?"

"No," said Rodenave.

"Because," said Waylock, "I intend to speak nothing in this matter except the truth: that you approached me in regard to your designs on The Anastasia, that you proposed a second dereliction from your trust—"

"That's enough," said Rodenave in a metallic voice. He touched a button. "There is no recording being made."

Waylock grinned and Rodenave had the grace to return a sheepish smile.

"I take it," said Waylock, "that your attachment for The Anastasia has not diminished?"

Rodenave said, "I am no longer a reckless fool, if that is what you mean. I don't care to be stoned by the Weirds." He eyed Waylock in frank speculation. "My folly is of no concern to you. Why are you here?"

"I want something. To get it, I must give you what you want."

Rodenave made a skeptical sound. "What do I want that you possibly could supply?"

"The Anastasia de Fancourt."

Rodenave's eyes became careful. "Nonsense."

"Let us say, one of The Anastasias, for after all there are several. It's been a week since the transition. Presently the cell opens; the new Anastasia comes forth. There are several remaining behind."

Rodenave's eyes were hard and hostile. "Well?"

"One of these surrogates is what I have to offer you."

Rodenave shrugged. "No one knows the location of her cell."

"I do," said Waylock.

"But you offer me nothing, really. Each of the surrogates is The Anastasia. If one of them repulses me, as you put it, they all will."

"Unless you use an amnesiac drug."

Rodenave stared at Waylock. "It is impossible."

"You still have not asked me what I want."

"Well then, what do you want?"

"You were able to remove one televector flake. I want others."

Rodenave laughed weakly. "Now I know you are mad. Do you realize what you're asking? What I would be doing to my career?"

"Do you want The Anastasia? Perhaps I should say, one of the Anastasias?"

"I could not aspire to anything of that nature."

"You were able to do so last week."

Rodenave rose to his feet. "No. Completely and definitely, no."

Waylock said grimly, "Remember you took not one but three televector flakes from here. In doing so, you did me a personal injury. So far I have made no complaint."

Rodenave sank back into his seat. An hour passed, during which he writhed and sweated, argued and blustered, trying to extricate himself from the situation. At the end of this time he had been reduced to criticizing the details of Waylock's plan.

Waylock would not be led away from his main theme. "I ask you to do nothing which you have not done before. If you co-operate with me, you gain what you lost the last time. If you refuse to co-operate, you will simply pay the penalty for your previous theft."

Rodenave at last slumped back in defeat. "I'll have to think it over."

"I have no objection. I will wait while you do so."

Rodenave glared at Waylock, and for five minutes there was silence in the room.

Rodenave finally fidgeted in his chair and muttered, "I have no choice in the matter."

"When can you get me these flakes?"

"You want only flakes for members of the Amaranth Society?"

"Correct."

"I'll have to run them out once, weigh them. I'll do this on one shift. Next shift, I'll bring in a package of film of this weight, density and size. Then I can bring flakes out past the screens."

"Today is Monday. Tuesday, Wednesday. Wednesday night then?"

"Perhaps not Wednesday. We're having a distinguished visitor—Chancellor Imish and his entourage."

"Indeed?" Waylock remembered his conversation with Imish; evidently the Chancellor had been aroused to interest. "Very well. Thursday. I'll come to your apartment to pick them up."

A spasm of anger crossed Rodenave's face. "I'll deliver them to you at the Cafe Dalmatia. And I hope it's the last I see of you!"

Waylock smiled, rose from his chair. "You'll need me to gain your reward."

Crossing the plaza on his way home, Waylock passed under the Cage of Shame. The outcast sat disconsolately, occasionally turning a desperate gaze down at those below. Waylock was in a state of reaction from his contest with Rodenave, and the picture of the miscreant lingered in his mind.

2

Waylock's work schedule was still unsettled and irregular, and on Wednesday he was dismissed at noon.

He crossed the plaza to the Cafe Dalmatia, ate a leisurely lunch, and read the late edition of the *Clarion*.

A terrible event had occurred the previous day at the town of Cobeck in the upper Chant Valley, near the border of the Reach. The inhabitants strove principally at the cutting and polishing of fine pink marble, and had lived the most unobtrusive of lives—until on the afternoon of Tuesday they lapsed into mass hysteria. A great gang boiled from the town, pushed howling to the border control. They stormed the door, set the building ablaze, destroying the control officer and the frontier guards who had barricaded themselves on the upper floor.

The electric barrier went dead for the first time in centuries. The mob charged out into Nomad country, where they were surrounded and attacked. A fearful battle took place in the forest and the villagers were wiped out. The Nomads swarmed across the borders of the Reach and down Chant Valley, spreading horror. They were finally driven back, but the destruction and loss of life were very great.

What had occurred to drive the men and women of Cobeck into the manic phase? Slope was hard to come by; work was slow and monotonous; there was no Carnevalle and the tension had been building up for years: such were the hypotheses. . . . Waylock glanced up from the paper. Into the plaza, normally barred to traffic, came a long gray and gold official car.

Chancellor Claude Imish slipped out, followed by his dark-visaged secretary. They were met by functionaries of the Actuarian; after a brief exchange of pleasantries, the party disappeared within.

Waylock returned to his reading.

3

Chancellor Imish stood on a mezzanine overlooking the Chamber of Archives, in the company of Hemet Gaffens, the portly Assistant Supervisor, two or three lesser officials, and Rolf Aversham, Imish's secretary. The room below them rang with a disturbing shrill singing, half-in, half-out of perception, rising and falling as the mechanism assimilated quanta of information. Gaffens looked down at the whale-smooth housings, the globes of vibrating metal, the suspended glass piezostats. "They can whistle messages to each other which no one else can understand."

Chancellor Imish shook his head. "I had not conceived the magnificent intricacy of this place."

One of the lesser officials spoke in a sententious voice. "It is the magnificent intricacy of our civilization in miniature."

"Why yes, I suppose that's true," said Imish.

Hemet Gaffens snorted under his breath. "Shall we continue?" He swung away and touched the plate on the door, which was a division-point between color zones. Their passes were inspected by house assassins.

"You are cautious here," marveled Imish.

"A necessary vigilance," Gaffens said curtly.

They passed through another portal marked:

EXOTRACKING LABORATORY
Televection.

Gaffens called over Normand Neff, the supervisor, and Vincent Rodenave, his assistant; introductions were performed.

"Your face is familiar," said Imish to Rodenave. "Of course I meet many people."

"I believe I saw you at the Biebursson Exhibition."

"Of course. You are a friend of the dear Anastasia."

"That is so," said Rodenave stiffly.

Normand Neff edged away, impatient to return to his work. He spoke to Rodenave. "Perhaps you'll show the Chancellor some of the projects in conception."

"I'd be delighted," said Rodenave. He stood fingering his chin, as if engrossed by a sudden thought. "Perhaps—well, the televector system."

At the door to the televector chamber they were once again halted by guards, then passed through the antechamber where the various screens, fields and gauges took inventory of their persons.

"Why such precautions?" Imish inquired in innocent wonder. "Surely no one attempts to break in here?"

Gaffens smiled stonily. "In this case, Chancellor, we guard the privacy of our citizens. Not even Director-General Jarvis of the assassins can request information from this room, unless the citizen in question is extant beyond his span."

Chancellor Imish nodded. "Eminently praiseworthy! I wonder—would you kindly explain the function of the device?"

"Rodenave perhaps will demonstrate it for you."

"Why yes," muttered Rodenave. "Of course."

They crossed the white tile floor to the façade of the machine. Technicians glanced at them, returned to their benches. The room foreman approached; Gaffens muttered a few words to him; they stood a little apart as Rodenave took Imish and Aversham to the great mechanism.

"Every person in this world radiates cerebral patterns as unique as his fingerprints. When he registers for Brood, the pattern is recorded and put on file."

Imish nodded. "Go on."

"To locate this person, the master station and two slave stations tune in his pattern, broadcast interference waves. There is a clash, a tiny disturbance, reflection. The directions are plotted as vectors, and appear as a black dot on a master chart. Hence—" He sought through an index, punched buttons. "Here is your personal index, Chancellor. The red outline on the blue coordinate represents the Actuarian. The black dot of course is yourself."

"Ingenious!"

Rodenave went on talking, glancing nervously toward Gaffens and the room superintendent. The name of The Anastasia once more occurred; as if casually, Rodenave keyed out her flake; then according to plan, arranged a throw-out for the entire Amaranth class. The flakes clicked into the hopper—a small gray block of film.

Rodenave's hands were shaking like palm fronds. "These," he stammered, "you understand, are Amaranth televectors— but of course they're blurred . . ." The packet slipped from his fingers and scattered across the floor.

Gaffens exclaimed in annoyance, "Rodenave, you're all thumbs!"

Chancellor Imish said good-naturedly, "No matter, let's gather them up." He bent to his knees and began to scrape up the glittering little flakes of film.

Rodenave said, "That's not necessary, Chancellor; we'll just sweep them into the waste."

"Oh, in that case . . ." Imish regained his feet.

"If you've seen all you care to, Chancellor, we'll move on," said Gaffens.

The group started back through the security chamber. Rolf Aversham lingered behind. He picked up one of the flakes, held it to the light, squinted at it, frowned. He turned to Gaffens, who was leaving the chamber. "Oh, Mr. Gaffens," called Aversham.

4

Waylock sat at the Cafe Dalmatia, toying with a glass of tea. He felt restless but could think of nowhere to take himself, and there seemed to be nothing that urgently needed doing.

From within the Actuarian came a muffled bedlam of alarm. Waylock twisted in his seat, looked across the plaza.

The great façade told him nothing. The alarm cut off. The people in the square who had paused to turn curious faces toward the Actuarian continued about their affairs; some, however, moved aside to watch the Cage of Shame.

Half an hour passed. The creaking of pulleys sounded; out over the square swung the Cage.

Waylock stared, half-rose in his seat. Inside the Cage sat Vincent Rodenave, and his gaze seemed to burn across the plaza into the shadows of the Cafe Dalmatia, into Waylock's brain.

XIV

AT MIDNIGHT the streets of Clarges were quiet, with only a vague subterranean hum to be heard. Few people were abroad.

Students at the vocational improvement classes had returned home to pore over exercise books and perfect their new skills with practice. There was small night life, only the cabarets and theaters catering to the glarks. Those who sought relief from tension had crossed the river to Carnevalle.

The plaza before the Actuarian was empty. Esterhazy Square spread dark as a wilderness. At this hour the Cafe Dalmatia would normally be almost vacant, with only a few dim figures at the tables—a late worker at the Actuarian, an assassin returning from an assignment, a person troubled by the angle of his slope and unable to rest, an occasional pair of lovers. Tonight the tables were all occupied by persons who kept their faces in the shadow.

A light fog had drifted in from the river, blurring the street lights. The Cage of Shame hung like some rusted ancient object, and the man inside sat stiff and brooding as an old iron weathercock.

Midnight was signaled by a far mournful hooting from the direction of the river. The Cage of Shame descended with a rattle; the bottom triggered open, Vincent Rodenave stood free on the pavement.

He faced the shadows of Esterhazy Square, and listened. They seemed to rustle. He took a slow step to the right. A rock spun in out of the gloom, struck him in the side. He stood back, arms and legs thrown wide. A low, hoarse cry sounded from the park; this was unprecedented, because the Weirds traditionally kept utter silence.

Rodenave sensed the new passion; he decided to make a quick escape. He ran for the cafe. A volley of large stones arched in from the dark like meteors. The Weirds were in a grim and savage mood.

A shape appeared in the sky, a dark object falling—an unlighted air car. It grounded; the door flung open; Rodenave tumbled into the cab; the car rose. Stones rattled on the hull; dark shapes raced out of the shadows, to stand staring into the sky. Then they turned and with cautious eyes examined each other, for never had Weirds ventured into the open before. They rumbled and muttered, melted back into the darkness and the plaza was once again empty.

2

Rodenave sat hunched forward, his eyes like bits of murky glass. He had spoken a few husky words, then had lapsed into silence.

Waylock parked the air car and led Rodenave up to his apartment. Rodenave hesitated in the doorway, looked around the room, then walked to a chair, sat down. "Well," he croaked, "here I am. Disgraced. Cast out. Destined." He looked at Waylock. "You don't speak, I notice. Does shame silence you?"

Waylock made no answer.

"You saved me," mused Rodenave, "but you did me no favor. What striving can I find? I will meet the terminator as Third. It means disaster for me."

"Also for me," said Waylock.

Rodenave croaked, "Where do you suffer? Your flakes are secure."

"What!"

"Temporarily, perhaps."

"What happened? Where are the flakes?"

Rodenave's expression became crafty. "Now I wield the lash."

Waylock considered him a moment. "If you keep your end of the bargain and deliver me the flakes, I will keep mine."

"I am proscribed! What use are lovely women to me?"

Waylock grinned. "The Anastasia's attention might help assuage your pain. And all is not lost. You are trained and talented; the world lies before you. There are other strivings with possibly more rapid slope."

Rodenave snorted.

"Where are the flakes?" Waylock asked gently.

The two men stared eye to eye; then Rodenave looked away. "They are behind the cuff of the Chancellor's coat."

"What!"

"That confounded secretary threw the alarm. He walked through the check station with a bit of blank film. The alarm went off and I had to dispose of the flakes; I took hold of Imish's arm and pushed the flakes behind his cuff."

"Then what?"

"Gaffens saw the flake. It was blank. He suspected me at

once. He went into the televection room and looked at the other flakes. All were blank. A number carried my fingerprints. The deduction was obvious, even to Gaffens. The assassins questioned me; threw me into the Cage."

"And Imish?"

"Went his way with the flakes."

Waylock jumped to his feet. It was one o'clock. He went to the commu, called the Chancellor's residence in the southern suburb of Trianwood.

After a lengthy pause, the face of Rolf Aversham appeared on the screen. "Yes?"

"I must speak to the Chancellor."

"The Chancellor is resting; he can see no one."

"It would be for no more than a moment."

"I'm sorry, Mr. Waylock; perhaps you'd care to make an appointment?"

"At ten tomorrow, then."

Aversham consulted a memorandum. "The Chancellor is occupied at that time."

"Very well, whenever you can get me in."

Aversham frowned. "I possibly can give you ten minutes at ten-forty."

"Excellent," said Waylock.

"Do you care to state your business?"

"No."

"As you wish," said Aversham. The screen went dead.

Waylock turned to meet Rodenave's gaze.

"You never told me why you want those flakes."

"I doubt if you'd care to know," said Waylock.

3

In her house on Vandoon Heights, The Jacynth Martin could not rest. The night was mild; she went out on her terrace. The city spread before her; she trembled, her eyes were moist with an indefinable grief. Magnificent Clarges must not decay; the human genius which had built the city must be called on to save it. Against the tides of unrest a counter-effort must be set up: a buttress of faith in the great traditions of Clarges.

On the morrow she would call upon The Roland Zygmont,

presiding chairman of the Amaranth Society. He was a sensitive man; he shared her disturbance, and already had acted with her against Gavin Waylock.

She would press for a conclave. The entire Amaranth Society must meet, discuss, decide and act, in order that the strange restlessness which pervaded Clarges should be soothed, and the continuity of the Golden Age reaffirmed.

XV

THE CHANCELLOR'S mansion was situated upon broad acres of lawn, among formal gardens and antique statuary. The style was old Bijoux, even more ornate than Contemporary. Six towers rose from the roof, each with an intricate crest of colored glass. Balconies ran between cupolas; the wide veranda was fringed with iron arabesques. A gate barred the only passage between house and landing plat, and a guard sat at the gate.

Waylock alighted from his cab, and the guard rose to his feet. He regarded Waylock with automatic hostility. "Yes, sir?"

Waylock gave his name; the gatekeeper checked a list, and let Waylock proceed to the manse.

Waylock crossed the terrace; a footman opened the twelve-foot door, and Waylock entered a formal foyer. In the exact center, directly under an immense old starburst chandelier, stood Rolf Aversham.

"Good morning, Mr. Waylock."

Waylock uttered a polite greeting, to which Aversham nodded curtly. "I must inform you," he said, "that the Chancellor is not only busy, he is indisposed."

"A pity. I will remember to offer my sympathy."

"As you may be aware, I am Vice-Chancellor. Perhaps you could transact your business with me."

"I know I would find you efficient and capable. But I wish to see my friend Chancellor Imish in any case."

Aversham compressed his lips. "This way, if you please."

He led Waylock through a fretted door and along a quiet corridor. A lift conveyed them to an upper floor. Aversham ushered Waylock into a small side chamber. He consulted his watch, waited an impressive thirty seconds, then rapped on the door.

Imish's voice sounded dimly, "Come in."

Aversham slid open the door, stood aside. Waylock entered the room. Chancellor Imish sat at a desk listlessly turning through an old folio. "Ah," said Waylock, "how are you?"

"Well enough, thank you," said Imish.

Aversham seated himself at the far end of the room. Waylock ignored him.

Closing the folio, Chancellor Imish sat back and waited for Waylock to broach his business. He wore a loose jacket of canary linen—definitely not that in which the flakes were concealed.

Waylock began, "Chancellor, I've come today, not as a personal acquaintance, but rather as a citizen—an ordinary man sufficiently troubled to take time away from his striving."

Imish sat up in his seat, frowning uncomfortably. "What is the difficulty?"

"It's a matter of which I don't have complete knowledge. It possibly might be considered a threat."

"Exactly what do you mean?"

Waylock hesitated. "I assume that you trust your employees implicitly? They are absolutely discreet?" He studiously refrained from glancing toward Aversham. "An eventuality might arise in which a word, a look, even a significant silence, might be serious."

Imish said, "This sounds like the sheerest nonsense."

Waylock shrugged. "You're probably right." Then he laughed. "I'll say no more—unless something happens to reinforce my suspicions."

"That might be for the best."

Waylock relaxed, sat back in his chair. "I'm sorry your visit to the Actuarian turned out so miserably. In a way I feel responsible."

"How is that?"

From the corner came the brighter sparkle of Aversham's eyes.

"In the sense that I suggested your visit."

Imish fidgeted. "Think nothing of it. An awkward situation."

"The manse is a wonderfully interesting place. But don't you find it—well, depressing?"

"Very. I wouldn't live here except that I'm required to."

"Just how old is it?"

"It predates Chaos by hundreds of years."

"A magnificent monument."

"I suppose so." Chancellor Imish looked suddenly toward Aversham. "Rolf, perhaps you'd better send out those invitations for the formal dinner."

Aversam rose and stalked from the room. Imish said, "Now, Waylock, what's all this talk?"

Waylock glanced around the walls. "You're protected against spy cells?"

The Chancellor's face was a comical mixture of doubt and indignation. "Why should anyone spy on me? After all," he gave a brittle laugh, "I'm just the Chancellor—next thing to a nonentity!"

"You are titular head of the Prytaneon."

"Bah! I can't even vote to break a tie. If I invoked the slightest of my so-called powers, I'd be certified either into a penal home or a palliatory."

"Possibly true. But—"

"But what?"

"Well, there's been a great deal of public dissatisfaction recently."

"It comes and goes."

"Has it occurred to you that behind this unrest there might be organization?"

Imish looked interested. "What are you driving at?"

"Have you ever heard of the Whitherers?"

"Naturally. A band of crackpots."

"On the surface. But they are inspired and led by practical intelligence."

"In what direction?"

"Who knows? I have been told that the office of Chancellor is an immediate goal."

"Ridiculous," said Imish. "I am secure in my place. My term continues for six years."

"Suppose there were a transition?"

"Such language is in extremely bad taste."

"Consider my question sheerly hypothetical: What would happen in such a case?"

"The Vice-Chancellor is Aversham. So how—"

"Exactly," said Waylock.

The Chancellor stared at him. "You can't imply that Rolf—"

"I imply nothing. I am making statements from which you are drawing inferences."

"Why do you tell me all this?" Imish demanded.

Waylock sat back in his chair. "I have a stake in the future. I believe in stability. I can help preserve this stability and at the same time make slope for myself."

"Ah," said Imish, mildly ironic. "Now it comes out."

"The Whitherer propaganda uses you as a symbol of luxurious living and automatic slope."

"Automatic slope!" The Chancellor laughed incredulously. "If they only knew!"

"It would be a good idea to let them know; to destroy this symbol."

"In what way?" said Imish.

"I believe the most effective counter-propaganda would be a visio-sequence—a historical survey of the office and a biographical account based on your career and character."

"I doubt that anyone would be interested. The Chancellor is nothing more than a minor functionary."

"Except in times of emergency, when the Chancellor must rise to the occasion."

Imish smiled. "In Clarges we have no emergencies. We are too civilized."

"Times change, and there's a spirit of unrest in the air. The Whitherer agitation is one manifestation. This visio-sequence I mention—it might puncture one or two forensic bubbles. If we successfully enhanced your prestige, both of us might gain slope."

Imish thought a moment or two. "I have no objections to a visio-sequence, but naturally—"

"I'd insist that you edit it," said Waylock.

"Certainly it could do no harm," Imish reflected.

"In that case, I'll start making notes today."

"I want to consider, talk the matter over before making a final decision."

"Naturally."

"I'm sure you exaggerate this thing. Especially the idea that Rolf . . . I can't believe it."

"Let's reserve judgment," agreed Waylock. "But it might be best not to confide in him."

"I suppose not." Imish sat up in his chair. "Just what do you plan for this sequence?"

"My primary aim," said Waylock "is to depict you as a man in the old tradition, aware of your responsibility, yet simple and modest in your habits."

Imish chuckled. "That might be a hard idea to put across. I am notoriously a good-liver."

"A matter of interest," Waylock went on thoughtfully, "would be your wardrobe—the ceremonial costumes, the various regalia."

Imish was puzzled. "I'd have hardly thought—"

"It makes a good introduction to the subject," said Waylock. "The human-interest touch."

Imish shrugged. "You may be right."

Waylock rose to his feet. "If I may, I'd like to visit your wardrobe, and perhaps make a few notes for this introductory sequence."

"As you like." Imish reached out. "I'll call Rolf."

Waylock caught his arm. "I'd prefer to work without Mr. Aversham. Just direct me; I'll find my way."

Imish was smiling. "It's incongruous using my wardrobe as counter-propaganda! . . . Well, for what it's worth . . ." He started to rise from his desk.

"No, no," Waylock insisted. "I'd prefer not to disrupt your life any more than necessary. And I work better alone."

Imish subsided. "Just as you like." He gave Waylock directions.

"I'll be back presently," said Waylock.

2

Waylock moved down the corridor. At the door Imish had designated, he stopped. No one was in sight. He slid back the door and stepped into the dressing room.

Imish's way of life, as he had admitted, was hardly austere. The walls were black marble, inlaid with malachite and cinnabar. The floor was white luster-foam; curtains of silk blew and rippled back from the tall open windows. Cupboards of waxwood with mother-of-pearl panels occupied one wall; opposite opened the door to the wardrobe.

Waylock hesitated only an instant, then entered the wardrobe.

He stood among racks, forms, cases, cabinets and shelves. About him were cloaks, robes, tunics, baldrics and mantles, breeches and trousers. Shelves held a hundred sets of shoes, pumps, boots and sandals. There were uniforms of twenty different orders, Carnevalle costumes; sport outfits. . . . Waylock's eyes roved back and forth, seeking the blot of scarlet which would mark the embroidered jacket of yesterday.

He moved along the aisle, touching, examining, peering. . . . On the second rack he found the jacket. He pulled it forth—and stopped short. At the far end of the aisle stood Rolf Aversham. He came forward slowly, eyes gleaming.

"I could not understand your interest in the Chancellor's wardrobe until—" He nodded at the jacket—"I saw what you were after."

"Apparently," said Waylock, "you understand my purpose here."

"I understand only that you are holding the jacket in which Chancellor Imish visited the Actuarian. May I have it?"

"Why, may I ask, do you want it?"

"Curiosity."

Waylock stepped around the end of the rack and reached to remove the flakes. He felt them but could not dislodge them. Aversham's steps sounded behind him; Aversham's hand reached forward, jerked at the jacket. Waylock gave a savage twist, but Aversham lunged forward and took a firm hold. Waylock struck at Aversham's face; Aversham kicked at Waylock's groin. Waylock seized the leg, hauled it up with tremendous force; Aversham went hopping, reeling back toward the windows. Clutching at the shinar silk, he gave a hoarse shout and fell backward out into space. Waylock stared in shock at the empty rectangle of light. From below came a jangle, another terrible call, a peculiar rattling sound.

Waylock ran forwad, peered down upon the body of Rolf Aversham, who in falling had impaled himself upon the lances of an iron fence. His legs, thrashing and kicking, rattled the loose iron, a sound which presently ceased.

Waylock came back into the room, feverishly tore at the jacket, extracted the flakes, then returned the garment to its rack.

A moment later he burst into the study. Chancellor Imish

hastily flicked off a screen upon which nude men and women cavorted in grotesque comedy. "What's wrong?"

"I was right," gasped Waylock. "Aversham came into the wardrobe and attacked me! He spied on us while we talked!"

"But—but—" Imish rose in his seat. "Where is he?"

Waylock told him.

3

Chancellor Imish, cheeks twitching, skin the color of stale milk, dictated a report to the Trianwood sub-Chief Assassin.

"His work had become faulty. Then I discovered he was systematically spying on me. I discharged him and engaged my friend Gavin Waylock in his place. He came on me in my wardrobe, attacked me. Luckily Gavin Waylock was at hand. In the struggle Aversham fell out of the window. It was acci-dent—sheer accident."

The assassin presently departed. Imish came wearily into the room where Waylock waited. "It's done," the chancellor said. He stared at Waylock. "I hope you're right."

"It was the only way," said Waylock. "Any other story might have involved you in a sordid scandal."

Imish shook his head, still dazed by what had happened.

"Incidentally," said Waylock, "when would you like me to commence my duties?"

Imish stared. "You actually intend to take Rolf's place?"

"Well, I have no love for the Actuarian and I'll do anything I can to help you."

"That's a poor way to make slope—jump from one job to another."

"I'm content," said Waylock.

Imish shook his head. "Secretary to the Chancellor is secre-tary to a nonentity—which is worse than being the nonentity."

"I've always wanted a title. As your secretary, I become Vice-Chancellor. Besides, you've told the assassins that you hired me to replace Aversham."

Imish compressed his lips. "That's no problem. You could refuse the job."

"I'm afraid it would be poor publicity. After all, we've got the Whitherers to think of—"

Imish went to his chair, dropped into it, stared with poignant accusation at Waylock. "This is a terrible mess!"

"I'll do my best to get you out of it." Waylock sat back in his chair. For long seconds the two men stared at each other.

"I might as well clean out Aversham's belongings," said Waylock.

XVI

A month passed. Autumn came to Clarges. Trees turned red and yellow, the dawns became gray, the winds brought a hint of approaching chill.

Clarges celebrated one of the great annual holidays. The people came out upon the streets to walk. In Esterhazy Square a man went into a sudden frenzy, and, mounting a bench, launched into a tirade, shaking his fist toward the Actuarian. Men and women stopped to listen, and presently his anger awoke resonance. A pair of apprentice assassins came past in their black uniforms, and the madman called a curse on them. The crowd turned to stare; the assassins veered away, and made the mistake of hurrying. The crowd roared and hastened after. The assassins, running fleetly, managed to escape. The speaker, overcome by excitement, sank to the ground, face buried in his hands.

Without a focus, the crowd lost cohesion, and dispersed into blank-faced components. But for a moment they had known mass anger; they had acted in concert against the static order. The news-organs, describing the event, used the caption: *Weirds in the Daylight?*

Waylock spent the day at his apartment on Phariot Way, where Vincent Rodenave had established himself. Rodenave had lost weight; his eyes peered from under his brows with demoniac intentness.

When Waylock called, Rodenave had worked halfway through the set of televector flakes. A large-scale chart hung on the wall, studded with scarlet-headed pins, each representing a cell where an Amaranth kept his surrogates. Waylock studied it with somber satisfaction.

"This," he told Rodenave, "could be the most dangerous sheet of paper in the world."

"I realize that," said Rodenave. He pointed toward the window. "There's always an assassin in the street. This apartment is carefully watched. Suppose they choose to break in?"

Waylock frowned, folded the chart, thrust it into his pocket. "Continue with the others. If I can get away this week—"

"If you can get away? Do you work?"

Waylock laughed sourly. "I do the work of three men. Aversham minimized his work. I make myself indispensable."

"How?"

"First, by enhancing Imish's own position. He had given up, was awaiting his assassin in Third. Now he hopes he'll make Verge. We go everywhere. He exerts his official status as much as he can. He makes speeches, champions good causes, gives interviews to the press, in general behaves like a man of importance." A few seconds later Waylock said in a thoughtful voice. "He might surprise us all."

2

Returning to Trianwood, Waylock went directly to the Chancellor's suite. Imish lay on the couch asleep. Waylock dropped into a chair.

Imish awoke, sat up blinking. "Ah, Gavin. The holiday, how goes it in Clarges?"

Waylock considered. "Poorly, I should say."

"How so?"

"There is tension in the air. No one rests. A running stream expends its energy, but when the stream is impounded, the weight builds up and becomes oppressive."

Imish scratched his head and yawned.

"The city is crowded," said Waylock. "Mr. Everyman is abroad, walking the street. No one knows why he walks, but he docs."

"Perhaps for exercise," yawned Imish. "To take the air, to see the city."

"No," said Waylock. "He seems wan and tense. He is uninterested in the city, he looks only at other men. And he is disappointed because they look back with his own face."

Imish frowned. "You make him sound so dismal, so tired."

"That was my intent."

"Oh nonsense!" Imish said bluffly. "Clarges was never built by men such as these."

"I agree. Our great days have come and gone."

"Why," exclaimed Imish, "our organization has never run so smoothly, we've never produced so efficiently, or consumed with so little waste."

"And never have the palliatories been so full," said Waylock.

"You're the soul of optimism today."

Waylock said, "Sometimes I wonder why I'm fighting for slope. Why rise to Amaranth in a world failing before one's eyes?"

Imish was half-amused, half-alarmed. "You're in a sore state indeed!"

"A great man, a great chancellor, could change the shape of the future. He could save Clarges."

Imish hoisted himself to his feet, padded over to the desk. "You teem with interesting ideas. At last," he smiled, "I understand the source of the talk I've been hearing about you."

Waylock raised his eyebrows. "About me?"

"Correct." Imish was standing by the desk, looking down at him. "I've heard remarkable reports."

"What do you mean?"

"You are said to trail a black shadow after you; wherever you go, horror follows close behind."

Waylock snorted. "Who is the author of this nonsense?"

"Director-General Caspar Jarvis, of the assassins."

"The Director-General passes his time at slander. Meanwhile the Weirds and Whitherers hang like an executioner's axe over our culture."

Imish smiled. "Now, then, it's hardly so serious, is it?"

Waylock had raised the Whitherers as a bugaboo merely for the entree it provided to the Chancellor's wardrobe, but now he was saddled with the issue.

Imish continued: "The Weirds are unorganized hoodlums, psychotics; the Whitherers are cloud-chasers, romanticists. The truly dangerous outcasts are all fled to the Thousand Thieves quarter at Carnevalle."

Waylock shook his head. "We know them; they are isolated. These others are part of us, here, there, everywhere. The Whitherers, for instance, work at low pressure. If they can communicate their central idea—that Clarges is sick, that Clarges must be cured—then they are content. Because then they have won a new Whitherer."

Imish rubbed his forehead in bewilderment. "But this is exactly what you were telling me five minutes ago! You are an arch-Whitherer yourself!"

"Possibly true," said Waylock, half-amused, "but my solution is not so revolutionary as some I've heard."

Imish was adamant. "Everyone knows that we live in a Golden Age. The Director-General tells me——"

"Tomorrow night," said Waylock "the Whitherers meet. I shall take you to this meeting and then you shall see for yourself."

"Where do they meet?"

"At Carnevalle. In the Hall of Revelation."

"That place of madmen? And still you take them seriously?" Waylock smiled. "Come and see."

3

Carnevalle was thronged; the avenues seethed with bright costumes. Faces masked and half-seen streamed past and were gone, like sparks from a forge.

Waylock wore a new costume, made of orange slave-light in tongues and plumes. A mask of scarlet metal clothed his face, reflecting the glow and flicker; he walked like a living flame.

Imish wore garb equally striking: the ceremonial costume of a Mataghan warrior. He tinkled with bells, shone with bright bosses, fluttered with black bristles and green feathers. His headdress was an enormous confection of luminous red, green and blue glass, shot with ribbons of white slave-light.

The excitement affected Imish and Waylock; they laughed and talked animatedly. Imish showed a disposition to forget the business which had brought them to Carnevalle, but Waylock was inflexible and led him past the temples of enticement. They walked under the enameled Bridge of Whispers, with its pagoda-like roof and heart-shaped casements. Before them bulked the Hall of Revelation. Blue columns supported a dark green architrave; a scroll inquired, WHAT IS TRUTH? Twin copies of an antique statue—a man cogitating a mystery with elbow on knee and chin on hand—flanked the entrance. Waylock and Imish tossed florins into the donation box and entered.

They were greeted by a confusion of sound and image. Along the walls, blank-eyed goddesses in archaic style held flaring torches; the ceiling could not be seen for shadow. Under each torch a dais had been built; on each dais stood a man or woman, more or less feverish, haranguing a crowd of greater or lesser volume. On one dais two men competed for the crowd's attention, until mutually frustrated, they turned upon each other and struggled with fists and knees.

"Who'll sail with me?" cried a man from another dais. "I've got the barge; I need money. The island, I swear it is mine; there is abundancy of fruit."

Waylock told Imish, "That's Kisim the Primitivist. He's been ten years organizing a colony for this island."

"We'll swim in warm water, sleep on the hot beach—it's the natural life, easy, free—"

"And what of the barbarians, the cannibal barbarians?" called a heckler. "Do we eat them before they do us?" The crowd laughed.

Kisim protested furiously, "They are innocuous; they war only among themselves! In any event the island is mine; the barbarians must depart!"

"With a hundred new skulls as trophies!"

The crowd roared at this near-obscenity; Imish grimaced in distaste. He and Waylock passed to the next dais.

"The Sunset League," Waylock told his companion. "Glarks for the most part."

"—and then at the end—oh brothers and sisters, don't turn away—because I say to you, the end is the beginning! We're going back to the bosom of the great Friend; we'll live forever in glory exceeding the Amaranth! But we must have faith, we must move away from earthly arrogance; we must believe!"

"—ten thousand strong men, this is our need and our goal!" came from the next dais. "There's no need to sweat and swelter for dear life here in Clarges. I'll lead you, the Legion of Light! Ten thousand of us in silver metal, with tools of war. We'll march through Tappany, we'll liberate Mercia, Livergne, Escobar. And then, we'll make ourselves Amaranth. Just ten thousand of us, the Legion of Light—"

On the dais opposite stood a frail woman with a white face. Black hair floated around her head. Her eyes, mild and wide, looked into a distance far beyond the knowing of those below her. "—fear and envy, they are with us, and with what justice? None whatever. Immortality is equally free to glark and to Amaranth; no one dies! How does an Amaranth live on? He emphathizes surrogates; he identifies with them completely. How will a glark live on? By almost exactly the same means. He identifies not with his surrogates, but with Man. All the people of the future are his surrogates. He identifies with humanity, and when the ultimate ultimate arrives, he transfers on, merges into a new life. He lives forever!"

Imish asked. "And who is she?"

"I don't know," said Waylock. "I've never seen her before. . . . Here are the Whitherers. Come. Listen."

A woman of striking mature beauty stood on the dais. "— any eventuality," she was saying. "It's hard to determine a trend, if trend there is. The participating public is superbly conditioned; it's hard to make any decisive impression. But the palliatories tell the story. A few patients are discharged, but a man is like a rope: both break at a definite strain. These 'cures' leave the palliatory; they return to the struggle, they encounter the identical tension which broke them before, and they're back at the palliatory.

"The solution is not splicing the rope; it's lessening the tension. But the tension increases, rather than decreases. So, as we agreed at our previous meeting, we must prepare for anything. Here is Morcas Marr, who has further information."

She stepped off the stand. Imish nudged Waylock. "I've seen that woman . . . That's Yolanda Benn!" He was astounded. "Yolanda Benn, think of it!"

Morcas Marr stood on the dais, a small knobby man with a rigid face. He spoke in a dead-flat voice, consulting a notebook.

"These are the recommendations of the Steering Committee. To simplify administration, we will continue with the present authority districts. I have here—" He held up his notebook—"the district assignments which I will presently announce. These appointments naturally are tentative, but in view of the popular temper, we thought it best to get our organization to its working efficiency as rapidly as possible."

Imish whispered into Waylock's ear, "What in the devil is he talking about?"

"Listen!"

"Each leader will organize his own district, appoint his own executive groups, schedule his own drills. I will run now through this list of appointments." He lifted his notebook. "Coordinating executive: Jacob Nile."

There was a small stir to one side of the crowd. Waylock saw Nile. Beside him stood a woman with a long nervous face, gaunt cheekbones, untidy roan hair: Pladge Caddigan.

Morcas Marr finished reading his appointments, and asked, "Now, are there any questions?"

"Yes, there certainly are!" The voice was close beside Waylock. In amusement and embarrassment he saw that it issued from the mouth of Chancellor Imish.

"I want to know the purpose of this massive semi-conspiratorial organization," Imish demanded.

"You are welcome to ask, whoever you are. We hope to protect ourselves and the civilization of the Reach in the cataclysm which quite clearly is approaching."

" 'Cataclysm'?" Imish was dumbfounded.

"Is there a better word for absolute anarchy?" Marr turned his attention elsewhere. "Any further questions?"

"Mr. Marr," said Nile, stepping forward, "I believe I recognize an eminent public figure." His tone was facetious. "It is the Chancellor of the Prytaneon, Claude Imish. Perhaps we can induce him to join our ranks."

Imish was equal to the occasion. "I might if I knew what you stood for."

"Ah ha!" exclaimed Nile. "That is a question no one can answer because no one knows. We refuse to define our position. And herein lies our great strength. All are zealots because each imagines the general conviction to be his own. We are linked only by the common question 'Whither?' "

Imish became angry. "Instead of talking cataclysm and bleating 'Whither?' you should ask, 'How best can I lessen the problems which beset our country?' "

There was silence, then a burst of spirited rebuttal. Waylock sidled away from Imish, to join Pladge Caddigan and Jacob Nile.

"I find you in distinguished company," said Pladge.

"My dear young woman," Waylock replied, "I *am* distinguished company. I am Vice-Chancellor."

Jacob Nile found the situation amusing. "And you two, our nominal heads of government—why are you here in such questionable company?"

"We hope to gain slope by exposing the Whitherers as conspiratorial subversionists."

Nile laughed. "You may call on me for any required cooperation."

Angry shouts interrupted them; Imish had stirred up an imbroglio. The evening was fulfilling Waylock's hopes.

"Listen to that ass!" muttered Nile.

"If you are not a party of criminal syndicalists," bellowed Imish, "why do you perfect this treacherous organization?"

A dozen voices answered him; Imish heeded none. "You may be assured of one thing. I intend to urge the assassins upon you; I intend to nail this insolent usurpation to the board!"

"Ha!" cried Morcas Marr in biting scorn. "Urge away! Who will listen? You have not the influence I have, you stomach, you loud voice, you bad breath!"

Imish pawed the air. He could find no words; he sputtered. Waylock took his arm. "Come."

Blind in his wrath, Imish allowed himself to be led away. At the Pomador, on the fourth deck of the fantastic Garden of Circe, they sat and took cooling refreshment.

Imish was numb, mortified at his retreat; Waylock kept a tactful silence. Together they looked out over the luminous paint-pot of Carnevalle. The time was midnight; Carnevalle was at its peak; the air sighed and vibrated.

Imish downed his drink at a gulp. "Come," he croaked, "let's move on."

They walked the avenues. Waylock once or twice suggested diversion, but Imish made curt refusal.

They wandered down to the esplanade. At the Argonaut they drank more liquor. Imish became a trifle ill, and decided to return home. They set out along the esplanade toward the air depot.

Carnevalle seemed vague, unreal. The lights and colors were absorbed by the water, crooked shapes moved through the murk. Some of these were revelers, anonymous as scraps of paper floating down the dark Chant. Others were Berbers, who, like the Weirds, took pleasure in dark violence. A group of these came from the shadows. They sidled up to Imish and Waylock, suddenly attacked, kicking and striking.

Imish squealed, fell to his knees, tried to crawl away on all fours. Waylock stumbled back, dazed. The shapes kicked Imish sprawling, beat Waylock's face with fists like hammers. Waylock fought back. The attackers fell away, then darted forward. Waylock was down; his mask came loose.

"It's Waylock!" came an awed whisper. "Gavin Waylock."

Waylock jerked a knife from a hidden sheath. The blade snapped out; he slashed at a leg, heard a scream. He hauled himself to his feet, ran forward, hacking and stabbing. The Berbers backed away, turned, ran.

Waylock went to where Imish was painfully rising. They hobbled down the esplanade, torn and disheveled. At the air depot they climbed aboard a cab, and were sped across the river to Trianwood.

4

Chancellor Imish was terse and moody for several days. Waylock performed his duties as unobtrusively as possible.

One bleak morning in late November, with black veils of rain hanging over Glade County, Imish came into Waylock's office. He settled gingerly into a chair. His ribs were still sore, his face was bruised and tender. There had been psychological damage as well: he had lost weight; lines had formed around his mouth.

Waylock listened while Imish struggled with ideas and sorted out words.

"As you know, Gavin, I am something of an anachronism. A Golden Age has no need for a strong leader. But still—" He paused and reflected. "We cherish security, strength to lean on in case of emergency. Hence the office of Chancellor." Imish went to the window, stood looking out into the stormy sky. "Peculiar things are happening in Clarges—but no one seems to care. I intend to do something about it. So—" He swung about, faced Waylock "—call Director-General Caspar Jarvis of the assassins, ask him to be here at eleven o'clock."

Waylock nodded. "Very well, Chancellor."

XVII

Waylock called the Central Cell in Garstang, and asked to be connected to Director-General Caspar Jarvis. The process consumed time and effort; he argued in turn with the switchboard operator, a public-relations official, the Cell Manager, the Assistant Director and finally won through to Jarvis himself—a bushy black-browed man crouched over his desk like a dog over a bone. "What the devil is it now?"

Waylock explained, and Jarvis became peculiarly cooperative. "The Chancellor wishes to see me at eleven then?"

"Exactly correct."

"And you are Vice-Chancellor Waylock?"

"I am."

"Interesting! I hope to see more of you, Vice-Chancellor!" He opened his mouth and laughed in small soundless gusts.

"At eleven then," said Waylock.

Jarvis appeared at ten minutes to eleven with a pair of aides. He strode into the ornate reception hall, halted at the reception desk, looked Waylock up and down, smiling as if at a private joke. "So now we meet in person, face to face."

Waylock rose to his feet and nodded.

"Not for the last time, I hope," Jarvis went on. "Where is the Chancellor?"

"I'll take you to him."

Waylock led the way to the formal council chamber, outside of which Jarvis posted his aides.

Within, Imish waited. In the massive old chair, with the escutcheons of former chancellors behind him, he achieved a certain brooding dignity. He greeted Jarvis, then signaled to Waylock.

"I won't need you, Gavin. You may go."

Waylock withdrew. Jarvis said with a kind of curt amiability, "I am a busy man, Chancellor. I assume you have something important to tell me."

Imish nodded. "I consider it so. I have recently been made aware of a situation—"

Jarvis held up his hand. "One moment, sir. If Waylock is involved in this matter, you might as well have him in here, because the blackguard listens by spy-cell in any case."

Imish smiled. "He may be a blackguard, but he listens at no spy-cells; there aren't any. I have had the room carefully inspected."

Jarvis looked skeptically around the room. "May I take the liberty of applying my own tests?"

"By all means."

Jarvis took a tubular instrument from his pouch, walked around the room, pointing the instrument, watching a dial as he walked. He frowned, made a second survey.

"There is no eavesdrop device in the room." He went to the door, slid it open. His aides stood quietly where he had left them.

Jarvis returned to his seat. "Now we will talk."

Waylock, standing in the next room with his ear to a hole he had forced through the sound-proofing, smiled.

"In a sense Waylock is involved," came Imish's voice. "For reasons of his own, he has shown me a subtle danger you may or may not be aware of."

"Anticipating danger is not my duty."

Imish nodded. "Perhaps it is mine. I refer to a peculiar organization, the Whitherers—"

Jarvis made an impatient movement. "There is nothing of interest to us there."

"You have agents among the group, then?"

"None. Nor in the Sunset League, nor the Abracadabrists, nor the Stonemasons Guild, nor the Unified Globe, nor the Vedanticizers, nor the Silver Thionists—"

"I want you to investigate the Whitherers at once," said Imish.

There was argument. Imish was quietly obdurate. Jarvis finally threw up his hands. "Very well. I'll do as you ask. The times *are* unsettled; perhaps we've been remiss."

Imish nodded, settled back in his chair. Jarvis thrust his heavy face forward. "Now—I have a very urgent suggestion to make. Drop Waylock. Get rid of him. The man is a blight, a dark shadow. Moreover, he is a Monster. If you have any regard for the reputation of your office, you will discharge him before we make our call."

Imish's dignity wavered. "Are you—ah—referring to the transition of my previous secretary Rolf Aversham?"

"No." Jarvis inspected Imish with a cold concentration. Imish squirmed. "According to your testimony, Waylock could not have been guilty."

"No," said Imish; "of course not."

"I speak of a crime which occurred several months ago at Carnevalle, when Waylock arranged the destemporization of The Jacynth Martin."

"What!"

"We have made contact with his accessory: a notorious Berber known as Carleon. Carleon will provide evidence sufficient to convict Waylock—for a consideration."

"Why are you telling me all this?" Imish asked stiffly.

"Because you can help us."

"In what way?"

"Carleon wants a pardon. He wants to leave Thousand Thieves and return to Clarges. You have the legal authority to issue it."

Imish blinked. "My powers are only nominal; you know that as well as I do."

"Nevertheless they are valid. I could go to the College of Tribunes or the Prytaneon for the same amnesty, but there would be publicity, awkward questions."

"But this Carleon—isn't his guilt equal to that of Waylock's? Why absolve one in order to punish the other?"

Jarvis was silent. Imish was not quite the pliant and amiable fool he had expected to find. "It is a matter of policy," he said at last. "Waylock is in the nature of a special case; I have had orders to apprehend him by any means whatever."

"No doubt the Amaranth Society is exerting pressure."

Jarvis nodded. "Consider the situation in this light. Two scoundrels, Waylock and Carleon, are both at liberty. By granting Carleon the amnesty we trap Waylock. This is clear gain."

"I see. . . . Do you have the necessary papers?"

Jarvis brought a document from his pocket. "You need only sign here."

Imish read the list of crimes from which his signature would absolved Carleon. He became indignant. "The man is depraved! You vindicate a creature of this sort in order to trip up Waylock, a saint by comparison?" He threw the document down.

Jarvis, with stolid patience, went over the situation again. "I explained, sir, that this creature lives free and untaxed at Carnevalle. We lose nothing by remitting him these crimes; we gain by prosecuting Waylock—and then, there are the wishes of highly placed persons to be considered."

Imish seized a pen, angrily scribbled his signature. "Very well, then. There it is."

Jarvis took the document, folded it, rose to his feet. "Thank you for your help, Chancellor."

"I hope I don't get in trouble with the Prytaneon," muttered Imish.

"I can reassure you there," said Jarvis. "They will never know."

Jarvis returned to the Central Cell at Garstang. Almost as he arrived a call came through from Imish.

"Director, I feel I must report that Waylock is gone."

"Gone? Gone where?"

"I don't know. He left without a word to me."

"Very well," said Jarvis. "Thank you for calling."

The screen faded. Jarvis sat a moment deep in thought. Then he punched a button and spoke into a microphone. "Carleon's pardon is ready. Get to him; arrange for a meeting —the sooner the better."

2

A man in a brass mask moved quickly along a narrow passageway, open to the sky. At a small steel door he paused, looked forward and back, entered, took three quick steps, stopped short. He waited two seconds while a trap of firelances struck out in front of him and behind him. They cut off; he stepped forward through the trap.

He went swiftly down a flight of stairs into a bleak room furnished with benches and a table. At the table sat a small man with a pinched face and great luminous eyes.

"Where's Carleon?" asked the man in the mask.

The little man nodded toward a door. "In his Museum."

The man in the mask went quickly to the door, opened it, passed into a long concrete-walled corridor.

He moved along this corridor in a peculiar fashion, walking for a space on the extreme left, then jumping across to the extreme right. At a seemingly blank spot, he brushed aside a door, entered a long room, furnished with overpowering opulence and shot with green light.

A large man with a round dead-white face looked up questioningly. One arm hung behind his back. His eyes shone when he saw the man in the brass mask. "Well?"

His visitor removed the mask.

"Waylock!" Carleon swung his arm around; it held a powerpistol. Waylock had been prepared; his own weapon was ready. It rattled; Carleon's lifeless body jerked back as if snatched by an invisible hook.

Waylock looked down the aisles of the "museum." Carleon had been a necrologue; the exhibits consisted of death in all its phases and stages. Waylock looked in surprise at the broken body of Carleon. This was the man who was to go free in order that Waylock be trapped! He had underestimated the determination of his opponents. . . .

He returned to the bleak lobby. The little dark man sat as before. Waylock said, "I've just killed Carleon."

The dark man showed no particular interest.

"Carleon wanted to cross the river," said Waylock. "He arranged with the assassins for a pardon."

The dark man flashed his luminous eyes across the table at Waylock. Waylock said, "I need a hundred men, Rubel. I have a great project in mind and I need help. I will pay five hundred florins for a night's work."

Rubel nodded solemnly. "Is there danger?"

"Some."

"The money in advance?"

"Half in advance."

"Do you possess this money?"

"Yes, Rubel." The Grayven Warlock, publisher of the *Clarges Direction*, had been a wealthy man. "You shall act as paymaster."

"When do you want these men?"

"I will let you know four hours in advance. They must be strong, quick, intelligent; they must be able to avoid common death traps. They must follow instructions exactly."

Rubel said, "I doubt if there are a hundred such in all Carnevalle."

"Then find women. They will suit just as well, and perhaps better, in certain cases."

Rubel nodded.

"One last caution. The assassins generally work through you, Rubel. You are their agent."

Rubel made a smiling dissent which Waylock ignored.

"Therefore you know the lesser informers. There must be absolutely no leaks. You will be held responsible. Do you understand?"

"Fully," said Rubel.

"Good. When next I see you I will bring money."

A little screen box buzzed; Rubel, with a cautious look at Waylock, answered. A voice spoke in Carnevalle cant, unintelligible to the plain citizen.

Rubel turned to Waylock. "The assassins want Carleon."

"Tell them that Carleon is dead."

3

The news was relayed to Jarvis; he reacted decisively. "Send the Special Squad to Carnevalle, every man. Their orders are to find Gavin Waylock and take him."

Two hours passed, and the reports began trickling back. "He's slipped us by." Jarvis sat back in his chair, gazed across the black roofs of Garstang. "Well, we'll find him. . . . A pity we can't use televection. . . . They tie our hands!" He swung around, volleyed a barrage of orders.

XVIII

THE AMARANTH SOCIETY had convened to its two hundred and twenty-ninth conclave. Each member sat in a chamber of his home, facing a curved wall, formed of ten thousand facets. Each facet showed the face of an Amaranth and his vote-indicator—a tiny bulb which could glow the red of vigorous dissent, the orange of disapproval, the yellow of neutrality, the green of approval, or the blue of vehement approbation.

At the center of the mosaic a tabulator integrated the votes and displayed the color of the group decision. Any member addressing the Society was depicted on a large central screen.

Tonight, ninety-two per cent of the Society was in attendance.

After the traditional opening ceremonies, The Roland Zygmont preempted the speaker's screen.

"I will waste no time on introductory flourishes. We meet tonight to discuss a matter which everyone has pretended not to notice: the violent destemporization of one Amaranth by another.

"We have ignored this matter because we deemed it shameful and not too serious: after all, why else are surrogates empathized?

"Now we must strike out boldly for our principles. The quenching of life is a fundamental evil; we must react savagely against any transgressor among us.

"You wonder why the topic arises now. The basic reason is the continuing and steady series of destemporizations across the years, the latest victim being The Anastasia de Fancourt. Her assailant ended his own life; neither the new Anastasia nor the new Abel have yet returned to us.

"There is one case, however, which exemplifies the evil which can come from disregard for another's life. The protagonist of the case is one Gavin Waylock, known to many of us as The Grayven Warlock."

From the mosaic came a quick hum of interest.

"I yield now to The Jacynth Martin who has made a study of the case."

The face of The Jacynth appeared on the central screen. Her eyes were wide and brilliant; she appeared overdrawn and tense.

"The case of Gavin Waylock defines the entire issue which faces us. Or perhaps I do him an injustice—because Gavin Waylock is a man unique!

"Let me list the violent devitalizations for which Gavin Waylock is directly responsible: The Abel Mandeville; myself, The Jacynth Martin. Speculatively, Seth Caddigan, Rolf Aversham. Only yesterday, the Berber Carleon. These are the events known to us. Doubtless there have been others. Evil follows Waylock.

"Why is this? Is it accidental? Is Waylock an innocent instrument of doom? Or is Waylock possessed of so massive an arrogance that he destroys to gain his selfish ends?"

Her voice had risen, her words were uttered at a staccato pace. She was breathing heavily.

"I have studied Gavin Waylock. He is no innocent instrument of doom. He is a Monster. His morals are those of the Jurassic swamp; they give him a remorseless power, which is directed against the people of Clarges. He is a physical threat to each of us!"

From the mosaic came a rustle, a buzz. A voice cried, "How so?" echoed by another voice and another: "How so? How so?"

The Jacynth responded: "Gavin Waylock ignores our laws. He breaks them whenever he feels so inclined. Success is contagious. He will be joined by others. Like a virus molecule, he will contaminate our entire community."

The mosaic hummed and whispered.

"Gavin Waylock's goal is Amaranth. He is candid on the subject." She leaned back, looked around the mosaic, scanning the thousands of minute faces. "If we felt so inclined, we could ignore the law of Clarges, and give him what he wants." She asked in a quiet voice, "What is your will on this?"

A dull sound like spent surf came from the speaker. Hands reached for the optators, the mosaic twinkled with color: a blue here and there, a few more greens, a sprinkle of yellows, a great wash of orange and red. The panel of the tabulating register glowed vermillion.

The Jacynth held up her hand. "But if we don't surrender, I warn you, we must fight this man. We must not only discourage and subdue him; this will not be enough. We must—" She leaned forward and spoke with concentrated brutality— "We must extinguish him!"

There was no sound from the mosaic; each facet hung like a painted tile.

"Some of you are shocked and uncomfortable," said The Jacynth, "but you must adjust yourselves to a harsh undertaking. We must destroy this man for the predator that he is."

She sat back; The Roland Zygmont, chairman of the Society, assumed the control plate. He spoke in a subdued voice. "The Jacynth has illuminated a specific aspect of the general problem. Beyond question Grayven Warlock is a clever rogue; he seems to have outwitted the assassins and laid low for seven years, then registered in Brood as his own relict, with the intent of making the climb once more to Amaranth."

A faint voice cried out, "And where is the wrong in this?"

The Roland ignored the question. "However in this larger matter—"

The Jacynth reappeared on the panel. Her eyes roved up and down among ten thousand faces. "Who spoke?"

"I spoke."

"And who are you?"

"I am Gavin Waylock—or The Grayven Warlock, if you prefer. I serve as Vice-Chancellor of the Prytaneon."

Across the great mosaic, faces shifted and moved as eyes scanned the ten thousand facets.

"Let me speak further. Chairman, give me the floor please—"

"I yield," said The Jacynth.

Waylock's face appeared on the central screen. Ten thousand pairs of eyes studied the stern face.

"Seven years ago," said Waylock, "I was relinquished to the assassins and convicted of a crime of which I was only technically guilty. By good fortune I am here today to protest. I petition this conclave to rescind the order of arrest, to acknowledge the mistake, and declare me once more a member of the Society in good standing."

The Roland Zygmont spoke in a voice burdened with perturbation. "The conclave is at liberty to vote on your petition."

"You are a Monster!" came an angry voice. "We will never submit!"

Waylock said in a steady voice, "I request your vote of acceptance."

The tabulator plate burnt ember red.

"You have defeated the proposal," said Waylock. "May I inquire—Chairman Zygmont, I call on you—why I have been denied?"

"I can only guess at the Society's motives," muttered The Roland. "Apparently we feel that your methods are reprehensible. You have been accused of irregularity, if not crime. We are annoyed by your aggressive approach. We do not find you qualified by character or achievement for membership in the Amaranth Society."

"But," said Waylock mildly, "my character is irrelevant, as it is with any Amaranth. I am The Graven Warlock, and I claim recognition."

The Roland yielded to The Jacynth Martin. "You are registered at the Actuarian as Gavin Waylock, are you not?"

"That is true. It was a matter of convenience, a—"

"Then this is your legal identity. By your own recognition, The Grayven is extinct. You are Gavin Waylock, Brood."

"I registered as Gavin Waylock, relict to The Grayven. This is a matter of record. However I *am* the identity of Grayven, and hence entitled to the same perquisites as if I were The Grayven himself. It is all one."

The Jacynth laughed. "I will allow the Roland to respond; he is the arbiter on such matters."

The Roland said shortly, "I deny the assertion of Mr. Gavin Waylock. The Grayven was Amaranth for only two years at the time of his trouble. He could not conceivably have brought surrogates to a state of full empathy."

"This is the case, however," said Waylock. "You may challenge me on any aspect of The Grayven's past; you will discover an unbroken continuity. You have acknowledged me Warlock's surrogate; I therefore petition for recognition as the new Grayven Warlock."

The Roland said uneasily, "I cannot receive your petition. You may be The Grayven's relict, but you cannot possibly be his identity, his surrogate."

The argument had resolved to interchange between these two, and their faces shared the screen.

"But," asked Waylock, "is this not your doctrine in regard to surrogates? Is not each of your surrogates the identity of you?"

"Each surrogate is an individual, until he is invested with the legal identity of the proto-Amaranth, whence he becomes the Amaranth."

Waylock for a moment had nothing to say. To the mosaic of faces, he appeared countered and thwarted.

"Then the surrogates are distinct individuals?"

"In effect, yes," responded The Roland.

Waylock asked the Society. "All of you agree?"

The tabulator shone bright blue.

"It occurs to me," said Waylock thoughtfully, "that in making this affirmation you admit to a vast and cynical felony."

There was silence across the mosaic.

Waylock continued in a stronger voice. "As you know, I am invested with certain duties. They are latent, but nonetheless real. In the absence of the Chancellor, I, as Vice-Chancellor, at least tentatively hold the Amaranth Society in violation of basic law."

The Roland Zygmont frowned. "What nonsense is this?"

"You maintain adult individuals in captivity, do you not? It is therefore my executive order that you desist from this violation. You must liberate these individuals at once, or suffer an appropriate penalty."

The mutter of indignation swelled to a roar. The chairman's voice shook. "You are mad."

There was little light in the chamber from which Waylock spoke; his face showed on the screen like a dark stone mask.

"It is by your own admission that you are incriminated. You must choose. The surrogates are either individuals, or they are identities of the proto-Amaranth."

The chairman averted his eyes. "I will gladly allow others of the Society to comment on these witless remarks. The Sexton Van Ek?"

"The remarks, as you say, are witless," said The Sexton Van Ek after a moment's hesitation. "Worse, they are insulting."

"To be sure," sighed the chairman. "The Jacynth Martin?" There was no response. The Jacynth's square of mosaic was vacant.

"The Grandon Plantagenet?"

"I echo the words of The Sexton Van Ek. This criminal's words are only to be ignored."

"He is no criminal until he is so adjudged," sighed The Roland.

"Just what is he after?" The Marcus Carson-Sce demanded peevishly. "Frankly, I am confused."

Waylock answered, "Bluntly, endorse me Amaranth, or liberate your own surrogates."

There was silence, then a few faint laughs.

The Roland said, "You know we will never turn out our surrogates. The idea is fantastic!"

"Then you recognize my right to be endorsed into the Society?"

The tabulator glowed first orange, then red. "No!" cried voices.

Waylock stood back, suddenly haggard. "You are beyond reason."

"We will not be hectored by you!" "We will not submit to extortion!" came faint calls.

"I warn you: I am not helpless. I have been victimized once, I have spent years in misery."

"How have we victimized you?" demanded the chairman. "We are not guilty of The Grayven Warlock's crimes."

"You dealt him the harshest possible penalty for a nominal offense—one of which hundreds of you have committed. The Abel Mandeville extinguished two souls—but he survives unscathed in his surrogates."

"I can only say," remarked The Roland, "that The Grayven should have guarded himself until his surrogates were ready."

"I will not be turned aside," cried Waylock in a passionate voice. "I insist on my due. If you deny me, I will act with the same ruthlessness that you have shown me."

The faces of the mosaic quivered in surprise. The Roland said in a half-conciliatory tone, "If you like, we will review your case, although I doubt—"

"No! I will use my power now—either in forbearance, or in retaliation. The choice is yours."

"What power is this? What can you do?"

"I can liberate your surrogates." Waylock looked across the mosaic with a harsh smile. "In fact, they are being liberated at this moment, for I anticipated your stubbornness. And there will be no stopping until you allow me my rights—or until every surrogate of every Amaranth is free."

The Amaranth sat numb. No sound came from the mosaic.

The Roland laughed shakily. "We may rest at ease then. This man—Gavin Waylock or The Grayven—can have no knowledge of our cells. He cannot do what he threatens."

Waylock raised a sheet of paper. "These are cells which already have been visited." He read:

"The Barbara Benbo
1513 Anglesey Place.

"The Albert Pondiferry
Apartment 20153, Skyhaven.

"The Maidal Hardy
Clodex Chandery, Wibleside.

"The Carlotta Mippin
The Sign of the Oaks
Five Corners."

Gasps of shock came from the mosaic. Faces jerked and bobbed as the Amaranth debated whether to stay or hasten to their cells.

"It will serve nothing to leave the conclave," said Waylock. "Only a certain number of cells are to be opened tonight— about four hundred. The job is half done now, and will be complete before interference is possible. Tomorrow four hundred more cells will be opened, and the surrogates sent into the world. And every day thereafter. Now—will you give me what is my right or must I make misery for all of you?"

The Roland's face was stark and pallid. "We cannot break the laws of Clarges."

"I ask you to break no laws. I am Amaranth; I wish recognition for my status."

"We must have time."

"I can give you no time. You must decide now."

"I cannot speak for the Society."

"Let them vote."

The Roland turned his head to the buzz of a commu, stepped aside. When he returned, his face wore a blank stunned look.

"It is true! They are breaking open the cells, all the surrogates are cast into the world, out of empathy!"

"You must concede me my rights."

The Roland cried out, "Let the Society vote."

The lights flashed, fluttered, wavered. The central tabulator glowed green, then yellow, then orange, back to green, finally a blue-green.

"You have won," said The Roland bleakly.

"Well, then?"

"You are hereby given official notification: I pledge you now, brother Amaranth."

"Do you withdraw all charges of criminal act and intent?"

"In the name of the Society, they are withdrawn."

Waylock heaved a deep sigh. He spoke into a shoulder microphone. "Halt the operation."

He turned back to the mosaic. "I offer my apologies to those who will be inconvenienced. I can only say that you should have dealt me justice to begin with."

The Roland's voice came coarse and gruff. "Clearly it is possible to storm into Amaranth, by brutality and bold deception. It is done. You are in. Now we will mend our laws; it will be——"

A chattering sound interrupted The Roland. As ten thousand eyes stared in shock and horror, the headless body of Gavin Waylock fell out of sight.

Behind him appeared The Jacynth Martin. She wore a ghastly smile, her eyes were wide and staring. "You spoke of justice; it has been done. I have destroyed the Monster. And now I am tainted with the blood of Gavin Waylock. You shall see no more of me!"

"Wait, wait!" cried The Roland. "Where are you?"

"The Anastasia's house. Where else is there an open seat to the conclave?"

"Then wait—I will come quickly."

"Come as quickly as you like, you will find only the corpse of a Monster!"

The Jacynth Martin ran out to the landing plat, where her silver Starflash waited. She plunged into the cabin, the car rose like a rocket, soaring high into the dark air. Clarges twinkled below, far north, far south, beside the great river.

The Starflash edged over the apex of its arc, plunged whistling down at the Chant.

Inside sat the woman, eyes glazed, face pinched and bleak. Clarges, beloved Clarges, lifted up past her; she glimpsed the oily black water, with faint tendrils of reflection glistening on the surface.

XIX

A CURIOUS placidity held the city. The morning news-organs made only cautious reference to the events of the night, uncertain what particular line to take; the population attended their usual strivings with only dim realization of the bold acts of Gavin Waylock.

Among the Amaranth, the name Gavin Waylock excited much stronger emotions—for as Waylock spoke to the conclave the despoliation of the cells had been completed. Four hundred vaults, aeries, strongholds, cellars, secret rooms, and isolated cottages had been forced open; Waylock's hirelings burst in, blinking when they saw the vats, the cushioned stalls, the naked simulacra. There was hesitation, then malicious glee. The simulacra were jerked from the stalls, guided out into the night, and sent wandering into the strange open world—seventeen hundred and sixty-two in all.

Many of the Amaranth, in retrospect, claimed that they knew to the instant when first the rude knocks sounded, so strong their empathic bond. Their agony was enormous. Now they were vulnerable, the interminable sessions voided, the cherishing wasted, the empathy destroyed. Eternity was at the mercy of chance.

Four hundred Amaranth, suddenly prone to mishap, reacted with psychotic exaggeration. They scuttled into seclusion, sweating in large rooms, fearing to stir into the open lest an air car fall on them, or they encounter a homicidal maniac.

The Council of Tribunes met to consider the case, but when interviewed by the press they made indecisive comments.

Chancellor Imish broadcast a statement disavowing Waylock. He emphasized that Waylock, in describing himself as Vice-Chancellor, had used the title inappropriately and in no wise expressed the official position.

The public assimilated the news and began to react. Some took alarm at the flouting of tradition, others felt secret pleasure. Waylock was variously regarded as a martyr and as a criminal justly despatched. Few could concentrate on their work. Thousands wasted time discussing the strange affair. Where would it lead? The hours went by, and the days, and Clarges waited.

2

Vincent Rodenave had also participated in the events of the dramatic night. In a rented air car he flew to the Souverain Uplands, forty miles north of Clarges, and landed beside an isolated little villa. After some difficulty he forced an entrance, and broke into the central chamber.

In blue satin stalls lay three versions of The Anastasia de Fancourt—simulacra of the original Anastasia. The shadowed eyes were shut; they lay in a state of trance, alike even to the curl of short dark hair.

Rodenave could hardly control the urge of his emotion. He leaned forward, hands trembling to caress the naked flesh.

The Anastasia whom Rodenave had touched awoke. With her awoke the other two.

They cried out in surprise. In modesty and confusion they looked right and left for covering.

"The Anastasia has transited," said Rodenave. "Who is senior?"

"I am," said one. The three reflections suddenly became one person and two reflections. "I am The Anastasia." She turned to her simulacra. "Return to the stalls, and I will go out into the world."

"All of you go out," said Rodenave.

The Anastasia regarded him with bewilderment. "This is not correct!"

"But it is," said Rodenave. He added in a hungry voice, "Since last The Anastasia visited you, she married me. You are now my wife."

The new Anastasia, the two simulacra, inspected him with interest.

"I find that hard to understand," said the new Anastasia. "You are familiar. What is your name?"

"Vincent Rodenave."

"Ah—I recognize you now. We have heard of you." She shrugged and laughed. "I have done peculiar things in my life. Perhaps I did marry you. But I hardly think so."

She was slipping into the character of the great mime, as if a disembodied intelligence were merging into her body.

"Come," said Rodenave.

"But we can't all go!" protested The Anastasia. "What of our empathy?"

"All must come," Rodenave said obdurately. "I shall use force if necessary."

They all backed away looking at him from the corners of their eyes. "This is unheard of. What happened to the previous Anastasia?"

"A jealous lover committed violence upon her."

"That would be The Abel."

Rodenave made an impatient gesture. "We must leave here."

"But," urged the senior, "if we all go, there will be three Anastasias! These others are as advanced as I. In fact, they are identical with me."

"One of you may be The Anastasia, if so you choose. Another will be my wife. The third may do as she pleases."

The three Anastasias looked at him with an unflattering deliberation. The senior spoke. "We do not care to attend upon you. If there is a marriage, it will be dissolved. We will go from our cell, if we must. But no more."

Rodenave went gray. "You shall come with me, one of you! So choose—which shall it be?"

"Not I." "Not I." "Not I." The three voices spoke with a single intonation.

"But your marriage, you can't ignore it!"

"We certainly can. And we intend to. You are not one whom we would touch with pleasure."

Rodenave said in a strangled voice, "All Amaranth, all scions and surrogates must leave their cells; this is the new ordinance!"

"Nonsense!" "Nonsense!" "Nonsense!"

Rodenave stepped forward, swung his hand; the face of one girl burnt red. Then he turned, marched to his air car, and rode alone back to Clarges.

3

The Roland Zygmont had known only indecision, conflict and anger since The Jacynth Martin had first brought the case of Gavin Waylock to his attention.

The Roland was a very old man, one of the original Grand Union group. He was slender and fine-boned; his face was thin, with a thin nose and jaw, pale gray eyes and fine golden hair. Time had mellowed him, and he had not shared The Jacynth's passionate zeal. After the apocalyptic night which had brought so much anguish, his first emotion was relief that the worst was surely over.

For the next few days, however, he was subjected to an aftermath of annoyances and vexations. The seventeen hundred and sixty-two surrogates posed the biggest problem: what should be the status of these new citizens? For each of the four hundred Amaranth whose cells had been despoiled, there were four or five versions extant—each with the same outlook, background, and hopes for the future. Each had every right to regard himself as Amaranth, with all the privileges and perquisites; it made for an awkward situation.

The issue was debated at the stormiest session of the Directive Council in The Roland's memory, and resolved in the only way which appeared conceivable: the seventeen hundred and sixty-two surrogates were to be accepted into the Society as Amaranth in their own right.

After the decision had been reached, the name Gavin Waylock inevitably arose. The Carl Fergus—one of those whose surrogates had been liberated—spoke bitterly. "It is not enough that this man has been executed, he should be resurrected and destemporized Nomad-style; then again; and again!"

The Roland, out of patience, made a sharp retort. "You are hysterical; you see the situation only in terms of your own trouble."

The Carl glowered. "Do you defend this Monster?"

"I merely note that Waylock was subjected to extreme provocation," The Roland replied coldly, "and that he fought back with the only means to his hand."

Silence lay uneasy in the chamber. Vice-Chairman The Olaf Maybow spoke in a conciliatory voice. "In any event the episode is at its end."

"Not for me!" roared The Car Fergus. "The Roland can easily display a smug sanctity; his surrogates are still safe in their cells. If he hadn't been so inept, so timid and vacillating—"

The Roland's nerves were already raw, and the accusation stung him past the limit of control. He leapt to his feet, seized The Carl's jacket, flung him against the wall. The Carl struck out with his fists; the two fought half a minute before the other members of the council could separate them.

The meeting dissolved into anger and factionalism; The Roland returned to his apartment, hoping to soothe himself with massage, a hot bath, and a good night's sleep. But the worst shock of the evening lay ahead of him. When he arrived, he found a man waiting in his foyer.

The Roland stood stock-still. "Gavin Waylock!" he whispered hoarsely.

Waylock rose to his feet. "The Gavin Waylock, if you please."

"But—you are extinguished!"

Waylock shrugged. "I know little of what occurred: only what I have read in the papers."

"But—"

"Why are you astonished?" Waylock asked in some irritation. "Have you forgotten that I am The Grayven Warlock?"

Enlightenment came to The Roland.

"You are senior of the surrogates set down by The Grayven!"

"Naturally. Gavin Waylock has had seven years to build up empathy."

The Roland slumped into a chair. "Why didn't I forsee it?" He rubbed his temples; "What a situation! What shall we do?"

Waylock raised his eyebrows. "Is there any question?"

The Roland sighed. "No. I will not revive that contest. You won, and the prize is yours. Come," he led the way to his study, opened a large antique ledger, dipped a quill pen in purple ink and inscribed the name GAVIN WAYLOCK.

He closed the ledger. "There. It is done. You are enrolled. I will strike you a bronze medallion tomorrow; you have already undergone the treatments; there are no further formalities." He looked Waylock up and down. "I will not pretend affability, because I feel none. However I will offer you a glass of brandy."

"I accept with pleasure."

The two men drank in silence. The Roland leaned back. "You have achieved your aim," he said heavily. "You are Amaranth; life extends before you. You have won a treasure —" He shook his head—"but how you have won it! Four hundred Amaranth must now keep to their halls; they must cultivate new surrogates, build new empathies. Some may meet accident; they may transite, and without their surrogates it is oblivion. Those lives will be on your conscience."

Waylock evinced no concern. "All this could have been avoided seven years ago."

"That is beside the point."

"Perhaps. In any case the climb up-slope is always at the expense of someone's vitality. I am relatively blameless. My victims are these two or three you mention; every other Amaranth has usurped life from two thousand."

The Roland Zygmont laughed bitterly. "Do you think that you have not cheated vitality from two thousand? The Actuarian will maintain the quota; your elevation is at the expense of the top Verge, and all the others below them!" He threw up his hands in a listless gesture. "Let's not wrangle; you are Amaranth, but you will not find the Society so exclusive, the perquisites so rich, nor the company so select."

"How so?"

"Each of the seventeen hundred and sixty-two is entitled to and has been granted Amaranth status."

Waylock snorted. "You *do* look after your own! And what of Actuarian quotas now?"

The Roland started to speak, frowned and hesitated. Then he said, "We can only do what we consider right."

Waylock rose to his feet. "I will bid you good night."

"Good night," said The Roland.

Waylock went out to the landing deck, where he had left his rented air car. High in the air he rose, high above the traffic lanes. Clarges spread below him, a teeming, antique city, rich, strange, various.

What now? thought Waylock. He might rest for a period, perhaps in the hills above Old Port, and there make plans. The urgency, the pressure, the danger were gone. He laughed aloud. He was The Gavin Waylock, with a future stretching into the haze of the infinite. No need to struggle or strain, no challenges to meet . . . no scheming, no calculation, no defiance. And, he thought ruefully, no longer the triumph when the schemes and calculations were successful.

Waylock felt a vague apprehension. He had won, the prize was his—but what was the value of the prize? What was the worth of the system, if a man could not dare the desperate glories he otherwise might shrink from? Amaranth were as timorous as glarks, and as ignoble.

Waylock thought of the *Star Enterprise*, which now must be refueled and ready for venture into the outer night. Perhaps he would make the trip to the Elgenburg spaceport and pay Reinhold Biebursson a visit.

XX

THE ROLAND ZYGMONT spent another hectic day with the Directive Council, but was able to disengage himself before his evening meal.

He ate in solitude, thankful for the quiet, and skimmed through the daily newspapers.

The Gavin Waylock's reappearance was the subject of excited bulletins, but the treatment was cautious and impersonal.

On the front page of the *Broadcast*, a newspaper with mass circulation among glarks and the Brood, The Roland read:

> The *BROADCAST'S* policy has been ever to avoid distinction between the phyle, never to single out any phyle as a target for criticism. Nevertheless, we are troubled by the Amaranth policy in regard to the 1,762 scions recently released into the world by the zeal of Gavin Waylock.

Admittedly these scions were identities of their respective Amaranth, and in this sense identical persons with identical rights.

However, 1,762 new Amaranth represent a 17.62 per cent increase in the phyle, and a correspondingly heavy drain upon the production of the Reach. It is notorious that each Amaranth, with his leisure, his opportunities for amassing wealth, consumes ten to a hundred times more of the gross product than a typical member of Brood.

In our opinion the Society could justify its exalted position of trust by registering the scions in Brood. The present course of action smacks of favoritism and special privilege.

The Roland smiled sourly and turned to the *Clarion,* a news-organ generally reflecting the attitudes of the upper phyle:

The city seethes with a peculiar excitement—one, in our opinion, quite out of proportion to its instigation: the formalization into the Society of the 1,762 surrogates so unhappily released.

We agree that the occasion is completely awkward, but how else may justice be served? Certainly by no will of the individuals involved were they ejected into the world. Each and every one of them is the identity of an Amaranth, and it would be cruelty to plummet these persons back into the lower phyle.

Let us all make the best of a disturbing situation, lick our sore spots and make sure that nothing of the sort ever occurs again.

How do the people of Clarges feel about the new Gavin Waylock? It is hard to know. The popular pulse has never beat so erratically. Actually, there seems more resentment against the Society in connection with the 1,762 newly formalized Amaranth. But then, the people of Clarges are an unknown quantity, and never more so than at this present moment.

Elsewhere he noted a cursory paragraph, but gave it no particular heed.

The Actuarian briefly halted report service this morning during evaluation of new information.

The Roland was committed for the evening to a social function from which he could not escape. He planned to make only a token appearance, but not until midnight did he find it possible to return to his apartment.

He opened a window. The night was clear and cold. He looked up into the sky where a pale moon rode.

The worst of the trouble was over, he told himself. The hard decisions had been made, only details remained to be worked out. These would be vexing, but could be delegated to others. He felt a sense of relief and relaxation.

The hour was late, the city was dark and quiet. The Roland yawned, turned away from the window and sought his couch.

The night passed, the moon sank behind the tall towers, dawn came to dilute the dark; the sun rose.

The Roland slept on.

Several hours passed. The Roland stirred, awoke. He had been disturbed by a strange sound, and for a moment lay trying to identify it. It seemed to drift in through the open window—a sound like a deep stream flowing.

He arose and went to the window. The street was thronged with people—a crowd dense as raisins in a box. They moved in a slow tide toward Esterhazy Square.

The commu signal sounded; The Roland turned away from the window like a man in a dream. The face on the screen was that of The Olaf Maybow, Vice-Chairman of the Society.

"Roland!" called The Olaf in excitement. "Have you seen it? What shall we do?"

The Roland rubbed his chin. "There is a great crowd in the street. Is this what you refer to?"

"Crowd!" cried The Olaf in a brassy voice. "It's a mob! A convulsion!"

"But why? What's the occasion?"

"Haven't you seen the morning news?"

"I've only just awakened."

"Look at the headlines."

The Roland touched a tab which projected a news resume upon the wall.

"Great Eternal Principle!" he murmured.

"Exactly."

The Roland was silent.

"What shall we do?" asked The Olaf.

The Roland reflected a moment. "I suppose something must be done."

"So it would seem."

"Although the matter is out of our province."

"Still we must do something. It is our responsibility."

The Roland said in a quiet voice, "In some terrible respect our civilization has failed. The race of man has failed."

The Olaf spoke sharply. "We can't talk failure now! Someone must issue a statement, someone must take charge!"

"Hm," muttered The Roland. "Now a good Chancellor might prove himself."

The Olaf snorted. "Claude Imish? Ridiculous! No. It is up to us!"

"But I can't contradict the Actuarian! No more can I consign seventeen hundred and sixty-two Amaranth to Brood."

The Olaf turned his head. "Listen to them, hear how they roar."

The crowd-sound rose suddenly—a sound laden with high-pitched overtones, like the moaning of beasts.

The Olaf cried out, "You must do something!"

The Roland stood very straight. "Very well. I shall go before them. I shall counsel reason—patience—"

"They'll tear you to pieces!"

"In that case, I shall not address them. And presently they will tire of this demonstration and return to their strivings."

"When their strivings no longer have significance?"

The Roland sat back in his chair. "Neither you nor I—nor anyone else—can control this situation. I can feel it; I know what it's like. The people were like impounded water. The dam has burst and the water must find its natural level."

"But—what will they do?"

"Who knows? It might be wise to carry a weapon when you walk about."

"You speak as if the people of the Reach are barbarians!"

"We and the barbarians are the same stock. We have known a hundred thousand years of savagery together, and only a few hundred years' divergence."

The Amaranth men looked bleakly at each other, then both started as the crowd noise once more became louder.

2

The events which brought the desperate surge to the streets of Clarges represented a culmination to the Industrial Revolution, to the defeat of disease in the twentieth century, to the Malthusian Chaos, to the Reach of Clarges itself. They were a product of civilization, and in this sense foreordained. But the immediate source of the trouble was the expansion of the Amaranth Society by seventeen hundred and sixty-two new members.

The information reached the Actuarian, was coded and integrated. Even those who strove at the Actuarian were startled by the effect. The ratio between the various phyle was fixed, by a formula which maintained the aggregate years of life per thousand population at a constant value. For the purposes of this formula an Amaranth's life was arbitrarily reckoned at 3000 years, and the phyle ration worked out roughly as 1:40:-200:600:1200.

The accession of seventeen hundred and sixty-two new Amaranth destroyed the established balance, subtracting life expectancy from the Brood by something over four months, and the other phyle accordingly.

The first effect was a spate of instruction to the assassins, ordering visits to a large number of persons whose lifelines had edged to within four months of the terminator.

In some cases the lifelines were on the point of breaking up into a new phyle—but bringing the terminator four months closer to the source negated the possibility.

These particular cases made the first protest. There was violence; assassins were flung into the streets. Excitement in many neighborhoods was already at a high pitch when news-organs described the full implications of the new adjustment.

Reaction was instantaneous. The population of Clarges boiled into the streets. Strivings were deserted; if a man's most concentrated effort availed only a subtraction of four months from his life, then why strive? Why not give up?

Many failed to join the surge because they lay supine in their apartments staring at the ceiling. Thousands of others discarded all inhibition and sense of responsibility. They shouted and cried as the crowd swirled toward Esterhazy Square.

The plaza before the Actuarian was packed dense with bodies. Faces shone from drab clothing like confetti on dark water. From time to time one of the number raised himself upon a parapet, and his voice bawled thinly over the mass. The faces turned; there would be restless motion, a throaty rumble.

An air car hovered over the Actuarian; it dropped to the roof. A man alighted and came gingerly to the edge. It was The Roland Zygmont, Chairman of the Amaranth Society. He began to speak, using an amplifier, and his voice boomed over the plaza and Esterhazy Square.

The crowd paid small heed to his words; they reacted only to the feeling in his voice, and became ever more tense.

A whisper arose and swept across the square, backward and forward in a natural resonance: "The Roland Zygmont! It's The Roland Zygmont of the Society!"

The whisper grew in magnitude, became a mutter, a roar. The Roland had made an unfortunate choice of podium; the Chairman of the Amaranth Society standing four-square on top of the Actuarian carried too much symbolical sting.

From one side of the plaza came a bellowed insult. The crowd gave a curious deep sigh. Another voice took up the scream, then another and another, in different quarters of the plaza. The sound rang through Esterhazy Square. In nearby streets people froze in their tracks, quivered, opened their mouths.

The scream rose from the city; all Clarges screamed a sound never heard before on the face of the Earth. On the roof of the Actuarian stood The Roland, limp and stunned, arms hanging at his sides.

He made an attempt to speak; his voice was overwhelmed. Fascinated he watched, and the crowd raised arms toward him, fingers grasping and groping.

The crowd gave a lurch forward, pushed toward the Actuarian.

They pressed back the doors with weight of their flesh; metal bent, glass shattered.

A group of custodians held up their hands imploringly; from the Public Relations Office came Basil Thinkoup, calling out for order and calm. The crowd moved over them. Basil Thinkoup's life ended.

Into sacrosanct areas pushed the crowd. Bars struck control

panels, refuse was flung into the delicate microwebs. Power crackled, smoke rose, components exploded. The great mechanism died as a man dies when his brain is wounded.

Outside in the square the crowd struggled, desperate in their urge to attack the Actuarian. Those who fell disappeared without a sound; their expressions were calm, as if they had been relieved of a terrible duty: the ordeal of the future. Over them marched a thousand others, intent to enter the Actuarian.

Through the portals they pushed, shoulder to shoulder, eyes looking right and left, earnestly seeking something to destroy.

A group came out on the landing where the Cage of Shame hung. They swung it out and cut it loose; it fell into the crowd and was torn to bits.

The crowd's passion showed no abatement. Looking down from the roof The Roland thought that never in all human history had there been such passion.

The Olaf seized his arm. "Quick, we must escape! They are out on the roof!"

The two men hurried for the hovering air car; they were too late, and were seized from behind. Kicking, struggling, yelling, they were carried to the edge of the roof and flung out into the air.

Something within the Actuarian exploded; up came a burst of flame, spouting high. The men on the roof danced and ran crazily, like beetles in a bottle, and at last were singed and overcome. Within the Actuarian a thousand more perished.

The crowd heeded nothing; they were listening to the wild voice of a man who had mounted a parapet. It was Vincent Rodenave, beside himself with emotion. His face burnt with fanatic fire, his voice was a thrilling sound. "Gavin Waylock!" he called. "This is the man who wrought so great a wrong! Gavin Waylock!"

Without complete awareness the crowd took up the cry. "Gavin Waylock! Kill! Kill! Kill!"

3

The Prytaneon met in emergency session, but only half the assembly appeared, and these were tired and disheveled. They spoke in gloomy voices, and performed what legislative duties they thought necessary without zest or spirit.

Bertrand Helm, First Marshal of the Militia, was instructed to restore order through the city. Caspar Jarvis was ordered to co-operate along with the entire force of the assassins.

"What of Gavin Waylock?" came a voice from the floor.

"Gavin Waylock?" The chairman shrugged. "There is nothing we can do to him." And he added, "Or for him."

4

Gavin Waylock was sought throughout Clarges. His apartment was ransacked, a dozen men of his appearance were given rough treatment before they could talk themselves free.

From somewhere came rumor: Waylock had been seen in Elgenburg. The avenues leading south streamed with chanting columns.

House by house Elgenburg was searched, every cranny and nook investigated.

Nearby was the spaceport, where the *Star Enterprise* stood waiting for departure. Tall and clean over the turmoil rose the beautiful metallic mass.

From every quarter of Elgenburg men and women converged on the spaceport. Outwardly they seemed more quiet, less frantic than those who had destroyed the Actuarian but, halted by the barriers, they showed their original fervor. Chanting and singing, they began to attack the gate, using a metal pole as a battering ram.

Down from the sky dropped a large aircar; it landed inside the gate and six men alighted; the Council of Tribunes. They advanced in a stern line, holding up their hands in admonition.

In the center walked Guy Carskadden, the High Tribune.

The crowd momentarily hesitated, the battering ram faltered.

Carskadden cried out, "This madness must stop! What do you want here?"

"Waylock!" came a dozen voices. "We want the criminal, the Monster!"

"Are you barbarians, destroying property and ignoring the laws of the Reach?"

The voices came back at him, stronger and more defiant: "There are no more laws!" And a single shrill cry: "There is no more Reach!"

Carskadden made a gesture of despair. The crowd surged; the barrier broke under the weight of ten thousand bodies.

Hot-eyed men and women came forward. The tribunes retreated slowly, holding out their hands, and calling, "Go back,
go back!"

Below the tall shape of the *Star Enterprise*, glinting in the
sad light of late afternoon, the tribunes formed a line, and the
crowd slowly approached.

Carskadden again sought to halt them. "Stop!" he thundered.
"Return to your homes, attend to your strivings!"

The crowd paused, sullen and muttering. "Waylock!" "The
Monster Waylock!" "He has eaten our lives!"

Carskadden spoke with all the persuasiveness at his command. "Be reasonable. If Waylock has committed crimes, he
will pay!"

"Our lives! Truncated! Wasted!" "We avenge our lives!"

The crowd moved forward, engulfing the tribunes. Up the
catwalk scrambled the frenzied men, bent on the open port
fifty feet above ground.

Within the ship was movement. Reinhold Biebursson stepped
out of the dark interior, stood on the landing in front of the
port. He blinked down at the crowd, shook his great head
in pity. He lifted a bucket, cast forth its contents.

A green gas boiled up; the crowd choked, cried out in guttural voices, swirled, pushed back away from the ship.

Biebursson looked up into the sky where a large air vehicle
was slanting down toward the ship, looked once more over
the crowd, raised his hand in a melancholy salute and disappeared within.

The cloud of gas had created a momentary lull, although
now the crowd, fed by all the streets of Elgenburg, had spread
across the entire expanse of the spaceport.

From somewhere in the rear a chant began. "Gavin Waylock—give us Waylock! Gavin Waylock—give us Waylock!"

The chant spread and rumbled with an enormous volume;
the mass began to shove forward once more, clinching in
against the great vessel.

The aircraft dropped, hovered; out on the deck stepped a
man of medium height with a broad humorous face, a head
of thick yellow hair, with a lank lock hanging to one side
of his forehead.

He spoke into a microphone; his voice rang from a loudspeaker, cutting through the rumble of the chant.

"Friends—some of you know me. I am Jacob Nile. May I

speak to you? I have words to say which bear on the future of Clarges."

The chant quieted; the crowd listened.

"Friends, you are exercised, you are excited, and rightly so. Because today you have broken the past, and the future is clear and wide.

"You came here seeking Gavin Waylock, but this is folly."

A quick rumble of anger came from the crowd. "He is within!"

Jacob Nile spoke on imperturbably. "Who is Gavin Waylock? How can we hate him, how can we hate ourselves? Gavin Waylock is ourselves! He has done as all of us have wished to do. He has acted without restraint, without discipline, without fear. Gavin Waylock succeeded, and we are furious, we are jealous at his success!

"Gavin Waylock has committed wrong. If you were to tear him to bits, this might be very close to justice. But again—what of ourselves?"

The crowd was silent.

"Waylock is not so guilty as the rest of us—this great nation, the Reach of Clarges. We have laid a stain on human history, we have wronged the whole race of men. How? We have limited human achievement. We have tortured ourselves with the image of life, held up this glorious fruit and then eaten ashes.

"The tension was insupportable; today came the explosion. It was inevitable; Waylock was no more than the catalyst. He accelerated history, and in this sense he must be thanked."

The crowd hissed restlessly.

Jacob Nile took a step forward, brushed back his lock of hair. There was nothing now of the droll or waggish in his face; his cheeks were lean and corded, his voice taut.

"So much for Waylock: he is unimportant in himself. What he has done is vast. He has broken the system. We are free! The Actuarian is demolished, the records are lost, each man is like his neighbor!

"How will we use our freedom? We can rebuild the Actuarian, we can locate ourselves among the phyle; we can imprison ourselves again like flies in a web. Or—we can break out into a new phase of history—where life is for all men, not just the one in two thousand!"

The crowd began to respond to Nile's fervor; they rustled and made small sounds of approval.

"How can we do this? We are told that our world is too small for men of eternal life. This is true. We must become pioneers again, we must break out into new territories! The men of old carved living space from the wilderness; we must do the same, and let this be the condition for eternal life! Is it not sufficient? When a man creates his living space and guarantees his sustenance, is he not entitled to life?"

The crowd made a throaty sound. "Life! Life!"

"Where is this living space, where can we go to find it? First, in all the various wildernesses and Nomad-lands of Earth. We must expand, we must take our way to the barbarians; but we must go as pilgrims and missionaries, not as soldiers. We must bring them with us. And then—when the earth is full—where is there living space? Where else?" Jacob Nile turned to the *Star Enterprise*, looked up at the sky. "When we shattered the Actuarian, we shattered the bar across the sky. Now, life, eternal life, is at anyone's demand. Man must move forward; this is the nature of his brain and blood. Today he is given the Earth; his destiny is the stars. The entire universe awaits him! And so, why should we quaver and hedge at life for all of us?"

The crowd was curiously silent. For long seconds emotions adjusted, intellects wrestled with the scope of Nile's words.

The crowd sighed. The sound rose, swelled, dwindled, as if at a prospect too entrancing to be possible.

"You people of Clarges," said Nile, "it is by your will that changes can be made. What is your will?"

The crowd's response was quicker, more enthusiastic.

A lone dim voice—was it that of Vincent Rodenave?—cried out: "But Gavin Waylock! What of Gavin Waylock?"

"Ah, Waylock," said Nile thoughtfully. "He is at the same time a great criminal and a great hero. Shall we not then, at the same time, reward him and punish him?" Nile turned to look up at the *Star Enterprise*. "There it stands, the great vessel of space, ready for the void. What better mission could it undertake than the search for new worlds for Man? What better destiny for Gavin Waylock, than to go forth with the *Star Enterprise*?"

Behind Nile, high on the staging, there was movement. Gavin Waylock came forth from the *Star Enterprise*. He stood facing the crowd, which roared vastly, and surged forward.

Waylock raised his hand; the crowd instantly became quiet. "I hear your judgment on me," said Waylock. He stood erect. "I hear and I welcome it. I shall venture into space; I shall seek new worlds for Man."

He gave a salute, bowed, turned and disappeared into the ship.

Two hours passed. The crowd moved back, and took up stations on Elgenburg Heights.

A warning siren sounded; blue fire trembled under the *Star Enterprise*.

Slowly it left the ground. Faster and faster it climbed into the twilight.

The blue fire became a bright star, then dimmed and was gone.